Kitaine Neris, Book 2

THE VANISH TIDE

Kitaine Neris, Book 2

A.J. Locke

Indigaris
Luneso
Yarachon
Nimbisu
Hanceoh
Sollunara
Keltin
Vonuis
Moonglade
Youne Wilds
Tropical Islands
Xislao
N
NW
NE
W
E
SW
SE
S

Chapter One

There was an island floating amid the clouds.

Looking up at it made me feel incredibly small. And awestruck. And maybe a bit concerned.

A bird released a piercing cry from one of the trees in the bordello's back yard before taking flight. I watched sunlight ripple across the cardinal's red feathers as it flew east, in the direction of the floating land mass. Eventually, the bird became a speck, but the island continued to loom. Its surface was long and flat, while the bottom was rugged and conical, as though it had been carelessly scooped out of the earth and flung up to the sky.

"Here, Kit." I turned at the sound of Marrik's voice. He offered me a glass of lemonade.

"Thanks." I took it and gave him a smile, feeling that pang of pain laced relief I was growing used to ever since we'd been reunited after I thought he was gone for good. Because a year ago I had accidentally Vanished him.

The swinging chair I was on creaked as Marrik settled next to me. We were alone on the porch, but the yard was full of people. My parents were chatting with Jiano and Rowan under the oak tree the cardinal had flown up from. Calla, Hye-Jin, Valentino, and a few other Hexes were lounging on picnic blankets conversing and snacking. Phinra was trying to stop her twin, Milene, from exiting the yard down the side path. Milene was prone to wandering off, and Phinra sighed in relief when Arjun jogged over to help. They steered Milene to one of the picnic blankets where a chocolate bar helped her stay put.

"You okay?" Marrik pressed a kiss against my temple as I snuggled into his side.

"What do you think is up there?" I nodded at the island.

Answer a question with a question when you don't wanna answer the question you were asked.

The island had appeared in the hours after the ley lines had some of their strength restored, after being drained for almost four hundred years by a group of overly ambitious witches. They'd wanted to grow their magic strong enough to do things like shift the stars across the sky. All they'd done was kill themselves and deplete the ley lines, leaving every generation of witches after them with only the small amount of magic we were born with. Some witches, like Jiano and I, had slightly stronger magic, and it was my stronger Vanish magic and a sense of vigilantism that had recently led me into some very dark places.

"Lots of abandoned homes and buildings," Marrik replied, sounding thoughtful. "Dead vegetation. Space debris, maybe?"

"Green guys with antennae?" My lips quirked though I continued to harbor an anxious feeling as I stared at the island. It wasn't the only one that had appeared, pulled down by Magnes Witches who, like all witches, had experienced a surge in their magic when the ley lines came back and temporarily lost control of it.

"Arjun has been sharing what he's learned from his coven," I said. "He said that the sky islands were a collaborative effort with Repel Witches who would repel them to the sky after Magnes Witches pulled them up from the ocean. Because stronger Magnes magic can manipulate gravity, the islands' stability was maintained using the gravitational pull of the moons. And they were kept above bodies of water."

This one wasn't above water though. Its presence had caused *a lot* of unease in the east.

"They were necessary because there were classes of Mutans Witches that thrived better there, right?"

I nodded. "Some of the aerial types needed higher elevation to feel their best, even in human form. And Calla said some flora Regen Witches used in their spell work only grew at the elevation of the sky islands."

"Witches lost a lot after the ley lines were drained," Marrik said. "I'm sure many things will be reestablished now."

"Yeah, especially since the ley lines' restoration means we can strengthen our magic again."

"I worry though." Marrik's tone was grave. "Those islands required specific conditions to be maintained. Once there were no longer strong witches to keep them stable, the islands were pulled out of earth's orbit by Aulura and Cebis."

Our two moons. One a soft lavender, the other a smaller, golden sphere.

"Right. Because what if the islands—"

"Kit, have you had any of the potato pies? They are a lot of work, but I made them because they're your favorite. Here, eat two." My mother bustled onto the porch and shoved a plate into my hands. The delicious scent of fried potato pie greeted me.

I smiled at her. "I had one earlier, Ma, with the full plate of food you fixed me."

"Well, eat some more, you must get your strength back." Ma put her hands on her hips and looked me over. My magenta top was almost the same color as her A-line dress. We had similar brown skin tones and the color looked good on both of us. She had a forest green headwrap wound around her kinky curls.

"Your thighs look smaller." She gave my bare thigh a little slap. To go with my cap-sleeved tank, I wore a flouncy, gold skirt.

"Ma," I groaned. "I wasn't in Elsewhere long enough to waste away, and there was decent food to eat. Doesn't Marrik look healthy? And he was there much long—"

I cut myself off and felt Marrik stiffen. Mixed emotions rose. I had Vanished Marrik. He'd been gone for a year before a blowback of my magic had reunited us in Elsewhere, a parallel world that could have been a paradise but was a hellish wasteland thanks to the powerful witch who'd created it and saved a portion of the ley lines.

Marrik and I were overjoyed to be reunited. But hoo boy were there complications between us. Where was the therapist who could help us work through one of us accidentally Vanishing the other?

"Yes well, you did come back with more muscles somehow." Ma squeezed Marrik's very toned bicep, right below a garish scar that cut across his dark skin.

"All that fighting and dangerous stuff you were doing," Ma continued.

Marrik ducked his head at her chastising tone.

"Though I suppose there was no choice." Ma looked from him to me. "Since that place was … was not safe." Her voice hitched and I saw pain flash across her expression.

It had been less than three weeks since Marrik and I had made it home and told everyone about Elsewhere. Paluna Montclair may have been the reason I'd ended up Vanishing myself, but she was also the reason Marrik and I had been able to make it home from halfway around the world. After two days in Tsunsama, the tiny island we'd ended up on after Elsewhere collapsed, Paluna had gotten us on a private flight and quietly brought us back to Sollunara.

And for good reason, as her husband would be very interested to come face to face with the witch who'd tried to Vanish him.

I shivered despite the warmth of the day. Ma and Marrik asked at the same time if I was okay.

"I'm fine, just a body tremor." A tremor that extended to my voice and wasn't missed by either of them. But I didn't want to talk about the inevitable hammer that was gonna drop when it came to the High Coven. I was about to say something to veer the conversation in another direction when Jiano did it for me.

"Would my darlings on the porch care to join us? We're about to get started!"

Marrik took my hand and offered the crook of his other arm to Ma, who tittered as we walked down the short flight of steps into the yard.

"Always such a gentleman," Ma said, patting his arm. "Eldrick!" Marrik and I startled at the sharp rise in her tone as she called out to my father. "Do pay attention, your ice cream is about to fall!"

Dad looked down in time to save his dollop of ice cream from meeting its demise on the grass.

"Gobble it up or I will, we've got to set the lanterns out," Ma said as she returned to Dad's side.

Dad was well acquainted with Ma's threats to eat treats right out of his hands, so he made quick work finishing his ice cream and sugar cone. Jiano and I shook our heads at our parents.

"Kitten." Jiano pulled me in for a hug. It wasn't a greeting, as I'd been at the bordello for hours already, but it was affection Jiano needed to give and I needed to feel. When Ji let go, my father clasped his hand around my forearm. A touch that said, *you're here, you're back.* Same as Ji's hugs and Ma's fussing.

The dark brown skin of Dad's forearms was graced by the cream and coral-colored scales of his Mutans creature; they appeared when he felt deep jolts of emotion. There were also scales across his brow, along with a ridge of four small, grayish-blue horns. They were absolutely adorable on the head of a muscular, middle-aged man. Dad had never been able to shapeshift horns before, so it was nice to see more of what his Mutans creature looked like after the surge strengthened his magic.

"First, let me say, everyone looks fantastic," Jiano started. "Showing out for the summer solstice, I know that's right!"

Everyone preened as Ji made a show of checking 'fits. Marrik and my father wore polo shirts, Dad with slacks, Mar with black jeans. Jiano's hair was pulled up in a sleek puff, they had neatly groomed facial hair around their jawline, and had done one of those cool eyeliner looks in white and yellow. Their strapless, citron dress with high side-slits looked lovely against the deeper brown their skin picked up during summer.

Rowan was stylish in white, high-waisted shorts and embellished crop top. Her stitch style braids were Ma's handiwork. Valentino was shirtless, as he liked to joke he was allergic to clothes, but wore loose, linen pants low on his hips that made him look photoshoot ready. All around there were colorful skirts and dresses, button downs with rolled up sleeves, and jewelry glinting in the sunlight. Calla, whose long, brown hair was braided over her shoulder, held a lacy parasol, which went nicely with her pinstriped romper.

We stood in a circle in the middle of the yard. Before Ji had called us off the porch, they and a few others had gathered the white paper lanterns we were going to release. Phinra had shyly suggested we decorate them, so we'd had an art session earlier, after which our efforts were praised or ribbed depending on the skill of the artist.

I'd stared at mine for a long time and hadn't known how to decorate it. Moments when my heart felt so heavy I didn't feel as though I could move came and went, and I hadn't been able to rally my mood while we were working on our lanterns. In the end all I could do was paint an italicized 'R' with as much flourish as I could manage.

R for Remi. Remington Glace. The ghost who'd helped us escape Elsewhere by sacrificing himself to destroy it. To extend his ghostly ability to decay anything he touched to its fullest, so not only Elsewhere and everything within it collapsed … so did he.

"Now, my darlings, as we celebrate the summer solstice, we have much to give to this joyous occasion." Jiano looked at me and I gave them a warning look.

"You said you wouldn't do speeches," I hissed. I had been wrapped up in love and relief from my family and friends for the last three weeks. I'd given thanks again and again that Marrik hadn't truly been Vanished from existence. But I didn't need to keep being the center of attention. Ji had promised!

"I say a lot of things, Kitten." Ji grinned and turned back to the others. My parents were smiling, but there was sadness in their eyes.

"Three weeks ago, when I saw Kit Vanish, I wanted the world to end," Ji started, their voice and face growing somber. "I wanted to wake up from the nightmare and I wanted to tear apart the person responsible for setting Kit on the path that took her from my family." Ji glanced at Ma and Dad.

"I still dunno how I feel about ole girl," Ji continued, meaning Paluna. "But all I wish to say, yet again, is how thankful I am that I have my sister back, and that Marrik is back as well."

Ji took my hand in a tight clasp. "The one hurt I could not heal was Marrik's loss. And the hurt no one could have healed for myself, Ma, and Dad, was being without you. But now those wounds have been cleansed and I do not have the words to express how much I am glad for it."

Their voice cracked. I squeezed their hand, feeling my throat grow tight.

"The moment I saw your face on that text message is the moment I came back to life, Kit. Now I know how it feels to lose you and I never want to feel that way again. I cannot endure it."

"Ji." I had known how my family would have felt thinking I was gone. It was the same pain I'd felt for Marrik. Pain I never wanted them to feel again. Nor myself.

"I never believed much in miracles," came Dad's even toned voice. Ji and I turned to him. He adjusted his glasses as he gave me a gentle smile. "I was never one to argue against an absolute, something I knew could not be changed no matter what I wished. But when Kit was gone ..." He stopped to clear his throat. Ma threaded her arm through his and rested her chin on his shoulder.

"When Kit was gone," Dad continued, "I wanted to push back. I wanted a miracle. I could not have had any ease for the rest of my days if you were gone for good. Could not have comforted your mother through the heartbreak of losing you. Could give no solace to the grief Jiano would carry without you. I didn't want to believe this was an absolute that could not be changed."

"And it wasn't." Ma wiped a tear. Tears brimmed in my eyes as well. Marrik put his arm around my shoulders and leaned his head against mine.

Dad nodded. "We got a miracle. I will be grateful always."

"Dad. Ma." I folded myself into my parents' arms. These moments took the edges off the shards of pain that felt embedded in my heart for all the things that had happened and those yet to

come. My parents hugged me tightly then let me go. When I'd first
fallen into their arms after stepping off the plane it was the first
time in my twenty-nine years I'd seen my father cry. I had wiped
tears from his cheeks and prayed I was never the reason for those
kinds of tears again.

"Well." Jiano clapped their hands. "Now that my family has
yet again made ourselves a spectacle of emotions, let us continue
with our little ceremony, yes? Everyone pick up your lantern."

We did, then resettled.

"It feels like an ending and a beginning." I hadn't meant to
speak but my emotions had welled up. "For a very long time
witches have been stunted from growing into our true power. The
higher abilities of our magic have been unreachable for centuries.
I hope that the rejuvenation of the ley lines can finally usher us
into a better place. That our generation can see our magic grow so
we can teach those who come after us. My heart is full of hope,
but there are shadows."

My voice wavered and I took a steadying breath. I looked at
the 'R' painted on my lantern. At my chest, Remi's amulet sat
against my skin under my top. He was no longer within it; I'd
tried several times to feed it a drop of blood off foolish hope, but
Remi never appeared.

"Marrik and I would not be here if it wasn't for Remi." What I
wouldn't give to hear one of Remi's flirty comments. To have him
whisk me around the room whether music was playing or not. To
listen to him talk back to the television at my apartment or pester
me about my cooking skills.

I wished I could have given Remi everything he wanted. Life.
Love.

"All the things I feel … they are still difficult to speak on,
especially when it comes to Remi. I want to tell the world about
him. About the beauty of his life, the tragedy of his death, about
how he still smiled through his existence as an amulet bound
ghost. Of the depth of emotion he carried within him. About how
brave he was in the end."

I pulled in a breath and let it out slowly. "I don't yet have the
words to do him justice. So for now I will release this lantern in

his memory and pray that he is finally at rest. Though my selfish heart wishes he were here."

There were sniffles all around and a few people wiped their eyes. I hadn't meant to plummet the mood, but I had scarcely been able to speak about Remi without wanting to fall apart. I needed, wanted, to honor his memory, his sacrifice, his love for me that had helped make sure Marrik and I made it home.

"For Remi," Ma whispered. "May he rest."

"That silly ghost," Jiano said affectionately. "How I will miss him."

"Remi," Calla whispered. She had adored Remi.

Arjun and Valentino lit the lanterns. The sun had finally bowed to the moons and early twilight wrapped us in soft shadows. The glow from the lanterns' light played against our faces as the mood lightened and we spread out to release them.

"Kit." Marrik kissed my temple. I knew he wished he could say the words to take my grief away but we both knew there weren't any.

"Ready to release your abstract art?" I put on a teasing tone to try and pull our moods up.

"Excuse me, this is a masterpiece, museum worthy!" Marrik said haughtily. His lantern was ... colorful. It was splattered with paint done in various brush strokes. Marrik was a skilled artist and had worked as a graphic designer. But I had to rib him that I didn't quite see the vision with his lantern.

I laughed. "Well, we should always be our own biggest fans, so yes, museum worthy, Mar." He gave me a little poke.

"Are you ready, darlings!" Jiano called. We chorused that we were, then lifted our arms and released the lanterns.

They looked beautiful as they floated away, their soft glow lighting up the yard. I kept my eyes on my lantern, on that letter 'R', as it drifted higher and higher.

I wished I could say it felt like a catharsis. Like I was letting go of Remi and would be on the path of healing, of growing around my pain. But I still felt tethered to him, like the chains of his amulet had wound around my heart. It was too soon; barely three weeks. I still couldn't believe he was gone.

I wanted a miracle. To push back against the absolute, like Dad had. I wanted what wasn't possible.

Marrik drew me against his chest. The lanterns looked like stars against the darkening sky.

"Do you want to—" Marrik was cut off by the sudden, blaring screech of a siren and the thunderous sound of a powerful engine. When the rumble sounded like it was right in front of the bordello, it cut off. Seconds later heavy footsteps pounded down the side path and I could barely give voice to my speculation that the hammer was dropping before people were pouring into the yard with weapons drawn.

They were dressed in black tactical gear from head to toe, with helmets, shields, and body armor like they were on the front lines of a battlefield as opposed to a yard full of witches who'd been picnicking.

"Kitaine Neris," came a booming voice. The beam of a flashlight swung in my direction.

Marrik made a growling sound and pushed me behind him. In front of me, Jiano was rooted, their body angled toward the officers.

"Kit!" My parents wrapped their arms around me.

"Don't worry," I whispered. "Paluna said don't worry." She'd said this exact situation was inevitable and I should brace for it, but she'd said not to worry.

But I was worried. My parents were worried. My sibling, boyfriend, and friends were worried.

No amount of hiding behind Marrik would help so I stepped into the light. My parents moved with me. Marrik tried to maintain his cover, but I stopped him.

"You raggedy sons of bitches how dare you step foot in my bordello's—"

"Ji." Jiano turned to me, rage and fear on their face. Rowan, Arjun, and Val looked ready to throw hands. Calla was shielding Phinra and Milene, who looked terrified.

"Don't worry," I said in a low voice. They were the only words I could offer because we all knew what was gonna happen next.

Several officers swarmed forward. Jiano was pushed out of the way and cursed. Marrik was shoved back and yelled. Two officers had to restrain him while three blocked my parents from reaching me. I was roughly grabbed, and my hands were pulled together with my palms flat against each other. Thick cord was wrapped around them.

"Kitaine Neris," came the steely voice of the officer who'd bound my hands. "You are under arrest for the attempted Vanishing of High Coven witch, Linton Gladstone."

I was marched out of the yard, down the side to the front where a behemoth of an armored vehicle was waiting, along with several military Jeeps.

My heart felt like it was trying to pound out of my ribcage. The shouts and screams of my friends and family echoed in my ears.

The hammer had dropped. They'd come for me. Paluna had warned me, but now that it was happening, I couldn't say my trust in her made me feel as though I would be sleeping in my own bed any time soon.

I was shoved into the armored vehicle and barely had a chance to turn my head and catch sight of Ji, my parents, and Marrik as they ran toward us.

"Kit! Kit!" Marrik sounded like he would tear the tank in half to get me out.

"Release my fucking sister!" Jiano yelled.

"Kit baby! Kit!" My mother's shrieks. Next to her, Dad was shouting, looking enraged.

But there was nothing they could do to save me. Nothing I could shout back to bring them any ease.

I looked up before the door slammed closed. The last thing I saw was a speck of orange from a lone lantern, high above.

Chapter Two

Pulling up to arrest me in a massive, armored vehicle was a tad overkill if you asked me. Though I guess I should be flattered the High Coven brought out the big guns to scoop me up. That must mean I was a code red, big baddie, final boss kinda deal.

The tank hit a pothole and the reverberation felt like my entire skeleton vibrated. My teeth clicked together as I jolted, though the very secure seatbelt kept me from knocking into my seatmate; one of the armor-clad enforcers who'd bagged my head shortly after we drove off. The cord wrapped around my hands was wreaking havoc on my blood circulation. I couldn't move them at all, and even if I tried to call up my magic all I'd end up doing was Vanishing myself since my palms were pressed together.

Been there, done that, didn't wanna go back.

Not that there was a 'back' to return to anyway. Elsewhere, the chaotic pocket world that had once dragged in anything that had been Vanished was gone. Now, using my magic would mean true disappearance. I had no desire to be on the receiving end of a Vanish blowback ever again.

Although maybe blipping out of existence would be better than whatever was in store for me now that I'd been captured for the very serious crime of trying to Vanish a High Coven witch.

I squirmed. I had to pee, inside the damn hood was sweltering, which made breathing difficult, and, oh yeah, I was scared out of my mind.

I'd spent the last three weeks feeling as though I was on the edge of a precipice and it was only a matter of time before I was knocked off. Now, I was falling, and I was terrified about where I would land. A few days after Marrik and I had returned to Vonuis, Paluna informed us that the micro-technology in Linton's Repel amulet had revealed that it had been activated at the bordello. Linton had been extremely drunk, but that didn't mean his memory was wiped, and his amulet's activation, along with what he remembered of that fateful night, had painted a damning picture with me front and center.

I'd wondered if Paluna would suggest she whisk me out of Sollunara and set me up with a new life and identity, but she hadn't. Not that I wanted to spend the rest of my life living in anonymity while the High Coven continued to try and sniff me out. I didn't want a prison cell either though, much as I was on my way to one right now.

I wasn't sure how long we'd been driving and that untethered sensation I'd had in Elsewhere, where'd it'd been dark with no way to track the passage of time, came over me, making me feel even more uncomfortable. None of the officers spoke, and the vehicle's insulation dampened noise from the outside, so I felt as though I was alone in a void. I tried to keep my breathing even and not slide into an anxiety attack, but my discomfort and fear were hard obstacles to overcome.

Once again I was in trouble, and once again there were people who cared about me left to worry.

We drove for so long I started to wonder if we'd left not just Vonuis, but Sollunara altogether. Eventually, the vehicle slowed down. After taking a few more turns it stopped, and seconds later I heard the door slide open and I was roughly pushed out. The hood remained on, so I was not-so-gently guided toward my destination.

They decided not to warn me about the steps, so I had a trippy good time up half a dozen steps before I was led into a building and the chill of an air-conditioner replaced the dewy humidity of outside.

After a short walk I was taken onto an elevator that headed down. And down, and down. Were we taking it all the way to hell? Would be a fitting place to face off against Gladstone. It stopped and I was ushered off. It was colder here, and though my sense of smell was dampened by the hood, a stale, musty odor was prevalent.

My journey came to an end when I heard a door open. I was pushed forward, then my arms were unbound. Before I had a chance to wonder why they'd unbind me, something was shoved onto my hands.

Gloves?

They were tight, and the interior felt as though they were lined with hundreds of tiny needles. A sensation I did not like at all spread through my body. After the gloves were on, my hands were wrapped in cord again.

So I couldn't remove the gloves. Wonderful.

The hood was finally yanked off and I was faced with three officers in the room and four beyond it. One of them pushed me back, as though to reiterate I was to stay put, before they filed out and the door slid closed.

That entire wall was glass, but as soon as the door closed, it went from clear, allowing me a view of the dismal hallway, to black.

I looked around. The small room was outfitted with everything you'd expect to find in a holding cell; an uncomfortable looking cot, and a metal toilet bowl attached to the wall, next to a small sink. There were no windows, but vents in the ceiling gave me the relief that I wouldn't suffocate. Two dim lightbulbs fixed to the gray walls were all that kept me from being in total darkness.

I lifted my hands. The gloves were white, made of some kind of synthetic material, with odd stitching that didn't follow normal seam lines. I'd never seen gloves like these, but it was pretty obvious what they were for.

I tried to call up my magic. Then gasped and stumbled back when my Vanish magic didn't respond. At all.

I'd expected the gloves to be a barrier against being able to Vanish anything. I hadn't expected them to null my ability to even access my magic.

Holy shit. The panic attack I'd been holding off slammed to the surface. What the hell kinda tech was this? I knew the High Coven had their toys and experiments, but they'd actually come up with magic suppressing gloves?

I dropped down on the cot, trembling as I tried again to awaken my magic. It didn't respond. I stared at my shaking hands and the awful gloves. My magic not responding felt hideously wretched. Never in my life had I been completely blocked from my magic.

Every time I tried to awaken my magic it felt like I was blowing into a balloon that wouldn't inflate. It was one of the most uncomfortable feelings I'd ever experienced and that was saying a lot given recent events.

My shoulders sagged as I slumped forward and made a sound of frustration.

I was yet again in a situation where I had to hope and pray someone else saved me. Where I had to trust someone else. Trusting Paluna had landed me in Elsewhere, and even though I had strengthened my Vanish magic there, in the end Remi had been the one to save me and it had cost him everything.

Now, I'd been arrested in front of Marrik, my family, and my friends, and I couldn't think of any way to save myself because the one resource I had was cut off from me.

I hated this. I'd used my magic to Vanish corrupt judges, murderous street enforcers, people who'd carve out your organs and sell them for profit, or slit your throat to help themselves to the goods on your truck. They were gone thanks to my magic, and my ability to plan a successful hit.

I needed a plan. But instead, I had to wait for a miracle.

Except that while I waited, I still needed to use the bathroom. I looked at the commode on the other side of the cell, then at my bound hands. And sighed. Maybe there was one thing I could do for myself, difficult though it might be. I got up and walked over to the toilet.

I managed to take care of business using moves that made me feel like a contortionist. I sat back down on the bed and looked at the blackout wall, wondering when they'd come back for me and what would happen next.

They knew I was a stronger Vanish Witch. Would they bleed me to death to use in their amulet experiments? I'd wondered if the ley lines regaining strength would cause the High Coven to back off from their witch killing, but Paluna had warned that it wouldn't be as simple as that. Beyond that she couldn't speculate what they would do; we'd have to wait and see. If Linton disappeared now, even if it wasn't by my hands, I would be the first one eyes fell on.

So Gladstone had to live. And I had to figure out how to stay alive too.

I lay down on the cot and stared up at the ceiling. It was so quiet in here the sound of my breathing was unnerving. One of the lightbulbs flickered and I prayed my only source of light held. They probably hoped these conditions would break me so I'd be nice and piteous when it was time to answer for my crimes.

Joke's on them though. This tiny, dark room sucked ass, but it was nothing compared to the hellhole Elsewhere had been. When Onyx, the powerful which who'd created Elsewhere, had shown Remi and I that she could have made it into a beautiful paradise, it made the dark, empty landscape full of unbound magic even more sinister. It was a fabricated wasteland, and it was scarier than anything I'd ever experienced.

This stupid little room wouldn't break me.

Enough time passed that I felt pangs of hunger even though I had eaten a lot at the bordello. I got up to use the toilet again, and after I'd been laying down for some time more, I started to doze.

It was probably late night or early morning by now. Might as well see what kind of rest I could get before the real fun began.

Oh great, I was even gonna dream of darkness.

It was one of those self-aware dreams, so I knew what I was experiencing wasn't real, but I was disappointed my subconscious had decided to chuck me into surroundings similar to the one I was resting not-so-comfortably in. It reminded me a lot of Elsewhere. Above, below, and all around me shadows stretched endlessly.

Everything was still and quiet. There was no hint of a wind and no sound I didn't make myself. I huffed and started walking for lack of anything else to do as long as the dream held.

"Kit."

I stopped. My eyes widened. I looked around, but nothing had changed in the landscape.

But I had heard that voice, hadn't I? It had sounded like—

"Kit."

"Remi?" My voice was a choked whisper. I had yet to dream of Remi. I'd wished I would, even though waking up to reality would have been bitter, but a dream would have at least been a temporary salve to the pain of losing him.

"Kit." Remi's voice was faint and strained. It made my heart ache to hear the sound of his voice again, even if it was in a dream.

"Remi, where—" I turned around and sucked in a gasp. A ghostly figure stood several feet away.

Remi.

My hands flew up to cover my mouth. Tears came to my eyes.

Remi looked the way he had the last time I saw him, like a desiccated corpse. He was emaciated, his brown skin ashen and dry, his eyes sunken in. His lips were thin and shriveled, and his once thick waves of dark hair were stringy and sparse. Even his clothes were rotted and hanging off him. He was moving from side to side as though he was nothing more than a tattered flag in the wind. When he saw me, something sparked in his eyes and his lips pulled as though he were trying to smile.

"Remi." Why did I have to dream of him like this? All it did was remind me of those final, horrific moments when Remi gave himself and his Wither magic over to the ley lines and could do nothing to stop himself from being affected by it.

This wasn't a dream; it was a nightmare. I could hear the noise of Elsewhere falling apart, hear my screams as I begged Remi to stop. Remembered the way he'd kissed me before he'd pulled his hand from mine and unleashed his magic.

I ran to him. He reached for me and I reached back. His hand was thin and brittle. It felt like the slightest pressure would collapse him into dust.

"Remi." It was just a dream, but it felt so real.

I saw his throat work and his lips shift as he tried to speak.

"Kit … I am …" He stopped, his face contorting as he wheezed, as though those three words had cost him everything to say.

"Remi, oh Remi." I stepped closer, making my hold on his hand a bit firmer. "I'm so sorry, Remi. I—"

I wanted to say so much. I wanted to apologize, to hug him, to cry, to beg the universe to bring him back because he deserved so much better than the existence he'd had.

"Kit … tell you …" His face looked so pained. I raised my other hand and cupped his cheek.

"I … am … I am …"

It was difficult for him to speak. His ghost was so translucent I could see through him. Ghosts weren't supposed to be able to feel anything since they no longer had nerves, but Remi looked like he was in agony, and I wanted to give him some ease, even within a dream.

Maybe this would be the catharsis I needed; speaking to Remi in my dreams, trying to convey … to convey … Shit, I didn't even know what.

"I'm here, Remi. And I want you to know I miss you, all the time. There's no one to accidentally Wither my office plants or tell me I'm being reckless going after my marks."

Well, there was Marrik, but Remi had always stood by me amid the danger, even though I could have left his amulet behind when I went out Vanishing scum. He told me he'd rather be with me even if he had to be confined in the amulet. When I'd ended up in Elsewhere, having Remi there helped me fare better than I would have without him.

"Kit … lis …ten …" I frowned, finally realizing he was trying to tell me something.

"I am …"

My vision started to waver. Was I waking up? Damn it, no, I didn't want to wake up yet!

"Kit …" Remi sounded desperate. He reached up and I felt the cold touch of his bony hand on my collarbone.

"Remi!"

My eyes flew open and I sucked in a breath, my vision settling on the dark ceiling of the holding cell. I sat up and looked around. Goosebumps covered my arms, and it wasn't just from the chill of the dank room.

I blinked as my eyes adjusted to the dim light. One of the lightbulbs had blown. Wonderful.

That dream had felt so real even though I wished it hadn't presented Remi to me like that. I wanted to see him whole, to see that roguish smile and have him quip at me the way he used to.

It had been good to see him. But it had also been awful.

I sighed and raised my bound hands to where his amulet lay against my chest.

I wished he was still …

I shook my head, trying to steer myself away from dead end thoughts I'd already spiraled through. I had fed the amulet blood more than a dozen times. Remi hadn't emerged.

But …

A gift, may you one day know how to use it.

Onyx had said that right after she'd touched Remi and he'd fragmented into motes of light around her hand. Then she'd touched Remi's amulet and held her hand against my cheek with her other hand.

I had felt something in that moment, but I couldn't understand what. Didn't know what Onyx had done to Remi or to me.

But she had done *something*, which was why I'd tried in vain to see if there was anything of Remi left in the amulet despite what I'd seen with my own eyes.

That frustrated feeling rose, tangled around the tiniest spark of hope. But hope for what?

I needed to figure out if Remi was truly gone. Because if he wasn't … if there were remnants of his ghost left—

A sound jolted me out of my thoughts and I turned to see the glass shift back to transparent as the door opened and five task force officers filed in. I stood up and steeled myself as one of them grabbed my upper arm and pulled me forward.

All this rough treatment was overkill, especially since I couldn't use my magic. But people with a power complex loved to go the extra unnecessary mile.

My head wasn't bagged this time, so I was able to appreciate the dismal view of the hallway. My emotions were somersaulting as I flitted through various scenarios that could await me. None of them were good, and all of them ended with me either back in that room or on a metal table waiting for my blood to be drained.

I was herded onto the elevator for the long ride back up. All the calming breaths in the world or hints that Paluna had a way out of this couldn't stop the anxiety and fear that had clamped onto me.

It was time to face the music for attempting to Vanish Linton Gladstone.

Chapter Three

As far as interrogation rooms went, this was one of the nicer ones. Not that I'd seen the inside of a lot of interrogation rooms, but the media always made them out to be small and musty, with a two-sided mirror and a good cop, bad cop duo to run their game in making you talk.

The one I was marched into had the typical table and chairs, but it was a wide, clean table and a cushioned chair in a room that didn't have any two-sided mirrors as far as I could tell. Unless some advanced tech was being employed. And well, given the magic suppression gloves I was wearing, there very well could be.

There were windows along the wall, but the blinds were drawn so I couldn't see out. The room was brightly lit by fluorescent fixtures on the ceiling. There were a couple plotted plants near the windows, and a table along the back wall was neatly arranged with books and knickknacks. The walls were covered in wallpaper with an abstract pattern, and the floor had the flat carpeting you'd find in office suites.

I was pushed onto a chair, then the task force officers filed out. I raised an eyebrow as I watched them leave. I'd expected at least a couple to remain.

That probably meant this nondescript room wasn't one I had any hope of escaping. Not through those windows and certainly not through the door. But I wasn't stupid enough to try and bolt when my hands were bound and my magic unusable.

All I could do was wait. So I slumped in the chair, looked around the boring room, and waited.

Eventually, I started counting in my head. It was a better train for my thoughts than my current predicament or the unsettling dream I'd had of Remi and my lingering thoughts about exactly what had happened to him in Elsewhere's final moments. I could hear the echo of him calling my name, a soft, strained voice in the back of my mind. The way he'd sounded and the way he'd looked kept bringing tears to my eyes.

I had almost counted to two thousand when the door opened and three people walked in.

Leading the way was Linton Gladstone.

It felt like a hundred years had passed since I'd been the object of his drunken attention at the bordello with my sights set on Vanishing him. He was a slender white man in his fifties with a forgettable face and graying hair above a high forehead, dressed in an expensive suit and shoes. His watery blue eyes were cunning though. Linton might not look like he had much presence, but the fact that he'd spearheaded a program that killed witches so their magic could be given to other witches made it clear how much influence he had as one of the seven members of the High Coven's council. There was no way I'd believe Gladstone was running those experiments without the other council members knowing. Which meant our witch leaders were festering with corruption. And that was very, very bad.

The urge to Vanish Gladstone was still there despite everything that had happened. He was despicable and I wished he didn't exist. Him and every single person aligned with him.

My hands strained in their snug prison as I watched Gladstone and the other two people approach. One of them was a heavy-set Black woman who looked a few years older than me and was dressed in a black skirt suit. Her eyes were a bit too wide, and she kept brushing aside the bangs of her shoulder-length wig in what seemed like a nervous gesture. The other person was a Hispanic man about Linton's age with a severe expression and long hair pulled back at the nape of his neck.

"Good morning," Linton said pleasantly, as though we'd met up for a leisurely brunch. At least I'd gotten some sense of the time of day. Even though I could see daylight through the blinds I hadn't been sure if it was morning or afternoon.

I didn't reply to Linton's greeting. He pulled a chair out and sat opposite me, clasping his hands in front of him. The fake little smile never left his face. I gave him back nothing but resting bitch face.

"Kitaine Neris," he began. "We finally meet again."

"Gonna try to get in my pants like last time?" I felt a touch of satisfaction when his smile momentarily slipped and the people behind him shifted uncomfortably.

"I'm happy to do whatever you want, I'm here to please." I mimicked the words he'd spoken in the Garnet Room at the bordello.

The man cleared his throat while the woman's eyes went wider.

Linton's expression could cut glass. "Are you aware of the dire circumstances you're under, Ms. Neris? You do understand why you're here, don't you?"

"Couldn't be for the lovely views given I haven't seen so much as a sun beam since I was dragged here." I made a show of raising my bound, gloved hands to tap my chin. "Couldn't be for a magic workshop seeing as I'm tied up and cut off from my magic. Gosh, why am I here? What could the reason be?"

The skin around Gladstone's eyes tightened. I was sure he'd been expecting me to cower. To whimper and beg for my freedom. But I'd be damned if I let these people see my fear. In Elsewhere I'd almost had my eyes carved out by a criminal I'd Vanished. Had my back shredded and my kneecaps fractured by people seeking vengeance against me. Had dodged the meaty fist of a terrifying underground fighter, and the sharp blade of a sickle that had been thirsty for my blood. And I'd survived.

Linton had a high hill to climb to get a visible reaction from me.

"Dario." He raised his hand and made a beckoning motion. Dario stepped forward and laid the item he'd been holding, a large tablet in a black case, on the table. After some rapid finger movements over the screen, Gladstone propped the tablet up and turned it to me.

My eyes widened when I saw the playback of Linton and I in the Garnet Room. I couldn't help the lurch in my stomach as I watched us getting cozy. He put a hand on my thigh, and I put my hand on top of his. I saw my magic emerge; curls of dark blue smoke wafted around my hands.

Then there was a bright flash when my attempt to push my magic into him activated the repel magic in the amulet he'd been wearing. When the light was gone, so was I. Linton had fallen forward onto the couch and was staring at the spot I'd been sitting.

I slid my eyes back to Gladstone as he gave the tablet to Dario. I had seen this video before, after wearing Jiano down, who hadn't wanted me to watch it. They'd wanted to scrub the video, but Paluna had told them not to because we didn't want to add a tampering charge on top of what they'd be coming at me with. We'd had no choice but to leave the footage alone with the knowledge that the High Coven would swipe it.

They hadn't needed to rely solely on Linton's memory and the tech in the amulet. They had cold, hard proof I had tried to Vanish him.

"Where did you end up, Ms. Neris?" Gladstone's question drew me out of my thoughts. His hands were steepled in front of him as he stared at me as though he could compel answers from me.

"It is clear that your magic returned to you and that you Vanished," he continued. "You were not traceable for several days, then suddenly you resurfaced. In the company of a man who'd been registered as missing over a year ago, no less." His eyes narrowed. "What effect did your Vanish magic have on you?"

I wasn't surprised at his inquiry. Of course he'd want to know what happened when all along we thought Vanishing something wiped it from existence. And to be fair, that was how Vanish magic was supposed to work. The only reason things changed was because the ley lines Onyx had saved in Elsewhere dragged in anything that was Vanished. Some kind of transference as opposed to true disappearance.

But I wasn't gonna explain shit about Elsewhere to Gladstone, so I merely blinked at him.

His eyes narrowed further as he lowered his hands and leaned back.

"How intriguing you are, Ms. Neris. I suppose it is of no consequence whether you explain yourself or not. I shall be well informed very soon."

The woman shifted at those words and my eyes flicked to her. If I had to guess, she was a Memoria Witch and Gladstone planned to make her read my memories. There were several issues with that. For one, it was unethical to read someone's memories against their will. The laws about memory reading were so rigid even Gladstone wouldn't escape consequences. Which he clearly didn't give a flying fuck about.

But if my memories were read, the gig would be up with Paluna and the subterfuge she'd been executing against her husband. He would find out everything.

Plus, reading my memories could reveal how many people I'd Vanished. Even though I'd gone after criminals and a lot of things had improved once those people were gone, I'd still broken the law by using my Vanish magic on people.

Attempting to Vanish Gladstone would only be the first item on my list of charges.

I tried not to squirm. That woman was less than ten feet away. I did not want her to dive into my mind and tell Linton things he didn't even know he'd want to find out.

"The attempt against my life is a grave crime that will carry a severe sentence," Linton said. He sounded like he would savor my punishment like it was a finely aged wine.

"You were not operating alone; this I am certain of. I am deeply interested in learning who you are aligned with and why you decided to Vanish me."

He wasn't gonna ask me to name names. Not when his Memoria Witch could snatch it from my mind.

A clammy sweat clung to me. My hands felt like they were melting inside these damn gloves. I didn't want anyone inside my head. I wasn't gonna be the only one incriminated.

"You took an unfortunate gamble." Linton's voice dropped to a menacing whisper. He turned his head and nodded.

"Tarena, if you could please proceed."

Tarena hesitated but started forward.

Shit. Should I get up and run? That would only stall things. There was no way I could escape this building on my own. Tarena looked uneasy as she approached. I was sure she understood how wrong this was, that she could face felony charges for doing it, but under Gladstone's command she could do nothing but obey.

"Wait, listen—"

I was cut off by loud, rapid knocks on the door followed by someone bustling in. A brown-haired woman in a gray suit rushed forward with her arm extended, a phone in her hand.

I glanced at Gladstone. He was watching her with a disdainful look. The woman stopped at the table and thrust the phone at him.

"Gizelle—"

"Sir, I would not interrupt except for circumstances of utmost importance." Gizelle was breathing heavily as though she'd run from very far to get to this room. She glanced at me before returning her gaze to Gladstone.

"You must take this call, sir," Gizelle pressed. Her green eyes were wide and frantic. Gladstone's eyes narrowed as he took the phone. He glanced at the screen, but something told me there was no number he could read. He lifted the phone to his ear.

"Yes?" A short, clipped word. His eyes settled on me once again.

Silence fell. Gizelle straightened and stepped back but kept her attention on Gladstone. Dario and Tarena exchanged hesitant looks.

As for me ... I was cautiously hopeful that this phone call would see me in my own bed tonight.

As Linton listened, I watched his eyes widen and his mouth fall open slightly. A twist of triumph eased the knot of tension that felt like a brick in my belly.

"I see." His tone was frigid. I resisted the urge to ease a smug little smile on my face as I watched Linton come to the realization that he was no longer in control of this little show.

"Your meaning is clear." If looks could kill I'd be cold and stiff. He lowered his arm and placed the phone on the table. Gizelle took a step forward and reached for it, then pulled back as though she wasn't sure she was allowed to retrieve her own phone.

It was so quiet I felt as though I could hear ghosts whispering from the Afterlife. The seconds stretched. My heart was a frantic beat in my chest. Dario and Tarena looked as though this event had veered way off script and they were out of a plane with no parachute.

Finally, Linton spoke. He cleared his throat, adjusted his tie needlessly, then pushed away from the table and stood up. His skin was flushed, and there was a tremble to his jaw.

This man was pissed to the high heavens. And scared.

"Ms. Neris will be allowed to go free with no further interference."

There were shocked gasps at those words. Gizelle was the only one who didn't look as though Linton's head had flown off his neck.

"Sir ...?" Dario took a step forward and angled his body to get a better look at Linton's face.

"Are you sure?" Tarena ventured. "I mean, she did—"

"Did you or did you not hear me?" Linton's tone rose sharply.

My hopeful feeling grew as I stood up. The flush on Linton's face darkened.

"Take her outside and release her."

"That must have been an interesting phone call." I couldn't help but poke the bear a bit.

"You are playing a very dangerous game, Ms. Neris," Gladstone growled. "But you should remember that on this board you are a pawn amid giants."

I smiled as Gizelle beckoned me to follow her.

"Pawns have been known to capture kings," I said slyly. I turned and followed the trio out of the room without looking at Gladstone again.

Was I as confident as I sounded? No. But I was gonna walk outta here like I was. I might be little more than a wisp of paper skirting a raging fire when it came to Gladstone and the High Coven, but the look on his face after that call let me know that the pawn had made a move that caused all the other game pieces to pause and reconsider.

Let's see if I could pull off a checkmate.

Chapter Four

I was walked out of the building with no incident. We passed by task force officers and various people who looked at me curiously but said nothing. My three escorts had formed a triangle around me. I chose to feel like a V.I.P instead of a criminal, if only to distract my thoughts with nonsense as I was taken onto an elevator to the first floor.

Everything that I could see of this place was nondescript; gray walls, flat carpeting, and dingy hallways lined with closed doors. It had the feel of an abandoned building that had been cleaned up enough to make it usable. Something told me there was no map that would show its location.

Relief flooded me when we finally stepped outside. Gizelle unwound the cord binding my hands. I waited to see if she'd retrieve the gloves as well, but all she did was step back and give me a curt nod.

I raised my hands and looked at them expectantly.

"You may keep those," Tarena said, barely making eye contact.

That punched a laugh out of me. I peeled the detestable gloves off and held them up.

"Are they supposed to be a gift? Gloves that suppress my magic? No thanks. Here you go."

"The High Coven wishes you to remain in possession of those gloves," Dario said. I could tell that my interrogation not going according to plan had thrown them off. All of them took steps back once my hands were free of the gloves.

"Your dealings with the High Coven are not over," he continued. "You are a classified high level Vanish Witch and though certain … circumstances may go down another path, you are now on the High Coven's watch list. Those gloves are new technology and though we cannot enforce that you wear them … yet," he flashed a thin smile, "you are to keep them in your possession and are to remain aware that they can be tracked so discarding them will be noted."

And why would I give two shits if they found out I tossed them? But I didn't say that. They needed a win, so I'd let them have one. I bunched the gloves in my fist, treating them with all the respect they deserved.

"Noted." I glanced at them, committing their faces to memory. "Well then, do enjoy the rest of your day. It's such lovely weather, maybe you can do a picnic lunch."

I walked away. I'd exited into a fenced-in parking lot with several of the task force's vehicles. A narrow, unpaved road was to the right, against a dense tree line.

I for damn sure wasn't gonna get a ride outta here. And my phone had been left at the bordello since I hadn't had my bag when I'd gotten nabbed. But my anxiety about how the hell I was gonna get home eased when I stepped onto the road and saw a car some ways down pull away from the curb and drive up.

It was my car. I almost collapsed with relief.

The car stopped a few feet away and Marrik emerged. He ran around and pulled me into his arms in a crushing hold that still wasn't tight enough.

A sob clawed up my throat as I clung to him, my face pressed against his chest, breathing him in, the woodsy scent of his cologne wrapping around me. He was warm and solid, and I finally felt grounded again.

"Kit, you're okay. Oh God." He sounded relieved, but there was an undertone of searing anger that I knew wasn't directed at me. He pulled back and looked me over.

"I mean, are you okay? Did they hurt you?" He was looking at me the way he'd looked at me when we'd been reunited in Elsewhere and he'd finally accepted that I wasn't a figment of his imagination compelled by Memoria magic.

"I was so fucking worried." He bent his head and kissed me, his lips molding to mine as his arms kept me pressed against him.

"I'm physically unharmed," I assured him when the kiss broke. "I just need to get proper circulation back to my hands." They were sore, numb, and almost as cold as a corpse's. Marrik took my hands and rubbed them. I shuddered at how good it felt to have his warm hands wrapped around them.

"Let's get the hell out of here," he said. That sounded like a fantastic idea. I was exhausted. Whatever sleep I'd gotten had been restless. So much had happened in so short of a time I felt as though I'd been spinning inside a cyclone.

We got in the car, and after Marrik had driven off he navigated with one hand and laced his fingers through mine with the other. Once I could no longer see that ugly building behind us, my brave façade finally cracked.

I cried. Sobs shook my body, and for a while I could do nothing but succumb to the feelings that propelled the tears. Fear, anxiety, shock, confusion, uncertainty. Linton Gladstone was a big dog and he'd been about to crush me. I'd gotten away for now, but my dealings with the High Coven were far from over.

Marrik made soothing noises and thumbed the back of my hand as I released my pent up emotions.

Finally, I calmed, and opened the glove compartment for the stash of supplies I kept there. I utilized some face wipes then slumped in my seat and dropped my head back.

"Something for you to eat in the back," Marrik said, giving my hand a squeeze.

Food! My hunger and thirst crashed over me. I grabbed the paper bag from the back seat. In it was a container of food from my favorite Tropical restaurant along with two bottles of water. I drained one of the bottles before I turned my attention to the food.

Rice cooked up with pigeon peas, stewed chicken, fried plantains, and baked macaroni and cheese. I ate mouthfuls and sighed contentedly.

"The best food comes from the Tropical islands," I said. "You're my savior, Mar. I haven't eaten or drank anything since I've been there."

"Those bastards took you over twelve hours ago." Which meant it was Sunday morning. I continued eating, feeling so much better once the edge was taken off my hunger.

After I was done, I cleaned up with some more wipes and put my trash on the ground between my feet. I then told Marrik everything that had happened since I'd been taken.

"He almost got into my head." I turned to Marrik. We were at a stop sign, and he'd linked hands with me again. "He was gonna have a Memoria Witch dive in and he would have found out everything about the plan to Vanish him. Paluna's goose woulda been cooked alongside mine."

Marrik shook his head as he returned his attention to the road and started driving again.

"Her call happened just in time then."

"She threatened to expose his experiments, didn't she?" That would have been the only thing she could have used against Gladstone that would guarantee my release.

Marrik nodded. "She called Jiano on an untraceable line after you were taken. We were all far from calm, but she sounded confident that she could get you out before anything dire happened. She said the best way for things to go would have been for you to get arrested."

"But this could have gone differently if they'd used Memoria magic on me as soon as I got there." I frowned. "Paluna probably guessed a Memoria Witch would have been in play, but she couldn't have known when Gladstone would have them access my memories."

"Which was why she ran interference. Apparently, that building is a secret outpost that's only occupied when it needs to be. Paluna says Gladstone moves carefully; you were nabbed first, and everyone else was set to arrive after you were secured. Her team monitored who Gladstone was mobilizing there and she disabled their vehicles, which brought you and her some time. She needed to make sure everything was in place to back up her threats after she made the call."

"That woman thinks a hundred steps ahead," I muttered. "I'm so damn relieved."

"She told me where to go to pick you up and what time to come. They took you all the way to Hanceoh."

"Damn, we're that far up north?" Hanceoh was over two hours away from Vonuis and was mostly farmland and forests. The woods and single road had lasted for a while, but we were now driving through a more residential area though the lots were big and the houses far apart. We'd driven past several corn fields; the most bountiful crop grown here.

"Yeah. Paluna has further plans, but she said she will tell us about them once you're back."

"She really is something else." My feelings about Paluna were complex. I was struggling with how resourceful and capable she was versus how getting tangled up in her crusade against her husband had caused me to Vanish. And if it wasn't for Elsewhere, I would have been gone for good.

But I was the one who said yes. I could blame Paluna, but I had chosen to work with her despite the risks. I was the one who'd trusted her and hadn't considered that Gladstone might have been wearing one of his experimental amulets.

And if I hadn't Vanished, I wouldn't have gotten Marrik back.

And wouldn't have lost Remi.

Why was everything so damn complicated? Everywhere in my life there were layers to peel back. Paluna was an ally on thin ice, Marrik was back in my arms but there was a tightrope beneath us and we might lose our balance. My parents and sibling had experienced traumatic grief because of my decision making, and my oldest friend, who'd had a brief life with a beating heart and tormented centuries without one, was no longer with me.

I wrapped my free hand around Remi's amulet as fresh tears fell. What could I make of my life now? What was I supposed to do?

"Kit, hey, talk to me," came Marrik's gentle voice.

"Where do I go from here, Mar? I—" Yelped as a chirping sound rang out, then realized it was Marrik's phone, which was in the console between our seats. He let go of my hand long enough to nudge the screen so he could see it, then his expression tightened as he regained my hand and focused on the road again.

"Who was it?"

He sighed. "Namira."

"Oh." My stomach felt like a ship was sinking within it. Namira was Marrik's cousin, one of the few members of his family he'd kept up with since a lot of them, including his parents, were in deep with an anti-witch organization. He had a close relationship with Namira but hadn't told her we were dating to make sure information didn't make it back to the haters among his people. A few weeks ago, Namira had sussed me out and confronted me at my coven house, accusing me of Vanishing Marrik and letting me know she'd put me on the High Coven's radar.

Namira pinging me to the High Coven had been enough for them to send a grab team after me. If I hadn't Vanished my assailants, I would have ended up bled dry for my stronger magic. After that close call I'd decided to work with Paluna to start toppling the experimental program by Vanishing Gladstone.

"She wants to meet up," Marrik said. He'd reached out to Namira some days after we'd gotten back. When he'd gone to his apartment building the very shocked superintendent had told him that his stuff had been packed up in storage by his family and his apartment leased to someone else. Namira was the one who'd stored his stuff, so he'd contacted her. She'd been overjoyed to hear from him, and they'd met up at the storage unit, but because Paluna wanted us to keep the story of Elsewhere close to the chest, Marrik had been withholding the truth of where he'd been.

But Namira was no fool and she wanted answers. She'd been calling and texting a lot. Marrik was staying with me, and I was sure if she knew where I lived she'd have popped up.

"She wants ..." Marrik cleared his throat and shifted in his seat. "She wants to have dinner with me," he continued, "and you."

"Ohhhh ..."

Marrik gave me an apologetic look. "I'm gonna tell her it's not the best time. With everything you have going on, you don't need this right now."

I chewed my lip as I thought that over. I did have an overflowing plate, but I wasn't the only one. Marrik had been in Elsewhere longer than I had, and I could see how difficult it was adjusting back. He'd spent most of his time in Elsewhere fighting the worst criminals our world had ever seen in a dark, desolate world full of dangerous magic waves. He hadn't even known where he'd ended up or if he'd ever get out. He was a year out from his life and couldn't transition back like nothing had happened. He'd lost his apartment, his freelance work, and he had friends and family other than Namira who'd want to hear from him.

Marrik was under as much stress as I was, if not more, but he was putting me first. But he was struggling. I could see it whenever he spoke or messaged Namira. How difficult it was to continue keeping her at arm's length when she'd been grieving him all this time.

I sighed. Deflecting her wouldn't push anything in a better direction. We had to face her and deal with whatever came. Marrik and I were still trying to grapple with the complications within our relationship, but our relationship wasn't the only one that needed attention.

"Call her and set dinner up."

Marrik glanced at me, looking surprised, but I could also see some relief there.

"Are you sure? I can—"

"My problems don't deserve more attention than yours. Namira is one of the few family members you're close to and she should get the answers she wants. I saw her pain when she confronted me. She spent a year trying to piece together what happened to you. And now you're back and you've been making her beat against a closed door because you're trying to protect me. And I love you for that. But I need to face Namira and we need to have everything out in the open. I want her to heal, and I want you to have her back in your life. Its murky waters but we'll navigate it."

He was quiet for a while. Finally, he lifted our hands and planted a kiss on the back of mine. An electric feeling fizzled in my belly, same as it always did from Marrik's touch.

"Thank you," he whispered, his lips brushing my skin before he lowered our hands.

"Of course." I was a twisted-up knot of nerves and trepidation at the idea of facing Namira and laying the story of Elsewhere out for her, but it needed to happen.

At least she couldn't threaten me with the High Coven again.

Those bastards already had my number.

I was having far too many tearful reunions with my family. I really had to stop putting them through a cycle of losing me then getting me back.

After a very long car ride, Marrik and I arrived back at Kiss and Hex and I'd been delivered into the waiting arms of my parents and Jiano, who'd done an outstanding job of expressing their relief while cussing the High Coven, with especially heated words for Linton Gladstone. Even my father, who wasn't much for swearing, dropped a few f-bombs.

After I'd been hugged to lengths that restricted circulation, I'd gone up to Jiano's room on the third floor to shower and change. I kept a drawer in Jiano's dresser, same as they had at my apartment, and changed into a slouchy T-shirt and denim shorts, pulling my freshly washed hair into a ponytail. Remi's amulet remained around my neck.

As for those terrible magic suppressing gloves … I'd been tempted to wreck them and toss them, but decided I didn't need another reason for the High Coven to reach out to me. I rolled them up and stuffed them into my purse, which had been waiting for me in Ji's room. I slung the small bag over my chest.

I stood in front of the ornate mirror that graced Ji's antique dresser and stared at my reflection. Physically, I hadn't changed; I'd been banged up quite a bit in Elsewhere, but I was healed now, mostly thanks to Regen magic Onyx had put into a pool of water Marrik and I soaked in. But I hadn't slept well since we'd been back, not to mention the less than restful night I'd just had, and my face showed it. Even when I smiled, I looked tired.

I looked haunted, grieved. Sometimes I felt as though I still had one foot in Elsewhere even though the contrast between that pocket world and the world I lived in was so vast it felt like Elsewhere had been one long, lucid nightmare.

One I wished I could wake up from. Especially since Remi was gone.

I touched the amulet. That dream …

"Remi, are you really gone?"

A knock came at the door. When I answered, my mother entered and flashed a smile as she came over.

"Can I do your hair?" Ma had taught Jiano and I a lot of hairstyle skills, but we weren't anywhere as good as she was.

"I don't think we have time? We're supposed to rendezvous with Paluna soon."

"I'll do something quick, two French braids?"

"Alright, thanks." We gathered some of Ji's hair products then I sat on the floor between Ma's knees while she sat on the plush stool in front of the dresser. Ma undid my ponytail and did a more thorough job than I did of adding leave-in conditioner, curl cream, and detangling my thick hair.

Tears rose as I felt Ma's hands work through my hair. There was a time in my life when my mother combing my hair was an everyday occurrence, nothing to get choked up about. But now, after Elsewhere, and after I'd kept her at a distance during the year Marrik had been Vanished, this moment of being under her care hit differently.

"I'm sorry, Ma." I sniffled and wiped my eyes.

"Whatever for, Kit baby?" The slender tip of the comb glided down the center of my head as she parted it to start the French braids.

"For keeping you away. After I Vanished Marrik I kept telling you not to come. And I wouldn't answer your calls most of the time. I knew how worried you and Dad were and I locked you out."

"We understood," she said gently. "Our presence might have been smothering, though not by intent. We were so pained for you."

"I know." I released a sigh. "It was denial. That was the only reason. If I allowed you to come, it would be acknowledging that it had happened and there were so many days where I could only get through by denying my grief. If you came, we'd have to talk about it. I'd have to lay in your arms and cry. I'd have no choice but to admit Marrik was gone and my parents were here to try and comfort me through it."

"And we knew that," Ma said. "Which was why I stopped pushing you. You don't have to apologize, Kit baby. We do what we can in those moments. We make the choices that bring us even the smallest amount of relief from the pain. You do not need to be held accountable for how you handled Marrik's disappearance."

Loving acceptance and understanding. My parents had always been that way. And all I could do was be grateful they were the kind of people they were.

"I missed you," I said. "I feel terrible that I kept you away only to Vanish and make you, Dad, and Ji endure that."

"We endure many things in life, don't we?" One braid was done, and she started on the other. "Joy, anger, sorrow, excitement. That's what it means to live, I think. We cannot create situations that always go according to how we wish them to. Where we only experience joy and safety. We can only accept the things that happen and handle them as best we can. Revel in the high moments and overcome the low ones.

"Yes, we did lose you, and I wanted to die, I won't mince my words on that. But," she lowered her hand and squeezed my shoulder before moving it back to my hair, "you came back. Marrik came back. And it has shown me what can emerge from the darkest, most painful moments. So now we rejoice and look ahead. And we stay as close as we can. Perhaps Dad and I will buy a home here, do you think they will sell us the rental?"

"Maybe not, but I'm sure you can find something." I wiped the tears her words had brought forth. After I returned, my parents extended their stay indefinitely, so Jiano had found them a house to rent that was walking distance from the bordello.

"All done," Ma announced. I stood up and looked in the mirror, turning my head to admire her handiwork.

"Thanks, Ma." I put my arm around her and squeezed.

"I tell you the Hexes have been putting me to work." Ma pursed her lips as we put the hair products away. "All of a sudden no one remembers how to braid their hair so they can put on their wig caps!"

I laughed. "Selective memory. When someone with magic fingers comes around, they can't help but forget how to do it themselves."

"I suppose that must be it." Ma was smiling. She adored the fact that everyone wanted her to do their hair. She'd braided Arjun's waist length hair in an intricate style last week. When he'd undone it a couple days ago his hair had retained a nice wave and he joked that his clients had fallen even more in love with him.

We made our way downstairs, to Jiano's office at the end of the hallway near the back door. Since it was Sunday, the bordello was closed to customers and the Hexes were scarce, enjoying their day off. Dad and Marrik were in Ji's office. Leftovers from the picnic were on the coffee table. Ma immediately put a plate of food in my hands.

"Thanks, Ma." I was no longer so hungry it felt like my stomach was eating itself, thanks to the food Marrik had brought for me, but I obliged Ma by nibbling one of the potato pies. Dad nodded approvingly. Jiano and Marrik stood next to each other with their arms crossed and expressions like they were ready to go to war.

"Twins," I commented, glancing between them. Jiano raised a sculpted eyebrow and glanced at Marrik, taking note of their similar stance. Their lips quirked.

"How are you feeling? Are you tired of being asked that?" Ji gave me a scrutinizing look. They were dressed in harem pants and a T-shirt, their hair pulled up in a puff.

"What's one more traumatic event." I waved my hand. My father made a choking sound. "Sorry." I put the plate down. Ma frowned and I patted her on the shoulder.

"When do we get to hear the rest of Paluna's plan?"

"Now," Jiano replied. "She called a short time ago. We are gonna shadow travel to her little spy chamber. Ma, Dad," Jiano gave them a stern look, "you wish to come, as you've made clear. But we know that the High Coven has the bordello under surveillance, and we need to maintain a front when it comes to our dealings with Paluna. It will also be preferable not to have too many people acquainted with her operation. The less you know, the less can be read from your mind should the High Coven decide to do the most. So please, stay here. Take a cold beverage and hang out in the yard. Don't give watching eyes a reason to think we're up to somethin'. Hold things down here please?"

Ma looked like she wanted to do anything but put on a front of normalcy for watching eyes, but I got the sense she and Dad had had this conversation with Jiano enough times for Ji to have worn them down.

"Very well," Ma said. Dad nodded, though he didn't look happy. "Don't be gone too long though. You leave us in the dark and we're gonna come looking for you."

"Can track much better now," Dad said, crossing his arms. I resisted the urge to comment that he, Ji, and Mar were triplets.

Dad's Mutans creature was a tracker and his senses had been enhanced off the ley line surge. I had no doubt he would attempt to sniff us out.

"We will be safe and we will be back soon," Jiano assured. I gave my parents hugs, took two more bites of food to placate Ma, then Marrik and I followed Jiano into the bathroom.

"Continues to tickle me that you anchored the shadow that will take us to Paluna's lair in the bathroom," I said.

Jiano flashed a cheeky smile. "Well, Paluna confirmed that the High Coven has their spy tech poking at our walls. They swiped that footage of you and Gladstone in the Garnet Room without having the decency to ask for it first. And they've been trying to tap our cameras and phones. Her team has been running interference so we're okay so far, but if there's one thing even the High Coven knows, it's that trying to get surveillance into a bathroom will get them strung up on lawsuits faster than they can blink."

"The bathroom is the safest place for subterfuge," Marrik said amusedly.

"Life continues to be strange." I shook my head. Jiano took a step forward and called up their magic. Shadows darker than the blackest black coated their hands and crawled up their forearms. The bathroom was huge, with room for an antique tub, standing shower, double sink, and a dressing area with an armoire and vanity mirror.

Ji touched one of their hands to the armoire's long shadow. It rippled like a stone thrown into calm waters. Ji quieted their magic and the inky shadows around their hands dissipated.

"One hand each, darlings." Marrik and I took hold of their hands, then followed Jiano through their anchored shadow.

Chapter Five

I could never properly describe what it was like moving through shadows, even though I'd done it a fair number of times with Ji, most of those times being when we were younger and Ji was testing the limits of their Umbra magic. Shadow travel was like stepping into a void of darkness so thick it felt like it coated my eyeballs. There was always a moment where I felt weightless, and it was accompanied by a spike of anxiety as though my brain thought we'd lifted off the ground and gone adrift. I knew Ji would take me through the shadows safely, but I could never relax until we were out.

It was only a few moments of walking in the thick, warm darkness before we emerged into light. Jiano led Marrik and I into Paluna's underground cavern and let go of our hands. We'd come out of the shadow one of the large monitors cast against the rocky wall. Ji's anchored shadow rippled then was still as we walked from behind the monitor. Before the surge, the distance between here and the bordello would have been too far for Ji to shadow travel. But they'd been nicely surprised when, after Paluna suggested trying to anchor a shadow here, it had worked.

This was the first time I'd been here since my visit a few weeks ago. It was as I remembered; a large space carved out from rock with tech I could name and many I couldn't set up everywhere. There were normal sized computers and behemoths, and a wall of offensive and defensive weapons and gadgets. A few wide, wooden tables were neatly lined with drones of various sizes, while other tables were dedicated to files and paperwork. There was even a snack area I hadn't noticed on my first visit.

There were about twenty people here by my estimation. Some nodded greetings our way, others remained focused on what they were doing; staring at a monitor, cleaning a weapon, fiddling with a gadget or tablet, or in small groups conversing.

"Hey, Jiano!" I turned to see a petite, South Asian woman wave to Jiano. She stood with a few others next to one of the drone tables.

"Hey, Jupiter!" Jiano called back. I recalled that Jupiter was the Umbra Witch they'd partnered with during the mission to rescue Milene. Just before I'd come back, the High Coven had attempted to abduct Phinra and Milene while they were on a grocery run and succeeded in nabbing Milene. With the help of Paluna's resources, Jiano had been able to rescue her before she'd ended up part of their deadly amulet experiments.

The three of us made our way across the cable strewn ground to where Paluna stood in front of one of the larger monitors. Two people sat at the table in front of it, each with a keyboard. They were clicking through photos of a derelict landscape.

Paluna turned at our approach. She wore tapered slacks and an icy blue blouse that sat well against her brown skin. Her hair looked like it'd been heat stretched and was up in a French roll with a swoop angled over her forehead.

I'd spoken to Paluna since we'd been back but hadn't seen her in person yet. Given the High Coven's scrutiny, Paluna was exerting caution with our correspondence. Hence her calls on an encrypted line and Jiano's anchored shadow that would get us here without having to come through her real estate office above.

Marrik gave my hand a squeeze. I was tense. And felt more than a little awkward coming face to face with Paluna again.

"Kitaine." She offered me a smile, her dark brown eyes shifting from me to Marrik. "And Mr. Laughton."

"You can call me Marrik," he replied, inclining his head. "Thank you again for what you did to get us back from Tsunsama."

The muscle in Marrik's jaw twitched, his tell-tale sign for conflicting emotions. We'd spoken at length about my dealings with Paluna and he'd admitted to complicated feelings, especially since we weren't out of the woods with the High Coven. But we were trying to focus on the good that had come out of the bad; I'd found him and we'd made it home.

"It was the least she could do." This from Jiano, whose tone didn't hide their shade, but lacked bite. From the look on Paluna's face as she flicked her eyes at Ji, it seemed she was used to these jabs.

"Yes, thank you." I continued to feel awkward. Should I go for a handshake, a quick hug? Were we gonna stick to smiles and nods?

Paluna's expression sobered. "Kitaine, the things I have felt these past few weeks I cannot fully convey, and I would not wish to overshadow what you've all endured." She moved her eyes over the three of us. "I am deeply apologetic for drawing you into my crusade and not being able to guarantee the safety I promised. Working with me brought pain to you and your family and I am committed to making amends. Please accept my apology and know that I remain aligned with keeping you safe. We've deep waters yet to tread."

"I appreciate it." Marrik's hold on my hand tightened, and I leaned into the support he offered. On my other side, Jiano was close enough for our forearms to brush and I felt strengthened by them as well.

"Elsewhere was harrowing, but if I hadn't ended up there Marrik may never have made it home. Nor the ley lines. Something was accomplished though wrong turns were taken."

Remi hovered in the back of my mind, as always. His loss was part of the wrong turns and was the one thing I wished could be undone.

Paluna's smile returned. "The ley lines returning is a gift no witch ever thought possible. To feel them so much stronger is wondrous."

Veins of the ley lines crossed below Paluna's lair. They'd been strong enough for Remi to gain tangibility but had felt very faint. Now, there was a constant, gentle vibration below my feet.

"The tide is turning, and I am invested in seeing how our leaders handle it," Paluna continued.

"I hope the experiments stop, but you said it may not be as cut and dry as that," I said.

Paluna shook her head. "Unfortunately not, so I will monitor whether they continue to abduct witches. For the time being it seems to have halted, and I am certain my recent threats will keep their finger on the pause button for a while."

"The plan to Vanish Gladstone is no longer on the table, right?" Jiano inquired.

Paluna nodded. "As much as getting rid of Linton would have started to shut down the experiments, if we Vanish him now, they will zero in on Kit and may not even care about the threat to expose their crimes. I won't put Kit or another Vanish Witch in that position again. Mistakes were made and we adjust. Linton can continue to exist. For now. Exposure of the experiments is our ace and we'll hold it as long as we can."

This woman was ruthless when it came to the man she'd engaged in an affair with then quietly married when his wife died. I knew she had no love for him, but to be strong enough to pretend, to play the role of his wife so perfectly he didn't suspect what she was up to … Shit, I couldn't do it.

"The look on Linton's face when he took that call was priceless." I couldn't help the smile that came to my lips. "His head looked ready to pop off. It was you on the line, wasn't it?"

"It was, with my voice disguised and the number untraceable," Paluna replied. "I called his personal assistant because I knew she would make a beeline for him. I sent her photos my team had gleaned of their experiments to make sure she understood I wasn't bluffing."

"She bustled into the room like hell hounds were after her. Linton let me go immediately after he hung up."

"That was phase one of my plan. Like I told you, the High Coven coming after you was unavoidable, and it would not have been the best route to send you into hiding for the rest of your life. On the contrary, I believe we should shine a spotlight on you. Make you so visible that the High Coven won't be able to try and silence you without the whole world knowing a hair on your head moved."

Ji, Marrik, and I exchanged tense looks.

"What exactly do you mean by shine a spotlight on Kit?" Marrik asked.

"And you as well," Paluna said.

"Me?" Marrik's eyebrows rose.

"I have scheduled a live, televised press conference for tomorrow," she said. Now my eyebrows rose. "I've invited members of the press, and the conference will be handled by my people. The host, the camera operators, the security team, everyone who interacts with you will be a trusted member of my network, including some of the reporters."

"Oh wow," I said. "You have that many connections?"

"I have operatives everywhere, not just in places like this." She indicated the spy chamber and its occupants.

"You keep making me wanna be impressed and I hate that for me," Jiano said flatly.

"It really is impressive," I said. "One day I wanna hear the full story of how you built all this."

Paluna smirked. "A story I will share one day." She looked from Marrik to me.

"I know an abundance of exposure is not what you relish, but I believe hiding in plain sight and garnering the support of the general public will keep the High Coven at bay when it comes to their desire to punish you for going after Linton." She beckoned to someone who came over and handed her a tablet. She tapped around for a few moments then showed us the screen. There were three rows of headshots with names under each photo.

"These are some of the people you'll see tomorrow." She pointed to someone on the first row, a pretty, East Asian woman with a short haircut.

"This is Inori Yamamoto. She will be leading the press conference. We have been working closely to plan everything."

"I recognize her, she's a top journalist at The Sparrow," Ji commented. The Sparrow was a witch run media conglomerate that spanned print, radio, and television. I'd heard of Inori as well; she was well-respected, was often on the front line of big news, and wasn't camera shy. That she was part of Paluna's network was amazing.

Paluna nodded. "The reason for the press conference has been kept secret, which has raised interest, as has Inori's involvement since she's known to break big stories. A lot of reporters have signed up to attend, including from the High Coven's media hub."

"Lovely," I muttered.

"And this." Paluna tapped her finger above the picture of a man in the second row. He looked to be of mixed race, with both Black and East Asian features. "Is Jamari Zhao. He is a Memoria Witch and if you permit it, Marrik and Kitaine, I would like him to read your memories during the conference."

That uneasy feeling strengthened. I'd almost had my mind read against my will today. Had already experienced it a few weeks ago when Milene used her Memoria magic to recreate a memory of Marrik around me while I'd been dancing with Remi at the bordello. Paluna was asking, not forcing it on us, but still.

"You want Jamari to read memories of what happened in Elsewhere and relay them as proof," Marrik said. His tone was neutral, but that jaw twitch never lied, and I saw it jump.

"Yes," Paluna replied. "While no one can refute that the ley lines have been strengthened, the truth of how it happened has yet to be revealed. We need to rise above speculation and give definitive proof that it was your actions in Elsewhere that brought the ley lines back. There are no downsides to publicizing this info, you will be lauded as a hero, Kit."

"That's a downside." My shoulders rose and fell as I released a breath. "Honestly, the real hero is Remi," my voice hitched around his name, "but I understand the angle you're playing and it makes sense."

"If Kit becomes the public's darling, the High Coven can't go after her without their reputation taking a hit, even if they reveal that she tried to Vanish Gladstone," Ji said, sounding thoughtful. "And all those eyes turned their way might make more of their dirty deeds come to light. I'm sure the amulet experiments are the tip of the iceberg."

"Exactly," Paluna replied. "So tomorrow, you and Marrik share your story. I suggest you explain that violence against the Elsewhere Witch ended her life and collapsed Elsewhere. I know the truth honors Remi, but it also gives the High Coven another edge as they will then be aware that your family has been in possession of a ghost amulet."

And we wouldn't want that. No one was supposed to be in possession of ghost amulets. I'd kept Remi's existence hidden save for Marrik and trusted friends at the bordello. I was lucky I hadn't been body searched yesterday. Even though Remi wasn't in it anymore, I wouldn't have wanted them to take the amulet.

"What about the fact that Kit Vanished dozens of criminals?" Jiano asked. "And ... Marrik."

I felt Marrik tense, but he quickly relaxed again.

"I know it may not sound like a good idea, but more of the truth will be better than less," Paluna said. "Marrik was a registered missing person for over a year and people in his life have already linked his disappearance to the Vanish Witch he was in a relationship with, right?"

"Right," Marrik replied.

"Therefore, we will tell the truth as far as Marrik is concerned," Paluna said. "His Vanishing was a tragic accident. But I don't think we need to lay bare all the criminals you Vanished. Regarding how you got to Elsewhere, we will have to obscure the truth since we don't want to reveal that it was because you went after my husband and he had a Repel Amulet on him."

"Yeah, that would be very, very bad," I said.

"But we can hint at their experiments since there have already been rumors about the grab teams and the amulet program," Paluna continued. "You can say you were targeted and attacked, and when you tried to save yourself, your magic backfired. If pressed on specifics, maintain that you are unclear how it happened. People are bound to speculate about the amulets being involved. And Linton certainly won't be the one to speak up and say that's not how it happened."

"That's a risk," Jiano said. "But it could work."

"A lot of truth with a sprinkle of lies," I commented.

"Kit." Paluna took a step closer and tentatively reached for me. When I didn't move away, she lightly gripped my forearm. "I'm sure this is overwhelming after what you've been through. I knew the High Coven would come for you and I gambled with getting you out before they could use Memoria magic on you, but I didn't anticipate it would be right before the press conference. You are surely exhausted and on edge and I'm sorry to lay all of this on you but—"

"It's okay." I couldn't hide that I was weary and my mind felt like it was full of spinning gears, but I did have clarity about the play Paluna was making. "I think it's a good plan even though I don't look forward to being thrust into the limelight. But you're right, hiding in the open is preferable to leaving my life behind. I appreciate all you've done to put this together and I hope it makes them back off all of us."

"The campaign about your time in Elsewhere will be ongoing," Paluna said. "The more we can keep public support in your favor the more the High Coven will be forced to rethink whatever they have planned for you." She beckoned to someone, and Jupiter came over with a few items in her hands, which she handed to Marrik, Ji, and me.

I made a choking sound as I held up the T-shirt I'd been given. Printed in the center was a stylish illustration of my face in between the words: Savior of the Ley Lines.

"Marrik, do you see what I'm seeing?" Jiano said in a rapturous whisper.

"I do." Marrik sounded highly amused. His lips twitched as he held up a coffee mug. There was flourishing word art that read: Replenish Yourself Like Kitaine Replenished the Ley Lines.

"Oh my God," I groaned.

"They're really well done," Marrik offered. "The art, the lettering, from a graphic design standpoint—"

"Don't you dare put on your artist hat about this!" I hissed. Marrik chuckled.

This *eats!*" Jiano exclaimed. I turned, with trepidation, to the tote bag they were holding.

"I Saved the Ley Lines and All I Got was this Lousy Tote Bag," Ji read the colorful word art. They clutched the bag to their chest and threw their head back, releasing a breathy exhale.

"I am nourished, my skin is moisturized, and all my problems are solved. My sister has honest to God merch, this is fantastic. I need two dozen of each delivered to the bordello immediately."

"That can be arranged," Jupiter said, after which Ji gave her a high five.

"Jiano!" Of course my sibling would be beyond tickled that I had merch.

"Kitten, come on," Ji drawled. "This is too good. Ma is going to keel over. I am taking T-shirts for her and Dad immediately."

"Oh, sweet baby Jesus she is never gonna wear anything else." I turned to Paluna, who looked amused at our reactions. "Merch? Seriously? This situation calls for something as kitschy as this?"

"The public loves a hero they can support with physical items, we've seen this time and time again," Paluna replied evenly. "I've gotten ahead by having some items prepared, but you are bound to see artisans put your face on things and try to make a buck off them after tomorrow. For us this isn't about making money, of course, but about keeping you elevated in the public eye."

I cringed. "But—"

"Kit." Her smile faded and she gave me a pointed look. "Don't ever forget that if it wasn't for your time in Elsewhere, we may never have gotten power back to the ley lines. Witch classes were dying out, we only had a few generations left before no one would be born with magic, or with so little nothing could be done with it. That you can claim responsibility for giving us back something no witch has thought was possible for almost four hundred years is no small thing. You may not have meant to position yourself as a hero, but you have done a good thing. We are presenting facts to the public that will be received with appreciation."

"It's like I've been telling you," Ji said, turning to me. "Even though I gave you a hard time about your vigilantism, you've done good. And when that Elsewhere Witch told you what you had to do to get home and release the ley lines, you did it even though it could have killed you and it took Remi from us. You've been focusing on your mistakes, your missteps, your losses, and that's fine, there are heavy things to process. But don't forget to focus on the good too, okay?"

I gave a slow nod as their words and Paluna's settled on me. I honestly hadn't focused too much on the fact that I had helped bring the ley lines back. I'd been too wrapped up in waiting for the HC to come after me and mourning Remi. But they were right, good things had come out of all of this. Marrik's return and the ability for the ley lines to benefit generations of witches to come.

"I think I'll be able to focus on the good when we've gotten past more of the bad, but you're both right and I appreciate the nudge to remember."

Paluna nodded. "I'd like you all to come here tomorrow morning, around nine. The press conference is scheduled for midday, but I want us to go over everything beforehand. I will be tuned in from here and you will be in good hands."

"Will Kit's increased magical strength be one of the things revealed tomorrow?" Marrik asked.

"No," Paluna said. "I think it is best to keep the extent of Kit's strength to ourselves. The High Coven already knows she's strong enough to Vanish people. We are trying to move Kit from under their thumb and knowing how strong she is will wedge her further under it. It may not necessarily be for deadly reasons, but we already know how heavily monitored stronger Vanish Witches are."

"But the covens are being tested in a couple days," Jiano said. "That Kit can Vanish things larger than in her files will be discovered."

"Shit, I forgot all about that," I said. "Reps are coming to the coven houses on Tuesday to reassess us since everyone got a boost when the ley lines strengthened. I'm gonna be spending the day Vanishing bigger and bigger things."

"Ah, yes. Even I must appear at my coven house to be tested." She gave me a speculative look. "How have you evaded them before?"

"When I Vanished a huge boulder in our yard when I was a kid, my parents realized my magic might be strong enough to Vanish people. They somehow acquired a couple human dummies, and I was able to Vanish one. Ma then made this disgusting Regen potion that weakened my magic and I couldn't Vanish the other one. They start magic assessment in high school, so she made the potion again and I avoided Vanishing the dummies."

"We haven't been able to grow our magic, so we haven't been tested in years," Ji said. "This assessment is gonna be a big deal."

"Hmm." Paluna tapped her chin. "What was the largest thing you Vanished in Elsewhere?"

"A huge warehouse. But Onyx implied that my magic had become strong enough to Vanish something bigger."

"It's unlikely they will have anything on the scale of a warehouse for the assessment," she said. "So they still won't know your limits."

"True. But they already aren't taking chances with what they do know about my magical strength. They gave me this, for starters." I fished the suppression gloves out of my bag and handed them to her. She spent a few minutes inspecting them.

"Tech I've seen before; my team has been aware that they've been developing this. It's been in the works for some years now and they aim to encourage their use with witches like you." She handed me the gloves and I stuffed them back into my bag.

"Encourage." I was unable to keep the bite from my tone. "I get the fear around the kind of magic I have, but these things don't just block my magic from reaching something I want to Vanish. I can't access my magic at all when I have them on. It's like my magic doesn't exist."

"That's despicable," Jiano said hotly.

"That is due to the spell work woven into them," Paluna said. "A much more powerful version of the stunting potion your mother gave you, and likely a result of Linton's experiments since strong magic is needed for something like this. Can they force witches they don't have detained to wear them? No, but I'm going to bet they're formulating a plan about it. All we can do is wait and see."

"They aren't going about this the right way, that's my gut feeling." I shook my head. "Suppression of strong magic instead of support. But that's a conversation for another day. Now—"

"Holy shit!" The exclamation came from one of the people who sat a few feet away in front of the big monitor. A short, stocky man with dark skin and a bald head.

"What is it, Titan?" Paluna asked as he pushed back his chair to face her.

"Part of the island fell off!" The person sitting next to Titan was tapping furiously on a tablet and several other people gathered around.

"The floating island off to the east?" I asked. On the monitor, I realized what was being shown was the island as seen from several drones. The screen switched between close up and long-distance views. Titan rewound some footage and when he pressed play, we saw a large chunk of the island break off from the left side and fall through wispy clouds.

"You've been monitoring the islands the Magnes Witches pulled down," Ji said. There was a murmur of nervous conversation around us. My anxiety spiked.

"As intriguing as their reentry into our atmosphere is, their appearance is concerning because variables aren't in favor that they will remain afloat or be released back into deeper space," Paluna said.

"The Magnes Witches do not know how to maintain them. The gravitational pull of Cebis and Aulura have been holding them up, but the trajectory of Cebis' orbit in a few days will weaken its hold on the islands. The other three that were pulled down are smaller and over bodies of water or a mountain range. This one will be dangerous. When it falls it will be a monumental disaster."

A beat of uneasy silence fell over us.

"What's below it?" I asked.

"Keltin," Paluna replied. Keltin was a large town in eastern Sollunara. "But like I said, the island is moving, so while Keltin may have received that fallen piece, they may not be the ones to bear the brunt of the island's collapse."

"They've been evacuating," Titan said. "We'll check to see what damage is reported from the chunk that fell."

"This is very-not-good-oh-so-bad," Jiano said. "That thing is gonna collapse on someone's head. On a lot of heads. What the hell can be done?"

"Get me up there and I'll see if I can Vanish it," I said. "Although let me make it clear that I have no idea if my magic is strong enough to Vanish something of that size. It is way, way bigger than a warehouse."

"And even if you could make it disappear, then what, you Vanish it from under you and fall to your death?" Jiano raised an eyebrow.

"Parachute?" I suggested. Ji rolled their eyes.

"Hmm." When I glanced at Paluna, she was giving me a speculative look.

"What?" I asked.

"Nothing." She shook her head. "This is dire, but the High Coven is on the ground in Keltin. My intel has revealed that they are assessing historical records of how those islands were maintained to see if they can stabilize them. They are sure to strategize some way to deal with it."

"Something to focus on other than me," I muttered.

"Did the people who were on the island leave?" Paluna asked Titan.

"Wait, wait, people were on the floating island?" I asked. Ji and Marrik made sounds of surprise.

"A couple people parachuted onto it this morning," Paluna replied. "My drones followed them as they did some exploration but lost them after a while."

"Adventure seeking morons," Ji said. "What would possess people to think jumping onto an island that's been orbiting space for centuries and is crumbling apart is a good idea?"

"Common sense is chasing them but they are faster," I quipped.

"They parachuted off several hours ago," Titan replied. "And made social media posts that have been going viral. We haven't seen anyone else land."

"Safe bet that others will try," Marrik commented.

"Idiots." A yawn came on and I couldn't suppress it.

"It's getting late," Paluna said. "And tomorrow will be a long day. Go get some rest. We will reconvene in the morning."

"Alright. Thanks again, Paluna. For all you did and all you're continuing to do."

Paluna offered me a smile and a nod. Marrik and Jiano said their goodbyes, then Jiano shadow traveled us back to the bordello where our parents were waiting with wide open ears. We spent some time telling them everything.

My mother's reaction to the T-shirt with my face on it was one for the record books. My father held my forearm and chuckled for several minutes before heading to the bathroom to put it on and model for Ma.

I decided they might as well get it in every damn color if they wanted.

Chapter Six

I was looking askance at the T-shirt, mug, and tote bag on my coffee table. My merch. I couldn't even think those words without cringing.

"I cannot believe you brought those home."

"Like there was a chance I'd leave them behind," Marrik replied with a laugh. He brushed his lips against my temple and I gave a disgruntled sigh as I settled against him. We were on the sofa, my chest against his back and our legs tangled. After coming home, we'd freshened up and changed; I'd thrown on shorts and a tank and Marrik knee length shorts and a sleeveless T-shirt. Ma had packed picnic leftovers for us, so we'd nibbled on some things before posting up on the couch.

Marrik had brought some of his records and his antique player from the storage unit. He'd put one on, and although I still felt wound tight with tension, the soft, melodic music was slowly pushing me toward a calmer headspace. Listening to music, wrapped in Marrik's arms, unearthed a wealth of nostalgic feelings as I remembered all the times we'd done exactly this before he'd Vanished.

But those memories contrasted with our present situation, felt like they were divided by a gulf too vast to bridge.

Would Marrik and I ever truly find our way back to each other after all we'd been through?

In Elsewhere, we'd gotten a few things out in the open, but we'd been in a dangerous pocket world trying to survive, and those weren't the conditions under which we could process much.

Now, we were back, but we individually had a lot going on, plus commonalities, like being thrust into the spotlight tomorrow.

Honestly, I didn't want to face any of it. I wanted to make believe. I wanted to carve out a paradise where everything in my life was okay and I had everything I wanted. Like Onyx's tremendous magical strength had been able to mold a world to her liking. But even so, she'd been trapped. A tired pawn in a game she'd lost a long time ago.

I couldn't wish for a magical solution. I had to do the work to fix what was broken.

"Tomorrow is going to be a lot." Marrik's words drew me out of my thoughts. "How are you feeling about everything?"

"I'm hoping for the best. I don't want to overthink and spiral because no matter what, something has to be done or the High Coven won't stop trying to nail me for my aggression against Gladstone. I've had nightmares about them deciding to use street gangs to knife me or something."

"Kit." His arms tightened.

"Paluna has people watching our backs, I know that. But anything can happen. We have to counter them and what Paluna put together seems like a step in the right direction. I just hate becoming so visible. But it's not only me, it's you too. How are you processing that?"

"If it will help keep you safe, I'll do anything. I'm maybe a little jealous Paluna didn't have merch with my face on it too." His tone was teasing. "Savior of the Ley Lines and Her Handsome Man would look good on a shirt, no? I have my tablet; I could sketch something and send it to her."

"What you have are jokes," I said flatly. Though I didn't miss that his answer had involved my well-being, not his.

I shifted so I could sit up and see his face. He was smiling, but he looked tired. I whispered my fingers across the stubble on his jaw. He'd wanted to go back to his barber, but in the efforts of keeping a low profile had gotten a cut and shave from Arjun last week. His face sobered and his honey brown eyes took me in as I looked him over.

His time in Elsewhere would forever be marked on him. So many scars lay against his skin. On his chest, and through the quarter sleeve tattoos on his arms. There was one that cut across his collar bone and partially up his neck. Each one with a harrowing story. And I didn't even know all those stories yet. Didn't know the full extent of what he'd been through in Elsewhere.

And everything he'd endured there was because I hadn't told him I was Vanishing criminals, which led to him following me when I went after a mark. Which led to him sneaking up on me, which led to a knee-jerk reaction where I Vanished him.

Tears pricked the corners of my eyes.

"Kit?" Marrik tugged me but I resisted falling back into his arms.

"Are you gonna give Namira a heads up about tomorrow?" I took a couple deep breaths to try and quell the tears.

He shook his head. "Since Paluna doesn't want details leaked before the press conference telling Namira wouldn't be a good idea. It kinda works out though, since we're supposed to have dinner with her in the evening. She is sure to see the conference and will be pissed I didn't say anything to her, but at least all the information she's been asking for will be out there and we can just talk it through."

"Tomorrow is gonna be another exceptionally long day." I rolled my neck to get the kinks out though the tension remained. Marrik gave me an apologetic look.

"I can re-schedule—"

"No, it's okay. The timing does work out well. It wouldn't be a good idea for her to see the press conference and hear about Elsewhere but still not be able to connect with you."

"Okay. Thank you, Kit. I know she doesn't have warm feelings toward you but—"

"But they are warranted and there's nothing I can do about it. Her suspicions were on point, and I lied to her. She's right to hate me, Mar. I could have taken you from her permanently had it not been for the ley lines in Elsewhere."

Marrik cast his eyes down as he gave a small nod. He looked sad.

"Do you think you will ever be able to forgive me?" I asked the question I'd been holding back for the last few weeks. Releasing the words made me feel like I was an arrow notched on a bow, pulled tight and finally released. But when I hit my target I might splinter into pieces.

Marrik's eyes widened. A pained looked flashed across his face.

"Do you think you can forgive me?" he whispered.

Answer a question with a question when you don't want to answer the question you were asked.

"Mar." One of my hands was against his chest. He covered it with his and squeezed. I moved so I could sit up more and he did as well.

"I kept our relationship a secret because my family is full of witch haters," Marrik continued. "I created the conditions under which you felt as though you couldn't tell me your magic was strong enough to Vanish people and that you were using it against Blights."

My lips twitched at the nickname the people of Elsewhere had given all the Vanished criminals, who were greater in number than just the ones I'd Vanished. Witches had been blipping bad people out of existence since the beginning of time. But after the ley lines were drained, they ended up transferred to Elsewhere instead of truly disappearing.

"I never feared your magic," Marrik said. He pressed my palm against his chest. "I know you don't lack control and I'm proud of how strong you always were and how much stronger you've become. We both held back things we should have been more open about and it took us to some terrible places, but we're back. Can't we focus on that?"

"Can we?" I challenged. "Sometimes it feels as though we're holding our breath around each other, Mar. I can see what a hard time you're having. You're trying to hide it for my sake, and I hate that. I want you to focus on yourself too, not just me. You were in Elsewhere so much longer. The adjustment back has been difficult and I wish you wouldn't pretend it wasn't."

"I'm not—"

"Don't lie, please."

He closed his eyes briefly, his shoulders rising and falling as he took a deep breath. When he opened his eyes, the look on his face was heartbreaking.

"I don't know who I am supposed to be other than the man at your side." His voice was soft and strained. "I spent a year in darkness, in chaos. The juxtaposition to what Elsewhere was like and this," he looked around the room, his gaze lingering on the window and the view of the glowing neighborhood lights beyond it, "is something I couldn't have anticipated I would struggle with so much. I thought my relief at being back would be all I felt."

"But it's not."

He shook his head. "I wasn't living in Elsewhere, I was surviving. If Onyx had kept it as a beautiful place, things would have been different. But there was nothing to do there but fight, scavenge, and evade terrible magic while trying to save people from it. I didn't rest well, not one single time. Every sleep was disjointed, full of dreams of you, of my life, that would shatter me when I woke up and realized where I still was.

"And before you showed up, I had no answers. Onyx never sought me out to explain who she was and that Elsewhere was her created world where she'd bundled a bunch of the ley lines. I had nothing to hold on to that could be called even the tiniest scrap of hope, so eventually I accepted that my fate would be to survive, and eventually die. A magic wave would shred me, or a Blight would put a bullet in me. Something in that hideous place would kill me and all I had to look forward to was my death."

Marrik ran a hand over his head. He'd been growing agitated as he spoke, but I was glad to see it because he'd been keeping a tight lid on his emotions these past few weeks. I needed him to feel his feelings.

"All I knew was that you Vanished me and I ended up there and my feelings were so, so complicated," he continued. "I understood enough that I didn't believe you'd meant for it to happen, but there were no other answers I could give myself about where I was or how to get out. So once I fell in with Arrow and the others and they started to see me as their leader I went with it. I let Elsewhere and its problems shape me into who I was when you found me. Someone who couldn't even believe it was you standing before me because I hadn't had any hope to begin with."

He made a frustrated sound and shook his head.

"And now I'm back, and I am so thankful to be back, to be with you in the world we belong in. But I don't know who I am anymore. I lost my apartment, my car was re-possessed after all the missed payments, and I don't have my freelance gigs. I've been wedged back into the real world and I don't have a purpose. I had one before, I had one in Elsewhere, and now —"

"Now, maybe you don't need one," I said gently. "At least not for a while." His words were heart shattering. He'd kept so much swallowed down for my sake.

"You should take time," I continued. "A lot of time, to do nothing. No one could expect you to come off being a mercenary in Elsewhere and immediately get back to illustrating gigs or catching drinks at the bar with your friends. Do nothing, Mar, give yourself time to readjust, three weeks ain't it. You know you're welcome here as long as you want; we'd been talking about living together, but that's a bigger topic we don't need to rush. You can get another apartment. Your bank accounts are intact, so you have your money.

"Tomorrow you'll start reconciling with Namira and you can reach out to other people as you feel like. I love you so, so much for standing by me and doing all you can to support me through the trouble I'm facing, but I want you to be more than the man at my side. But who you want to be and what you want to do won't come to you overnight, so give yourself time. Maybe you'll get back into your art, maybe you'll veer into something else. If you still feel the urge to use the skills you used in Elsewhere perhaps you can talk to Paluna about joining her team in some capacity."

A thoughtful look came over him. "I hadn't thought about that. But I will now."

I smiled and he gave me one back. "We have big steps to take, starting with the press conference tomorrow, but whenever we can, let's take smaller ones too, okay? A slower pace. Let's not put ourselves on a clock and feel as though time is running out for us to cross some kind of finish line. I know I can't do it. My life feels alien to me too, in a lot of ways. On the other side of Elsewhere I feel far too changed to pick up my life like nothing happened."

"We'll take it slow." He raised my hand and kissed my palm. Warmth spread through me at the touch of those soft lips. His eyes remained on mine as he nuzzled my palm. "Thank you, Kit. I needed … I needed to talk."

"*We* needed to talk. Neither of us have answered the forgiveness question."

He sighed, and the tickle of his breath across my skin spiraled maddening sensations through me and caught my breath.

"Can we do less talking now?" His tone was lower, suggestive. I bit my lip. We'd finally opened up about a lot of things. It would be a good idea to keep the conversation going.

"But—"

"Baby." The word eased from between his lips as he leaned forward, causing me to move until I fell onto my back. I uncrossed my legs and they slid around his body as he propped himself over me. The hand he'd been holding was behind my head, his fingers laced through mine.

"Less talking." He dropped his head to my neck and nipped. "I want to do other things with my mouth now." His lips dragged along my skin, his tongue darting out for a taste. My breath was coming in short, sharp bursts as my arousal increased.

"Marrik," was all I could gasp out before his mouth claimed mine. And he was hungry. The kiss was a deep, consuming clash of lips and tongue, the wetness of his brushing against mine, circling it like a savored candy. I yielded to the aggression of the kiss, let him take control as he grazed his teeth over my bottom lip, making a sound in his throat that made me grind my hips against him.

He released my hand and sat up, straddling me. I was breathing hard, my arms flung behind my head, my eyes half closed as I watched him cross his arms over his body and drag his shirt off, tossing it to the ground. He tilted his head to the side, a sultry smile tugging the corner of his mouth as he slid his hands up my stomach, pushing my shirt up.

The look on his face said he was in control. That I was at his sweet, sinful mercy.

And I loved it.

His hands reached my breasts. My back arched as his palms slid over them. He pushed my shirt all the way up and pulled it over my head. I watched him bite his bottom lip, a heady look in his eyes as he roved his hands over my tits, fingers working my nipples and making me moan.

He licked his lips tantalizingly as he lowered his head and drew my tit into his mouth, using slow, languid strokes of his tongue and a gentle rake of his teeth. His hand drifted down my body and into my shorts. When he touched between my legs, he made a ravenous sound at my wetness and bit down on my breast as he slid two fingers inside me.

Oh, those fingers were magic. Marrik worked me to the cusp of an orgasm. He could tell when I was about to come and slid down my body, pulled the rest of my clothes off, and latched his mouth around my pussy, bringing me over the edge with a few deep strokes of his tongue.

"Not done," he whispered. His hands slid up to cup my breasts.

"Come again, baby, I know how hard you can buck when I eat you deep. Give it to me again."

"Marrik." Every nerve felt like it was on fire. The orgasm ebbed but Marrik stroked my arousal right back up as he ate me out. My back arched, my head pressed into the couch as my hips moved in rhythm with his lips and tongue.

Marrik flipped me over, nudging me toward the arm of the sofa. I draped my upper body over it and he hitched my ass up. I cried out at the feel of his teeth biting down on my ass before he licked his way back to eating me out.

He made me come again, his mouth lapping up my release, his tongue trailing down my inner thighs.

"More." My voice was a desperate plea.

I felt him move. Moments later I felt the press of his dick and made a craved sound that released a dark chuckle from him.

He gripped my hips as he entered me. I moaned as he filled me up, as he pushed me to the limits of how much of his length I could handle. But I was always greedy when it came to him. I thrust back and inched more of him into me, releasing a grunt from him. He shifted his hands to my ass and squeezed in a way that was so painfully good.

He started to pump and pleasure spiraled through me. The drag of his dick over my clit was fireworks to my nerves, an intense build up that would have the most satisfying payout.

Marrik pulled me up and I ended up turned around and straddling his waist, inching back down on his dick. The arch in my back pushed my chest in his face and he took full advantage, ravaging my breasts with that hot, hungry mouth.

I rode him hard. His hands were tight at my hips, helping me move, giving control to the deep strokes. He thrust up to match my movements. His lips recaptured mine and one of his hands moved up to anchor the back of my neck, holding me close as we tongued and fucked. The air around us felt warm and charged, more biting and electric than any magic.

"Kit, Kit." The way he said my name was so damn erotic it drove me wild. His body shuddered as he came. His mouth tore from mine and he dropped his head back as his pleasure consumed him.

"Can't fuck me back anymore?" I whispered deviously. "I haven't come yet. Where's mine?"

He'd already given me two mind blowing orgasms, but like I said, I was greedy.

Marrik growled. Lifted his head and latched his eyes onto mine. His hands returned to my hips. He pushed and we were off the couch and on the ground. His hands slapped against the floor behind my head. A smile curled my lips as I followed the lines of his arms, rigid as they held him up, to the look on his face that said he'd accepted my challenge.

"I'm going to fuck you so hard it will be called a sin." Intense desire clenched my belly at those words.

Marrik bent my knees up and pushed my legs wider. He pulled out, leaving the teasing tip at my opening, and slammed back in, making me scream at the pleasure edged pain.

"Harder," I ground out. "Own me." He was controlling the strokes, but I let my body dance with him, and our combined movements took the fuck to the levels of an inferno.

Marrik pulled out. Gripped my calves and squeezed. I wrapped my hands around his forearms and anchored myself as he gave me the bruising satisfaction I was demanding from him.

The orgasm I experienced was nothing short of euphoric and I made sure Marrik heard every octave of my bliss. He collapsed onto me, breathing hard. I wrapped my arms and legs around him and kissed and nipped every patch of sweaty skin I could reach. He rolled to the side with his arms around me, his panted breaths pulsing against the side of my neck.

"Well, I've certainly been owned and I am okay with it."

Marrik pressed his lips against my neck; a soft, hot kiss.

"You own me, always," he whispered. "No matter what. My heart, my body, my soul, is yours, Kit. I love you."

"I love you too." His words and the way he held me were salves to my heart. We kissed, our bodies pressed together, my chest feeling tight with emotions.

We were not healed yet, but we weren't completely broken.

Chapter Seven

All eyes were on me.

Well, they were on Marrik as well since he was sitting next to me on a low stage in front of a sea of eager-faced reporters, cameras, and video recorders, as well as my friends and family.

I took a deep breath and let it out. Marrik sat in an identical, plush white chair to my right, while Inori Yamamoto was to my left in a dark blue chair. She was giving opening remarks to get this show started. I was trying my damned best to keep a neutral expression and keep my butt in the chair. The urge to get up and bolt was *strong*.

I looked around. The large room was located on the twenty-fifth floor of one of the skyscrapers uptown. Floor to ceiling windows ran the length of the wall behind us, letting in bright daylight and giving a fantastic view of the city. The building that headquartered the High Coven, the tallest building in Vonuis, was visible, and I was sure that was no coincidence. Paluna knew what she was doing when she'd chosen this spot for the press conference.

She also knew what she was doing with the aesthetics. Dark blue was the accent color, a shade almost exactly the color of

Vanish magic. Marrik and I had been messaging with Jiano this morning, who relayed suggestions from Paluna on how to dress. Mar looked exceptional in a charcoal gray suit and dark blue button down, while I wore one of my favorite maxi-dresses of dark-blue mud-cloth with a pattern of ginkgo leaves. Jiano, my parents, and several Hexes, including Phinra, Milene, Calla, Rowan, and Arjun, occupied two rows to the left and were well dressed with shades of blue accenting their attire.

"And now I'd like to explain the reason this press conference has been put together." Inori's words drew me out of my thoughts. I took another steadying breath. I'd moved my arm to the armrest, and Marrik was close enough to cover a few of my fingers with his. I relaxed a bit, comforted by his touch.

Inori stood up. She was poised and professional, with a strong, clear voice amplified by her mic. She was dressed in a slim-fit, navy-blue pantsuit, and looked every bit the top-ranking journalist she was.

"This is Kitaine Neris." Inori gestured at me. "And Marrik Laughton. They have an incredible story to tell, but before that, there is a revelation I want to make you aware of regarding them."

The room fell silent. Every single member of the press, who were to the right, strained toward us with their cameras up or their hands poised over notepads or tablets.

"Kitaine and Marrik are responsible for returning what has been calculated as fifty-five percent of the ley lines' strength," Inori announced. "And they did so by collapsing the parallel world the ley lines had been gathered into for almost four hundred years. I will be fielding questions, but first, I'd like Kitaine and Marrik to tell you all about their time in that parallel world, known as Elsewhere."

There were sucked in breaths and sounds of shock. Cameras flashed and notes were taken. Marrik's fingers tightened around mine and I wished I could Vanish from my seat and wind up somewhere else. Now would be a great time to be able to tap into a higher level Vanish ability that would allow me to transfer myself far, far away.

Back to the white sand beaches of Tsunsama, maybe.

"Marrik was in Elsewhere for about a year," Inori was saying. "And although how he ended up there was due to a tragic misstep of Kitaine's magic, which also informed her own journey to Elsewhere, this is a story with a triumphant ending." She turned to us and nodded encouragingly. "Kitaine, Marrik, the floor is yours."

Marrik and I exchanged looks. We'd gone over the specifics of what to say several times with Paluna this morning. I was still wound up tight with anxiety though, especially because the story revealed that I could Vanish people. But that was already known to the people who could condemn me the most. I was also worried that this would make witch haters zero in on me. Paluna had acknowledged that was likely, but along with all the other variables we had to consider regarding how to keep me safe from Gladstone, shining a light on me was still the best option.

There was no going back now. Good and bad would come from this press conference. Paluna kept assuring me she'd keep me safe from the bad, but I would never fully be at ease about any of this.

Marrik and I stood up. He gave my hand a squeeze then let go but stayed close.

Following Inori's prompts, Marrik and I took turns talking about Elsewhere. We explained who Onyx was and what she'd done, and how Elsewhere collapsing had allowed the ley lines to flow back to where they belonged. We described the unbound magic and the plethora of criminals who were equipped with all the weapons we'd Vanished. As we'd agreed, we'd said nothing about my responsibility for some of the criminals there. When I spoke about how there was almost four centuries of Vanished garbage in Elsewhere, there'd been some chuckles from the crowd.

The conversation steered clear of any mention of Remi. I'd reluctantly left his amulet at home and felt off without the weight of it against my chest.

I don't think I'd ever talked so much in one go in my entire life. I was buzzing with nerves, keenly aware that this was a live broadcast and the entire world now knew who Marrik and I were and that I was a stronger Vanish Witch. I knew the High Coven was tuned in. While we'd been standing in a closed off area to the side of the room before things had started, Inori had indicated which of the reporters were part of the HC's media.

Finally, the tale of Elsewhere was out. After we'd finished speaking, a hush had fallen over the room. I felt extremely exposed. Eyes were wide, cameras had stopped flashing, jaws were dropped.

Yeah, if I'd been on the listening end of this story my disbelief would be sky high.

"Now," Inori's voice broke the silence. "We understand that this may come across as a tall tale, even with the evidence of the stronger ley lines to support it. Still, it is not a reach to ask 'is this really how the ley lines were restored?' An explanation of a parallel world created by perhaps the strongest witch to ever exist may not be a story you can accept without critique. Thus, I would like to provide additional proof."

Inori beckoned and Jamari Zhao stood up. Paluna's Memoria Witch had been sitting at the end of the front row my friends and family were on. He buttoned his dark blue blazer and smiled as he came onto the stage to stand next to Inori.

"Jamari Zhao is a Memoria Witch," Inori explained. "Kitaine and Marrik have agreed, in properly filed paperwork, to allow him to read their minds in order to verify if everything they said is true. Now—"

"How's that supposed to verify anything?" one of the reporters called out. I looked over and saw that it was one of the High Coven's people who'd asked. A middle-aged, heavy-set man with a keen look in his eyes.

"The work Memoria Witches do is highly accepted as credible in many facets of life, is it not?" Inori said, seeming unperturbed by the interruption. "We use them to draw facts out for court cases, for example. Jamari has worked with the legal system for many years, using his magic to successfully close cases."

"That doesn't mean that's what will happen here," the man returned. Several other reporters murmured their agreement. "This smells of careful orchestration, Yamamoto. Your pretty face hinting at a big story only to bring us here and tell us things that absolutely can't be true."

"But is it true that the ley lines have been strengthened, Capaldi?" Inori asked smoothly. I could tell Inori wouldn't break a sweat easily. Capaldi looked like he enjoyed making people sweat to dehydration, though.

"Is it?" Inori prompted, when Capaldi didn't reply.

His eyes narrowed. "The ley lines' rejuvenation has been confirmed by credible sources," he finally said. Credible sources being the High Coven and their assessment of the surge and its aftermath but not the people who'd brought them back. Sigh.

"And how do you surmise they were strengthened?" Inori asked. "Out of the blue, after over three hundred years of being weakened. The specific event of Kitaine and Marrik tearing down the walls of Elsewhere brought the ley lines back with such force that we are still dealing with the effects, aren't we? All witches are a bit stronger than we were three weeks ago. Why, my vegetable garden has never fared better."

There were polite chuckles from the crowd. Inori was a Regen Witch like my mother and Calla, so her magic extended to healing and growth magic. No one could deny the surge had happened when there'd been so much collateral damage. Repel Witches had blasted cars through buildings and repelled trees into houses. Regen Witches had wreaked havoc on plant life, turning neighborhood gardens into mini jungles. Magnes Witches had pulled those floating islands down. Jiano could now make beastly shadow cats when previously they could only conjure a tiny kitten, and well, that was cool as fuck.

"Even so," Capaldi said. "You and whoever helped you organize this are pulling all the strings with whatever you're trying to accomplish here. You could make a show of Zhao tapping their memories, but he could tell us whatever the hell he wants, right? I bet there's already a script to follow."

Marrik and I glanced at each other. My palms were clammy and my heart was racing. Marrik had his emotion-hiding neutral expression on. There was a buzz of conversation throughout the room, and I saw a lot of hesitant looks. Only my people looked encouraging. And pissed. Jiano was looking at Capaldi as though they were considering conjuring a shadow beast to maul him. Next to Ji, my mother looked ready to spring out of her seat and get to defending me, and I'm sure it was only Dad's arm across her lap that kept her still. Scales rippled across Dad's forehead, which relayed his agitation despite his calm expression.

We were supposed to garner public support. I was supposed to be seen as the 'Savior of the Ley Lines' as much as that title made my skin crawl. If instead we were accused of putting on a farce and wasting everyone's time, Marrik and I wouldn't have public support to help bolster us against the High Coven's laser focus. Inori and Jamari's reputations would take a hit as well.

All of which would undermine Paluna's plan and leave the High Coven with more room to maneuver when it came to dealing with me, even with her threats to expose the amulet experiments.

We were following a script, but I'd bet good money Capaldi was too. He was probably tapped into people watching off scene. Once our story was revealed, he and the other High Coven press had probably been instructed to poke at us.

"I'm not saying I don't believe the information you've presented," another reporter spoke up. A young woman who looked fresh out of college. She wasn't one of the HC's reporters. "But there is merit to the fact that unless all of us are allowed to have a trusted Memoria Witch read their minds, we cannot verify their story with complete accuracy."

Multiple Memoria Witches reading our minds? I exchanged an alarmed look with Marrik. Oh no, hell no. I would never agree to that. Marrik neither.

Others were echoing what Capaldi and the other reporter said, and the buzz of conversation was rising. I was being given more and more apprehensive looks.

Marrik inched closer and eased his hand into mine. Things were sliding sideways, and I wasn't sure how we were gonna right this ship. The criticism was valid, because only Jamari would see what was in our minds, but we had no other way to prove our time in Elsewhere was real. We—

My train of thought was broken as I felt a sudden pressure in my head that tore a gasp from my throat. The pressure was accompanied by a touch of magic and my head whipped to where Jamari was standing. Memoria magic was being used on me. But Paluna had said Jamari's mind reading was done with physical contact. So it couldn't be him.

There was only one witch I knew who could memory read without physical contact.

My eyes widened and I turned to the crowd as the Memoria magic pulsing into my head made me cry out and stumble forward, bringing all eyes back to me.

"Kit?" Concern laced Marrik's voice as he put his arm around me. My gaze landed on Milene. She and Phinra sat between Jiano and Calla. Milene's eyes were on me, the expression on her face more intense than I'd ever seen. She was once again using her Memoria magic on me without my consent.

"Stop—" The press of Memoria magic got so strong I dropped to my knees. Marrik came with me, holding me and calling out to me, sounding helpless.

And then people started to shout, sounding shocked. When I raised my head to see why, I could not believe what I was looking at.

An image formed in the space between the audience and the stage. It shimmered into existence like a mirage. There was a transparent quality to it, but it was visible, and in shock I realized that it was a memory that had been pulled from my head.

And it was clear, impossibly clear, that I wasn't the only one who could see it.

The image was of the inside of Onyx's bar, as seen from my perspective as I sat across from her.

"Oh girl, I know all about this world," Onyx said. She wore an old-fashioned dress, colorful headscarf, and beaded accessories. *"It's a putrid, horrible wasteland of unbound magic, people who scrape out a bleak existence, and no shortage of the worst contenders of your world's population."*

"Can you help us escape?" Since it was my memory, there was no representation of myself, but the question I'd asked was heard. As was her reply.

"Of course I can. I created this place, after all. So it stands to reason I can help you escape it."

The memory of my conversation with Onyx continued. A hush had fallen over the room as every single eyeball stared at the memory, which looked like a projection onto the air. Marrik was deathly still beside me and all I kept spiraling on was the fact that the memory was visible to everyone. That shouldn't be possible.

Unless Milene was stronger than we thought.

"You created Elsewhere?" Memory-Kit was saying.

"I am one of those responsible for the collapse of the ley lines," Onyx replied. *"We wanted more power. I was a strong Mutans Witch who could shapeshift into half a dozen beasts. Elegant or fearsome creatures."*

Then came the explanation of what she'd done.

"In the moment of our demise I felt what I was becoming, felt the magic and what was possible with that level of power. But I knew naught would come of it because I would be torn asunder. I had not been trying to save myself though. I felt the ley lines draining. We had opened a wound we could not close, but all was not lost yet. I pushed, used my will, used power I should never have gotten a touch of, and I created a ... space? Another realm? A tear in the world I knew that led to one I made?

"Even now, I do not fully understand it. But what I do know is that when everything was going wrong, I tried to save whatever I could. I pushed the ley lines into the tear I made and I fell into it as well. Ended up in a void. There was nothing but darkness and magic and I was still burning. But my thoughts now had the power to shape the world. I knew it. I felt it. So I released the magic I had absorbed and I used my will to mold the void I had fallen into.

"I hardly knew what I was doing and did not expect to survive. I was bursting out of my skin. Shifting forms over and over, unable to control it. The chill of the grave clung to me. I watched my limbs vanish and reappear. All manner of debris kept being drawn to me then repelled away. I was being assaulted by every kind of magic there was.

"I survived because I released so much of it. Used magic like clay and sculpted a world that kept a portion of the ley lines safe. Closed the tear

I made. And here I have been ever since. I suppose I have magic to thank for the fact that I have not aged nor died. I have done my best, but Elsewhere is not entirely stable. So much powerful magic from my fellow witches was dragged in as well, and that I cannot control."

The memory abruptly disappeared and everyone sucked in a collective breath. But Milene's magic was still lanced through my mind and seconds later she pulled out another memory and recreated it where the first one had been.

It was the warehouse fight where I'd found Marrik again.

"I want her to hurt so badly she will beg for the release of death." The words were spoken by Gemira Monto, a tall, ruthless woman with pale skin and hair who'd robbed cargo trucks and spilled a lot of blood.

"We will each have our pound of flesh, won't we?" This from Conrad Belligra, another one of my marks.

The image rippled briefly and shifted to a further point in that memory.

"Marrik." I heard the whispered disbelief of my voice as Marrik appeared. Scarred, his hair grown out, weaponed up and wearing tactical gear with a hard look on his face. In the background were several of the people Marrik had fallen in with, who'd helped rescue Remi and I from those Blights.

"Marrik, it's me, Kit! It's me!"

Next to me, Marrik made a pained sound and his grip on me tightened. I was holding him tightly, suspended in the grips of Milene's magic and the emotional upheaval of what was playing out before the room.

Milene's magic in my head spiked again. The warehouse memory dissipated and another one took its place.

Oh shit. The memory was Onyx teaching me how to strengthen my magic on the ley lines.

We weren't going to reveal how strong my magic was!

"Right now, you have the power of the ley lines outside of you and your magic within you," Onyx said. *"That alone gives you a boost, but you need more. You must let the ley lines in so they can latch on to your magic and nurture it. It's like watering a plant. You feed it and it will grow. But if you overwater a plant, what happens?"*

"It dies," came my reply.

"Exactly. So you need to be very careful with how much of the ley lines' power you let in. Its magic will always be stronger than yours, remember that. The ley lines are veins of magic that existed before anything else in the world did. I've heard that they were bound to the earth by entities we have no names for. They want to make magic stronger, but they are all or nothing. If you stay closed off to them, you gain nothing. But if you open yourself to them, they will rush in with strength you may not be able to handle. Send your magic into the ground. And when the magic from the ley lines respond, when you feel some of it flow into you, shut your magic down."

There was a ripple in the image as Onyx crouched down in front of me.

"How do you feel?" Onyx's keen, amber eyes glowed brightly even in the faded memory image.

"I feel powerful," came my reply.

The image faded. Memoria magic pulsed through my skin like a drum was beating on it from the inside. A new memory took shape.

The memory of Elsewhere collapsing.

"Well done," said Onyx. These were her last moments as she was gripped by Remi's Wither magic. Her skin brittle, her hair and teeth falling out. She looked like a long dead corpse.

"You will be free and so will I," Onyx said. *"All you had to do was destroy me. I am Elsewhere, and Elsewhere is me. One cannot exist without the other."*

The memory disappeared. Milene's magic finally receded and the raging headache eased. I gasped like I'd been unable to breathe, and only Marrik's arms kept me from collapsing. My eyes were wet with tears as all the emotions I'd experienced in Elsewhere knotted inside me again.

The room was quieter than the depths of an empty grave. When I looked at Inori and Jamari, they were staring wide eyed at the spot the memory recreations had been, shock etched into their expressions.

"Milene!" Phinra's piercing cry broke the silence, and I snapped my attention to her. Jiano moved in time to catch Milene, who pitched forward, her eyes fluttering closed. My parents and the other Hexes gathered around Milene as Jiano scooped her up in their arms and turned to face me.

The look on Ji's face was stoic but I could tell they were rattled. This press conference had careened off the tracks. I was certain Inori did not have a contingency script for something like this.

With Marrik's help I stood up. He kept his arm around me as I wiped my eyes and tried to calm down, to keep some kind of composure.

Once again, all eyes were on me. They had seen it. Every single thing Milene had pulled from my mind, they had seen.

Every eye was wide, every mouth had fallen open like they were doors on broken hinges.

"Well then." Inori's strong, clear voice made us all jump. My heart would not stop racing. Inori flashed me a smile before she turned away and stepped forward.

"It seems Memoria magic was the way to go after all, if not exactly in the way we'd intended," Inori said. "You were all able to see what Jamari would have told you had he read Kitaine and Marrik's minds."

Conversation erupted throughout the room.

"Who the hell did that?"

"Was it that girl over there who passed out?"

"Holy shit, Memoria magic can do that?"

"I guess what those two told us was real, unbelievable!"

"There's no way Memoria magic can do that, maybe it was a projection?"

"That was Memoria magic, didn't you feel it? What projection can recreate the feel of magic?"

There was speculation and whispers of disbelief and awe. And while I caught snatches of people expressing hesitation to believe what they'd seen, it appeared that Milene's recreations of my memories had swayed the majority to believe us.

Were things actually gonna work in our favor?

"You have witnessed the Elsewhere Witch!" Inori said. Her voice was a little shaky, but she was regaining herself faster than I was. Reporters had to be ready for anything.

"You saw exactly what Kitaine and Marrik told you and you saw the moment Elsewhere collapsed and returned the ley lines to us. Should you continue to dispute their story I will have to question your ability to think logically when presented with substantiated facts." She said that last bit while looking directly at Capaldi, whose skin flushed and mouth still hadn't found its way to close.

"So," Inori clapped her hands, "does anyone have any questions?"

Almost every single person raised their hand.

Chapter Eight

That press conference lasted a thousand years.

To put it less dramatically, that had been the longest five hours of my life.

But it was over now.

We were back at the bordello, and though there was *a lot* to unpack from the conference, one of the biggest things to figure out was sitting in the crook of her sister's arm on the chaise in Jiano's office.

Milene.

"I wanted to help," came Milene's soft voice. She was worrying at her fingers in her lap, her head bent. Phinra's face showed a lot of concern for her twin.

Jiano, Calla, and I were the only ones here since we didn't want to overwhelm Milene. Jiano had taken Marrik to Paluna's spy lair to debrief and would bring him back soon. My parents were with others in the bordello's front room having a drink. This had been the kind of day that needed to be topped with drinks. Lots of drinks.

"Milene," Jiano said gently. They were perched on the chaise next to the twins. I was sitting on the coffee table in front of them, while Calla was on the adjacent armchair.

"They weren't going to believe," Milene whispered. Her voice was strained, as though she spoke while holding her breath.

Her fingers twisted around each other. She drew her bottom lip into her mouth and hunched her shoulders. Her pixie-cut was growing out and the bangs of her red hair fell into her eyes as she dropped her head. Phinra and Milene were petite; just a few inches over five feet. Milene leaned toward baggier clothes, and I couldn't help the piteous feeling as I looked at her in her dark blue dress over a white tank. The too big clothes made her seem smaller. The dress had huge pockets on the front, and she shoved her hands into them as Phinra gently patted the shoulder her hand was wrapped around. Phinra turned her worried expression to Ji.

"Madame, please don't—"

Jiano held up a hand. "I never indicated that anyone was in trouble. I know you two have had a tough life and I tend to have a firm hand with you, but my first priority is to take care of you, not punish you."

Phinra shifted her eyes to Calla. Calla was Jiano's second in command when it came to the twins since running the bordello kept Ji so busy. She was still healing from the abuse she'd suffered under the former Madame, who'd allowed clients to carve her up and watch her Regen magic heal her. But Calla had come a long way, and her experiences made her a good support for Phinra and Milene.

Milene's stronger Memoria magic had been exploited by their adoptive parents, who made Milene recreate whatever perversions people wanted. Phinra was forced to scout prospective clients. The girls had eventually run away, and several Hexes had saved them the first time the High Coven tried to snatch them for their amulet experiments and brought them to Kiss and Hex.

Calla gave Phinra an encouraging smile. "We are here to talk."

"I wanted to help," Milene said again.

"You did help," I offered. "Because everyone was able to see what you pulled from my mind, they believed our story. But—"

Milene flinched. There was a lot I could tack on to that 'but.' But we hadn't planned to reveal that I had strengthened my magic on the ley lines, for one. That information had been blown wide open and I was not looking forward to the coven reassessment tomorrow. Plus, I was worried about the memory with Gemira and Conrad. It could easily be interpreted that their antagonistic words were because I was responsible for Vanishing them into Elsewhere.

"But you went into Kit's mind without permission," Calla said. "You may have been allowed had you asked. You must remember that it is not right to enter someone's mind against their will."

Milene gave a small nod, still looking down.

"We tried to get her to stop but it didn't work," Ji said. "We couldn't break her focus."

I'd once seen a video where a group of friends took turns filling up a glass drop by drop to see whose drop made it spill over. The water at the rim seemed to defy physics as they carefully added drops. That's how I felt right now; full to almost overflowing yet tethering on the edge, unable to spill over.

I had to keep it together. Couldn't spiral.

"When did you realize that your memory recreations could become visible to more than just the person you used your magic on?" Ji asked.

"Um—"

"She didn't mean to do it," Phinra spoke up. "Milene sometimes uses her magic on me. I don't mind," she added quickly, "she can't help it most of the time. Um … but … last week when we were at the community garden with Calla, we were sitting on a bench and Milene's magic pulled a memory of our childhood dog from my mind. It was nice to see Bini but then … um …"

"Someone else saw the dog as well," Jiano said. Phinra nodded.

"A little girl saw Bini and ran over to play with her but the memory broke and Bini disappeared," Phinra said. "The kid looked a little confused but ran off. So that was when we realized that um, other people could see things too."

Jiano gave a weary sigh, pinching the bridge of their nose. "And why didn't you tell Calla or me?"

"We didn't want to cause trouble since there are a lot of important things going on with Kit," Phinra said.

Jiano and I exchanged looks. Yeah, the last few weeks had mostly been about Marrik and my return from Elsewhere. The care and concern was wonderful, but I was reminded again that my problems seemed to be eclipsing everyone else's. I felt terrible that Phinra and Milene had kept quiet about this development in Milene's magic for my sake.

"And ..." Phinra sounded even more hesitant.

"And?" Ji prompted.

Milene raised her head and looked at Phinra. They maintained eye contact for a moment, then Milene gave the barest nod. Phinra nodded back then looked at Jiano again.

"It's not only memories," Phinra said. "A few nights ago, I woke up in the middle of the night and our room was full of ... of fairies."

"Fairies." Ji, Calla, and I said in unison. You would think after the last few weeks I couldn't be more shocked than I already was.

Phinra looked sheepish. "Milene was awake, sitting up on her bed. There were these balls of glowing light everywhere and soft, musical laughter. When I looked closer, I realized the balls of light were fairies."

"Phinra, darling, are you sure you weren't dreaming?" Ji asked.

"I wasn't dreaming." Phinra's tone was insistent. "The fairies were from one of my dreams the night before. Milene had seen my memory of the dream. She said she thought it would make me happy if she recreated them for me."

"I see." Jiano looked at Calla, whose stunned look mirrored theirs. Ji turned back to the girls. "So, to be clear, you're saying that not only can Milene do memory recreations that everyone can see, she can also do dream recreations that are visible to all?"

Stronger Memoria magic could recreate dreams as well as memories. Even things you'd imagined if they'd taken strong root in your mind. I'd experienced that when Remi and I had been caught by a terrifying wave of Memoria magic in Elsewhere. It had made us see a daydream from Remi's mind of us living as a couple in my apartment.

Milene's magic was strong enough to do what that massive wave of raw Memoria magic had done. The surge had boosted her magic *quite* a bit.

"Yes," was Phinra's reply. "One of the fairies slipped under the door and I heard someone make an exclamation about it. All the fairies disappeared shortly after, but I'm pretty sure the one that went into the hall was seen."

"I believe you," Jiano said. "This is some damn development. I knew your magic grew stronger off the surge. I witnessed it when you helped us escape the High Coven's goonies who took you. But this is something else," they shook their head, "incredible for sure, but—"

"We are out of our depth," Calla said. "We need a Memoria Witch who can guide Milene. There are plenty within the coven houses, but we aren't ready to enroll them in a coven, right?"

"Right," Jiano said. "But we will need to find someone who can work with them." They considered Phinra.

"And what of your magic?" Ji asked. "How much stronger has it become off the surge?"

Phinra looked down and shrugged. "I don't know. I haven't used my magic in a long time. Because I … I've just wanted to look out for Milene. I know she causes trouble with her magic sometimes, so I didn't want to—"

"Oh, Phinra." Ji patted her knee. I felt a little ache in my heart. Phinra was putting Milene first. It was great that the twins were close and looked out for each other, but Phinra needed to prioritize herself too and not only be Milene's protector.

"We'll get help for both of you," Ji said. "Milene's magic is stronger than yours, but you should also explore your abilities."

"Yes, Madame," Phinra said shyly.

"Jamari Zhao perhaps," I suggested. "He's one of Paluna's people and that might be a better route to go than the covens. Paluna might be able to get us access to literature that expounds on Memoria magic too."

"Good idea," Jiano said. "We could all use more info on our magic, honestly."

Truth. There was more Vanish magic could do. Like Vanish things from a distance, or transfer things from one location to another, the way the ley lines had dragged Vanished things into Elsewhere. I'd wondered if I was strong enough to tap into either of those abilities, but I had absolutely no idea how to do them.

"I'm sorry," came Milene's soft voice. She raised her head. She looked tired. At the conference, she hadn't passed out for long, so Jiano had foregone taking her to the hospital and brought her home where Calla and my mother's combined Regen magic had produced a soothing tea for her and Phinra.

"There's nothing to be sorry for," Jiano said. "Having strong magic is a good thing, and we will do what we can to help you learn everything you need to know. For now, I would like you to focus on making sure you do not enter someone's mind without their consent, okay?"

"You can do it to me all you want," Phinra said. "If you feel the urge, focus on me. That should help."

The love between the sisters was clear. I could relate. Jiano and I always looked out for each other no matter what.

"I ain't happy about the fact that the strength of your magic was blasted worldwide," Ji said, shaking their head. "The HC already wanted to snatch you up, we gotta make sure another attempt isn't made."

"Having to dodge and weave the people meant to lead and protect us because we have stronger magic continues to be insane," I said bitterly. "As is having to hope the strengthened ley lines makes the High Coven back off from taking magic from us."

If witches couldn't trust our leaders and had to deal with haters from the Normie population, where did that leave us but screwed every which way?

"Will they come for me again … will they …"

Shit. Milene's eyes were wide and she was breathing in short, rapid bursts like she was about to hyperventilate. Phinra looked terrified again. Maybe I should have kept those thoughts internal given what the twins had already endured.

"If you believe nothing else, believe that I will keep you safe," Ji said firmly. "We may have unfriendly eyes looking our way, but no one is going to use and abuse you again."

Milene's breathing became more controlled and some of the tension eased from Phinra. I was glad to see the impact of Ji's words; it meant the twins had a measure of trust in them.

"Sorry for scaring you," I said. "I'll protect you too. I promise."

The girls nodded. Phinra even offered a small smile.

"We can talk more later," Calla said, standing up. She walked around the table and extended her hands to the girls. "Come and let's see about dinner, then you can pick the movies we'll watch tonight."

Phinra took a hand and stood up. Milene hesitantly reached for Calla's other hand after staring at it for a few seconds. Something inside me warmed even as it ached. The scar around Calla's wrist from when a client had tried to slice off her hand to see if her Regen magic would regrow it was stark against her pale skin. In the aftermath of the abuse, Calla had been severely touch-averse, but she'd come a long way.

"Let's go." Calla and the twins left Ji's office. Once the door closed, Jiano flopped back against the chaise and released a sound of exhaustion. I moved from the coffee table to sit next to them.

"Oh, Kitten," Ji said wearily, throwing their forearm over their eyes. "What have our lives become?"

"Chaos." Understatement. I drew my legs under me and pulled one of the chaise's pillows into my arms.

"What an absolute riot of a day," Ji said. "I'll tell you what I could use right about now, a scotch and a good fuck. No less than six rounds."

I smirked. "The bordello is opening soon, no?" I glanced at the clock on the nearby wall.

"Yes, and I do have a darling of a gentleman on the schedule," Ji said salaciously. "One of my favorites. Capital 'F' freak. Booked two hours. I have a wonderfully filthy night ahead."

"Love that for you," I said before my face sobered. "The press conference went completely left and revealed more than we were aiming for, but it did end up working in our favor overall."

"You are the Savior of the Ley Lines, the people's darling." Ji turned to me with a smile. I grimaced.

The Q&A had gone favorably, then Marrik and I had had to endure a meet and greet with the press who all wanted exclusive comments. The members of the public who'd been invited wanted to meet us as well, and there'd been a lot of awe directed at us. Everyone wanted more tidbits about Elsewhere and couldn't stop talking about how the ley lines had been revitalized. Many of them wanted to talk to the Memoria Witch who'd been strong enough to recreate my memories, but Jiano had quickly whisked Milene out of the room.

"Well, we moved our game piece across the board. Wonder what Linton and the rest of the council will do."

"We are sure to find out tomorrow," Jiano said. "Assessment day. I bet they're gonna bring something huge to test you with."

"I mean, it wouldn't be terrible to know the limits of my Vanish magic. Guess we'll see."

"Indeed, we will." Jiano reached over and squeezed my knee. "You doing okay? It's been quite an ordeal these past few days."

"I'm hanging in there. Maybe tonight I'll scream into a pillow before I fall asleep, but before that I've gotta get through dinner with Namira."

Ji made a cringey face. "Oh yes, that's right." They huffed out a breath as they stood up. "To that end I suppose I should retrieve Marrik." They started walking toward the bathroom and turned back to me. "I know she's Marrik's cousin but if she acts up, I can have a shadow beast gather her real quick."

I flashed a smile. "I'll keep that in mind."

Namira Kimell didn't like me. But, to her credit, she was trying not to show it.

Marrik, Namira, and I were ensconced in the booth of a Thai restaurant. I was glad it wasn't crowded; I needed a reprieve from the highly visible day I'd had. It was a stylish place; the wall our booth sat against had a pretty leaf pattern, and there was even a waterscape in the center of the room, which was a great backdrop for pics. The lighting was dim and atmospheric, coming from the fixtures on the walls and the round bulbs strung across the ceiling. The scents that accompanied the sizzling sounds from the kitchen were mouthwatering, but I felt too nervous to eat.

Marrik and I sat across from Namira. I hadn't wanted to show up in the press conference clothes, so we'd made a pit stop at home to change. I'd swapped my dress for black jeans and a sleeveless, light blue blouse with a pattern of peacock feathers, and pulled my hair up into space buns. Marrik had ditched the suit jacket, swapped the slacks for jeans, and rolled up the sleeves of his button down.

Namira still had her hair in Fulani braids, same as the last time I'd seen her. She wore a black halter dress that flattered her curvy figure, and a matte, purple lipstick I would have complimented her on if we were homies.

"So, you've had *quite* the day." That pointed statement was directed at Marrik with a raised eyebrow. Marrik sighed and straightened his posture. One hand rested on the table while the other lay on my thigh. His proximity to me and the location of his hand hadn't missed Namira's perception and I'd seen her struggle not to scowl.

"I'm sorry I didn't tell you sooner and personally, Mira," Marrik said. "It's been difficult adjusting back and I needed some time before I could get all of this out."

"And you got it out in front of the entire world before me?" Namira crossed her arms over her chest.

"There were circumstances that made it necessary to do things that way," Marrik said.

"Circumstances—"

"I'm sorry, Mira." Marrik's voice was firm. "There are things going on that endanger Kit and can't be talked about and they relate to the way things went today. Again, I'm sorry I couldn't tell you first. But you pretty much know the entire story now."

"Do I?" Her gaze shifted between us before settling on me. "You lied to my fucking face." Her voice was warm with anger. Marrik stiffened, but before either of us could say anything, our waiter came over for our drink order. I was tempted to tell him to plop a bottle of wine next to me and stick a straw in it but settled for a less messy order of sparkling wine. After he smiled and departed, the tension ratcheted back up.

"I hadn't meant to Vanish Marrik and I lied to protect myself, I won't hedge around that." I met Namira's less-than-friendly stare.

"There was not a day that went by after Marrik was gone that I didn't suffer. I was heartbroken, I hated myself, I honestly did not know how I would continue to live with the pain of what I'd done. I knew that I had removed Marrik not only from myself but from you. From everyone who cared about him and had no closure on what happened to him. And I know how painful the fear of not knowing is. To have questions no one could answer. And then you found the person who could answer them and I lied. I'm sorry, Namira. Vanishing Marrik was a terrible accident, and the incident is not indicative of a lack of control of my magic—"

"Oh?" She leaned forward. "You Vanish Marrik, and somehow yourself, and you think you have control? Especially since now you're apparently even stronger?" She looked at Marrik. "Are you sure it's a good idea to stay so close to her, Mar?"

"Namira." Threads of frustration crept into Marrik's tone.

"She's dangerous," Namira pressed. "She Vanished you! And you're still up under her? Like, come on—"

"You have all right to be concerned but let me make it clear that as long as Kit wants me by her side I will be there." Marrik's tone was steely. "So if your plan tonight was to rail at Kit and suggest we break up, Kit and I can leave right now because as you've seen, we've had a very long day."

Namira pressed her lips together and regarded Marrik, spearing me with a brief glance. "I dunno what to make of all this," she finally said. "That you were gone for a year, your return, everything that came out in that conference."

Her expression slipped and under the anger I could see her worry. She loved Marrik, I knew that the day she showed up at my coven house and confronted me, telling me the lengths she'd gone through to trace Marrik's disappearance and track me down. It wasn't great bearing the brunt of her dark emotions, but I understood.

"We can talk things through more." Marrik's voice was gentler. "I promise I won't keep you locked out, but please give me some grace. I'm still trying to get my legs under me after what I endured in Elsewhere."

Namira's expression softened. "Fine," she huffed. "I don't feel great about your relationship, but I know you well enough to know there ain't shit I can say to make you do anything you don't wanna do." She paused and seemed to be struggling with some inner thought. "I wanted to meet you for dinner for all the obvious reasons but also for something else."

Marrik tensed. As did I.

"What is it?" Marrik asked.

"The family." Namira released a sigh and closed her eyes briefly. She uncrossed her arms and placed her hands in her lap. "After you were gone I was so mad, so stressed, so worried, I took my findings on Kit to them. To … your parents."

Marrik sucked in a gasp. I felt like my heart had turned to ice. There was no hiding my place in Marrik's life after the press conference, but to hear that Namira had personally delivered me to Marrik's witch-hating family …

Vanish me off this planet right fucking now, please.

"Namira, why? Why would you—"

"I wanted justice!" Namira said, a little too loudly. The waiter, who'd been heading over with our drinks, faltered, but regained his smile and came over to place our glasses down and cheerfully tell us he'd give us a few more minutes before taking our food order.

"No, you wanted them to harass Kit, to target her, bully her, maybe carry out violence against her because you know very well how our family operates against witches," Marrik said, hardness creeping back into his voice. "You wanted vengeance, not justice."

"I wasn't the only one worried about you, you know!" she spat. "Uncle Barrett and Aunt Fallon wanted to know where you'd gone too. They were losing their shit over your disappearance, Marrik!"

Marrik flinched hearing his parents' names. They were a topic he carefully avoided and the layers of his feelings when it came to his parents were complex. He didn't speak to them, but they periodically tried to reach him. He'd had to change his number a couple times and I knew how much he hated the way he had to deal with his own parents.

Marrik might have been swayed to the anti-witch agenda had his grandparents not stayed close to him and helped him move out when he was a teenager. But I could always see the conflicting emotions within him about his frayed familial ties. He would never embrace their prejudice, but it hurt that he couldn't have a relationship with his parents and so many other members of his family.

"You gave them my current number," Marrik said flatly. Several voicemails and text messages over the past couple weeks had been from his parents.

"I'm sorry." Namira ducked her head. "Maybe it wasn't my place to do that given your relationship with them, but I figured they deserved some contact after their son blipped out of existence for a year then miraculously returned. They're your parents, Mar—"

"My parents who have spent years organizing hateful campaigns against witches, seeking to oppress an entire group of people simply because they exist. You knew and understood why I removed myself from them and you gave them a direct line to me and made them aware that I've been dating a witch."

Namira turned away. Marrik made a frustrated sound.

"So now they know where I am, and that Kit Vanished me. My witch hating family knows that, Mira. Thanks to the press conference, but also thanks to you."

The wine I'd been sipping felt like it was turning to sludge in my stomach. I was so damn tired of feeling like there was a target on my back. The last thing I needed was witch haters coming for me, but I had to be prepared for that now that I'd been thrust into the spotlight as the 'Savior of the Ley Lines.'

"Look, I … I can't undo what I did. I'm sorry I gave them your number without asking and that I put Kitaine on their radar." She glanced at me. "I'm really trying here, which is why I'm gonna warn you to be careful. Normies First have been acting like their heads are on fire ever since the ley lines got stronger and they realized all witches got stronger as well. The fear is high with the anti-witch groups and our family thinks they have a personal stake to save you from Kit for reasons I'm sure I don't have to explain. That press conference blew your spot wide open. Y'all need to understand that they may try to fuck with you."

"Fucking hell." Marrik dragged his hand down his face. I remained silent but my thoughts were churning and my anxiety was high. Normies First were the biggest hate group and the one Marrik's family was a part of. His parents held leadership roles and wielded a lot of power. All witches had been aware of how the haters had reacted to the return of the ley lines. Sollunara was a witch territory, so we tended to have relative safety, especially since the High Coven was headquartered here, but we weren't exempt from protests and targeted violence. We'd all gotten the feeling that something was simmering these past few weeks, but it had yet to boil over.

It might soon.

"I'm sorry," Namira said. "It's my fault for bringing Kit to them, although they would have found out about her anyway, given the press conference—"

"Namira—"

"Not the point, I know." Her chest rose and fell off an exhale. "I don't know how much I can do but I guess I'm the only buffer between you and them. I'll do what I can to warn you if I hear whispers of anything going down."

"Do you think your parents will come here?" I couldn't mask the anxiety in my voice. Marrik's parents and most of his witch hating family lived in Yarachon, a Normie territory on the west coast.

"No." Marrik shook his head. "It would be too obvious, especially if they are planning to move against you specifically. Coming to Sollunara ahead of something big going down would incriminate them. They won't risk the visibility no matter … no matter what."

No matter how much they might want to see their Vanished and returned son, was the thing unsaid.

"Makes sense." What Marrik said was probably true, but there was no comfort in knowing they'd probably not leave Yarachon to come here. Because danger still loomed and strikes from a distance could still devastate.

"Like I said, I'll do what I can to look out for you, but I'm not sure how much intel might come my way."

Marrik and I exchanged a look. I was sure he was thinking the same thing I was: Paluna. Namira would keep an ear out for Marrik's sake, but we could also utilize Paluna's resources to ensure that knifed-in-an-alley fear I had didn't come to pass at the hands of Normies First.

"I appreciate it." Marrik's voice was clipped and his hand on my thigh was tight.

I resisted the urge to heave a huge sigh. Yet another thing to worry about. I was still a small pawn on a board with behemoths. I was becoming more and more afraid that one of them was gonna topple me.

And as strong as my Vanish magic was, I had to reckon with my use of it and the fact that I couldn't always Vanish my problems away.

Although I sure as shit would to avoid the knife of a hater.

The waiter returned for our food order, which we hadn't paid any attention to, so we paused our conversation long enough to peruse the menu for the very patient waiter. The restaurant staff had recognized us off the press conference and had seemed very pleased that our post-revelation dinner was happening at their establishment. Something told me a snap of us might make it to their social media pages. One of the waiters even had Paluna's merch, the T-shirt, and asked me to sign it.

Her merch was already on the street. Paluna moved faster than the freaking speed of light.

After the waiter left, Namira looked at me. Her face was less hostile.

"I … I guess I should try to get to know you better."

My eyebrows rose. I glanced at Marrik who looked surprised as well. I hadn't expected this kind of progress.

"That would be nice." I offered her a smile.

She gave a curt nod then turned her attention back to Marrik.

"Now," she declared, "I've got a ton of questions about this Elsewhere place so wet your throat and prepare to talk."

Marrik gave her a strained smile but raised his glass of water to his mouth.

Chapter Nine

I don't think I'd ever seen this many witches in The Bramble at the same time. Even when we had communal events, our gathered number had never been this strong.

It was nice though, even if there was an air of nervousness as witches converged on the sprawling, downtown neighborhood that housed our covens. The Bramble was one of my favorite places with its colorful, cottage style coven houses covered in ivy. All the shops, food spots, and street vendors were witch run, and there were several parks and gardens as well as a sizable pond fed by one of the city's rivers.

I'd arrived with Jiano, Rowan, and Calla, but all the bordello witches would be here for the reassessment.

"You know, I fully expected the haters to be out in full force," Rowan commented as we walked down the cobblestoned pathway that cut through one of the parks. It was lined with tall trees whose robust foliage formed a shady canopy over the path. Dappled sunlight shifted across the stones as the leaves moved with the wind.

"So did I," I replied. Rowan was on my left, and one of her stunning, crimson wings brushed my arm as she flexed her back muscles. Before the surge, Rowan could shapeshift feathers across her body with her Mutans magic, but the magical boost had made her strong enough to shapeshift wings. She'd been working with Valentino to strengthen her back muscles in the hope that she'd be able to fly. She wore an orange halter dress with a short, flouncy skirt and low back so the wings, which curved down to the ground, would have no obstruction. Her braided hair draped over her shoulders.

Looking around yielded a view of dozens of witches, many of whom called out to me thanks to yesterday's press conference, but there were no protesters.

"That we're being reassessed today wasn't exactly blasted to the public, but the hate groups have their ways of finding out when we're gathering in larger numbers," Ji said. They were on my right, wearing denim shorts, a bright yellow tank top, and gladiator sandals similar to mine. A summer hat with a broad, curved rim was perched on their head.

Ji and Ma seemed to be in a hat mood, as Ma had tried to plop one on my head when I'd arrived at the bordello, but it hadn't sat well since my hair was still in space buns. It was nine in the morning, but the day promised to be a hot one, so I was wearing high waisted shorts with a white tank top tucked into it.

"I'm sure they knew we'd be gathering today," Ji continued. We'd exited the park and were walking down the road that ran past the river. A warm breeze ruffled our hair and clothes and again tickled Ro's feathers against me.

"I'd like to think the task force has been so diligent they've thwarted any attempts the hate groups made to get at us, but I don't think it's in my best interest to be so optimistic," I said. Thinking about the conversation last night with Namira and the revelation that Normies First was particularly stirred up against me was nerve-wracking. But I couldn't hole up at home and cower. We'd spoken to Paluna about it, and she assured us her people were monitoring all the anti-witch groups.

I continued to feel uneasy about always having to rely on Paluna for intel and protection, but I had to admit that it was much better that I had her as an ally than not.

"I agree," Ji said. "I can't quite shake the feeling that their lack of presence right now doesn't mean we're in for a calm day."

"I don't think calm was ever on the agenda," Rowan said. "This is the first time so many of us are gathering after the surge. The assessment will be a pain, but showing off our stronger magic will be exciting."

"Which is why you already have those beautiful wings ready, hm?" Ji said, to which Rowan flashed a cheeky grin.

"I hope Phinra and Milene are okay," said Calla. She was on Ji's other side, in a champagne-colored shift dress. I noticed she'd added ruffled cuffs at her wrists. They hid her scar, and a lacy bolero over her upper body cut visibility of the other scars she bore from clients with blades. At the bordello she was comfortable enough not to cover them up, but she usually did whenever she had to venture out.

"I'm sure they're alright," Ji said. Since the girls weren't aligned with a coven they weren't here, so Jiano asked Paluna if someone from her team wouldn't mind hanging out with them. Jupiter had volunteered, and created her own anchored shadow in the second-floor bathroom in case an emergency arose, so the twins were as safe as we could leave them.

"Speaking of showing off." My attention had been drawn to the river, where over a dozen aquatic Mutans Witches were swimming.

"I know that's right! Look at you, Emricka!" Rowan cupped her hands to her mouth and called out to one of the swimmers.

Emricka turned at Rowan's shout and waved, laughing. She'd just made an impressive jump and dive into the water, the sunlight glinting off the pink and gold scales that covered much of her dark brown skin. There were gills at her neck, dorsal fins fanned out above her elbow and on either side of her calves, and a webby coronet arched down the middle of her head through her short curls.

"This is really nice to see," Rowan said. "Emricka's magic wasn't strong enough to shapeshift fins or gills, or that many scales. She was naturally a good swimmer, but now she can breathe under water, and all those scales will help insulate her so she can be in the water longer."

"They're all fantastic," Ji said. We'd stopped so we could watch the Mutans Witches swim. There was one whose arms had shifted from elbow down into what reminded me of crab claws. They were indigo blue and huge, and propelled the witch through the water at top speed as he swam freestyle. Another witch's lower body from her mid-thigh down was a beautiful tail with pastel-colored scales and billowy flukes. She and Emricka were racing each other.

"They look great, it's wonderful." I felt a little choked up as I remembered what Paluna and Jiano had reminded me; that despite everything, strength returning to the ley lines was a good thing. I would never stand on a pedestal about it, especially when Remi had been the one who made it possible in the end, but I hadn't allowed myself much time to be warmed by the truth that witches could now grow stronger and become capable leaders for future generations.

Seeing all these examples of what was possible with stronger magic; sky islands, witches who could fly, breathe under water, or conjure magical beasts like Ji's shadow cats, made it clear what a watered-down existence we'd had for so long. I was excited about stepping into this new era and seeing magic thrive again.

"Guess the water assessment already began," Rowan said as we continued walking. On the riverbank stood several witches I recognized as Guardians, our coven house leaders. There were also people who were easily identifiable as being from the High Coven. They had a tablet or a clip board and were making notes as they surveyed the witches in the water.

"Do you think they will ask you to fly?" Calla asked Rowan.

"They'll be disappointed if they do," Rowan said, clucking her tongue. "I can move them a bit, but I've still a long way to go. Strengthening my back muscles is one thing, but there's a lot involved with learning how to fly. I'm hoping my Guardian will have helpful resources."

"I hope so too," Jiano said.

"I wonder if my Mutans creature was the type that thrived better on one of them islands," Rowan said. The floating island was visible in the distance.

More of it hadn't fallen, but the news about the island wasn't improving. It was starting to move faster and was no longer over Keltin. I really hoped the High Coven's team figured out how to send it back out or bring it down safely.

"I could put on performances up there," Rowan continued. "Dance and fly through the clouds in next to nothing. A crimson-feathered fallen angel ready to make people sin." She gave a wicked little laugh.

"Don't get the wheels in my head spinning, darling," Jiano said. "A bordello in the sky? You know I'd make it happen."

"Would put a fresh spin on the phrase 'mile high club,'" I quipped.

"I would love to fuck on a sky island," Jiano said dreamily. "Turn someone out while clouds tickled my ass cheeks, oh yes!"

I snort laughed.

"Me too," Ro agreed. "I just know they did all kinds of kinky shit up there."

"How crass you all are," Calla said with mock airs, turning her nose up disdainfully. "They grew sky-herbs and lived peaceful, family-friendly lives up there and—"

"Now, Calla," Ji said. The three of us paused and turned to her with flat expressions. She regarded us, then smiled.

"And probably got naked and nasty a lot," she finished, giggling. We laughed.

Speculation of getting freaky on a floating island was titillating, but we all agreed this particular island might be bringing more pain than pleasure.

"Anyway, I'm looking forward to seeing who else can create shadow beasts among my Umbras," Ji said.

"No shadow beast cage fighting," I warned.

Ji gave a sly grin. "Not here, at least. But after hours …"

I shook my head.

We walked, chatted, and greeted witches until we needed to part ways and head to our coven houses. I walked down the street that led to Celestine, feeling another warm feeling in my chest as the familiar, ivy-covered house came into view. I hadn't been here since returning from Elsewhere, hadn't done much other than lay low with Marrik and my family.

And now I'd done a complete one-eighty and was probably the most visible witch in the world.

Cool, cool, cool, cool, cool.

Nevertheless, it was nice to be folded back into a normal part of my life.

"Kit!" Tau spotted me and waved, giving me a big smile. She was standing near the door with several other Vanish Witches, including Indira and Elliot. As soon as I reached my coven-mates I was swarmed with hugs and questions.

"Oh my God, that press conference yesterday!" Indira exclaimed, her eyes wide. "Kit, I had no fucking idea you'd Vanished! Into a parallel world? Holy shit!"

"A parallel world that ate up everything we Vanished and had some of the ley lines stored?" Elliot said, looking awestruck as he brushed aside the bangs of his brown hair. "I am still bowled over by that. It may look like I am standing, but trust me, I am flat on my ass."

"Pretty much how I felt when I realized where Vanished stuff ended up," I said. "All the weapons, all the garbage—"

"All the *people.*" Tau raised a pierced eyebrow at me. Her green eyeliner looked great against her dark skin. "Kit, girl, all this time you were strong enough to Vanish people and ain't none of us knew? Bad ass."

I smiled. Something inside me eased and I realized I'd been worried about how my coven-mates would respond to seeing me. But everyone seemed amiable. My back was getting a little sore from all the friendly slaps.

"Thanks," I said with a laugh. "Honestly, it was harrowing, as you heard. A pocket world full of almost four hundred years of Vanished items and people was," I shook my head, "a lot, to put it lightly."

"And your boyfriend," Indira said. "Who, let me just say is extremely fine, good job on that pull." That elicited some laughs and comments about how good-looking Mar was. He'd be amused to hear this later. He was hanging out with Namira today and I was glad they'd be getting some one-on-one time after that intense dinner last night.

"But I feel for you, Kit," Indira continued, her face sobering. "You accidentally Vanished him and you didn't even know that he wasn't truly gone."

"And you never showed it," one of my other coven-mates, Jeon, said. He was looking at me with a mixture of awe and sympathy. "You're really strong, Kit."

"I tried my best, but it wasn't easy." Nor was it easy to talk about this with my friends, but I'd had to brace for that since we'd laid the tale out for the whole world. Naturally, people would want to talk about a story as sensational as this one.

"You hid the boyfriend even before though." Tau crossed her arms over her chest and gave me a shady look. "We coulda double dated so many times!" Tau's girlfriend was a Repel Witch whose coven house was two blocks over.

"Well, yeah, sorry about that." I sheepishly scratched the back of my head. Marrik and I keeping our relationship low profile because of his witch hating family weren't details my coven-mates needed.

"By the way, how's Rohan, Indi?" I asked not only to steer the conversation elsewhere but because I was genuinely concerned. Indira's cousin was a reporter the High Coven had assaulted right as he was on the verge of releasing a report on their witch abductions and amulet experiments.

"He was released from the hospital a little over a week ago," Indira said. "He's gonna be okay, but he never should have been hurt in the first place. And it pisses me off that no one will be brought to justice for it."

"It's really fucked up." Finding out about Rohan's attack had been one of the things that propelled me to work with Paluna to Vanish Gladstone. I knew Paluna wasn't ready to expose the experiments, but I couldn't wait for the day the HC was held accountable for their murderous deeds.

"Is he going to—" I was cut off by the coven house door opening and our Guardian, Reshmi, stepping out. She was South Asian, with graying hair cut short. She was wearing a long, mint colored skirt and matching blouse with embroidery around the round neckline.

"Elliot, what's our number?" She had a no-nonsense tone and wasn't prone to small talk though she was generous with her time and teaching.

"Twenty-five," Elliot replied. "Most are at the park, as you instructed."

"Good, let's all head there." Reshmi took a step forward then paused when she saw me. She smiled and placed a hand on my shoulder.

"Welcome back, Kitaine. I'm rather surprised by yesterday's revelations, but I'm glad you're safe and have returned to us. We will talk later, yes?"

"Of course."

Reshmi nodded, then moved forward to lead our little group.

"Why are we heading to the park?" I asked Elliot. The coven house was large enough to hold all of us.

"Apparently the things we're going to be assessed with are arriving via the river," Elliot replied. "Our testing won't be taking place in the coven house."

"Oh." My eyebrows rose.

"They're gonna be bringing things bigger than what's already been logged for us," Tau said. "Tryin' to fit all of us, plus a bunch of junk for us to Vanish inside Celestine is a recipe for disaster."

"Yeah, facts." I'd been threading nervousness all day and couldn't squash it. That I could Vanish people was already known. And, thanks to Milene, it was also known that I had grown the strength of my magic off the ley lines.

I wondered what the largest thing I'd be asked to Vanish would be.

"Have any of y'all tried?" Jeon asked. "I gave it a go and Vanished my sister's aerobic step. She was pissed. Couldn't Vanish anything that big before."

Reshmi gave him a disapproving look. Vanishing things willy nilly was frowned upon.

Not that I had any stones to throw in that regard.

"I ain't tried," Tau said. "Been too busy helping Fang repair the damage to her parents' house. The surge made her Repel everything in the living room. Place was wrecked. The television went straight through the wall."

Jeon whistled. "Damn. Heard a lot of stories like that. Also heard the surge made a lot of people spontaneously Vanish whatever they were touching at the time. So far I haven't heard that people were accidentally Vanished, so maybe the surge didn't power us up that much."

I'd been checking reports on the aftermath of the surge, especially curious about how it had affected Vanish Witches. Jeon was right, so far, Vanished people hadn't been reported, but that didn't mean it hadn't happened. I hoped it hadn't though, since there was no Elsewhere anymore and Vanishing now truly meant non-existence.

I let the chit chat of my coven-mates distract me as we headed to our destination, finally arriving at one of the parks that ran along the river. I'd expected it to be laid out with tables full of items for us to Vanish, but there wasn't anything Vanish-able that I could discern. It was full of people though. There were four Vanish covens in The Bramble, each with about two dozen witches, and we were all gathered here with our Guardians.

"So where's the shit we gonna be tested with?" Tau asked as we entered the park.

"Um, could that have anything to do with it?"

I looked where Indira was pointing and my eyes widened when I saw a huge, yellow shipping container coming down the river on top of a barge.

"That is where the assessment will take place," Reshmi said. "It contains items of various sizes, including human dummies."

That got a murmur of nervous conversation going.

"It is going to be a taxing day," Reshmi continued. "The size increase of the items you'll be asked to Vanish will be incremental and everything will be recorded. The HC reps will share the new data they log with the Guardians. I will be tested too, of course."

There were sighs and groans among us. Vanishing items with incremental size increases sounded tedious as fuck. The body dummies were sure to make a lot of people anxious. If anyone was strong enough to Vanish a dummy, they'd join the rest of Vanish Witches who were heavily monitored.

This begged the question of what the approach to strengthening our magic would be, but that was a headache for another day. Though something told me the High Coven wouldn't exactly be giving their blessing for Vanish Witches to power up too much.

We milled around and chatted for a while, watching as the shipping container finally docked. People filed off the barge and they needed no introduction to be identified as the HC's reps. There were about a dozen people in their business casual best, and a few people who looked like assistants. The assistants were carrying tablets.

The Guardians went to talk to the High Coven witches while the rest of us watched the barge crew open the front of the shipping container. I could see tables along the sides neatly arranged with various items.

After several minutes, Reshmi came back over. "They'll do two covens at a time," she said. "We're up first along with Aura, so let's go."

"This is gonna be remembered as a very strange day," Elliot said as we walked toward the ramp that led up to the barge. Once on board, we greeted the crew and headed into the shipping container along with the witches from Aura.

About half of the High Coven witches and their assistants had come with us while the rest stayed outside. They stationed themselves behind the tables.

"Bigger in here than I thought it'd be," Tau commented, looking around, same as I was. There were holes peppered around the top of the container which let light stream through. The main light source was from bulbs strung along the walls that were probably powered by a small generator hidden somewhere.

"There are the body dummies," someone said in a hushed voice. I caught sight of them at the back, draped over a table. They looked like crash test dummies.

"They're even diverse, how nice," someone else said, which made us snicker. The dummies varied in skin tone.

"The Celestine witches will be at the tables to the right, the Aura witches to the left," one of the HC witches announced. "You will give your name to one of the assistants, who will pull up your file. What has already been recorded as the capabilities of your Vanish magic will inform which objects you'll start with. Let us commence."

We moved accordingly and lined up to wait our turn with an assistant. I was strong enough to Vanish this shipping container, what exactly would be my starting point?

"Ms. Neris." I startled at the sound of a voice behind me and turned to see the HC witch who'd made that announcement. An older white woman with brown hair and glasses perched at the tip of her nose.

"Your testing will be different from your coven-mates," she continued. "There will be another container arriving shortly with larger items for you to start with. The shipping container will also be part of your test."

"Ah." I squeezed out a smile. "Got it, thanks." Honestly, I wasn't surprised they were putting a shipping container up for me.

"You may have a seat so as to stay out of the way." She indicated stools at the back, near the dummies.

"Cool." I made my way to a stool, glancing at the dummies and thinking I'd come up with outrageous names for them to share with my coven-mates when they made it over here. I pulled my phone out and saw a few texts from Marrik, checking in and letting me know what he was up to with Namira. Apparently, they'd gone to a park and several people had flocked to Marrik after recognizing him from the press conference. Marrik said one of them announced that they were a social media influencer with a big following and would be posting the selfie they took with Marrik. That text was accompanied by several crying emojis.

I smiled as I texted him back, congratulating him on his new social media fame. Then I answered a text from Ma about what she should cook for dinner. We were gonna be eating with my parents at their rental house. I'd kept telling Ma she didn't have to cook so much, but she insisted, and when Jiano nudged me to understand that my mother needed to mother me, I backed off. I had kept her at arm's length for a year after Marrik Vanished, then she'd almost lost me. She could cook for me all she wanted.

I gave her some suggestions, after which she texted five thumbs up emojis. I was about to answer a few more messages when elevated voices drew my attention to the front of the shipping container.

Just in time to see the doors slam closed.

Seconds later an explosion erupted. It hadn't occurred inside the container, but the force of it rocked the entire thing. The ear-splitting sound made me feel like I'd taken a mallet to the skull.

"What the hell?" I jumped up only to fall when another explosion resounded, and it felt as though I was standing on a trap door that suddenly opened.

The container dropped as though the barge under it had disappeared. I heard a booming sound and couldn't get my feet under me as the container tilted. All the dummies fell off the table, many of them landing on top of me.

I didn't understand what the fuck was happening, but I knew it wasn't good.

The doors had been closed, there'd been explosions, and the container was clearly in the water.

Oh shit. The river. We were in the river.

And water was rapidly pouring in.

Chapter Ten

The container had fallen sideways, so water was pouring in not only from the seams but from the holes that ran along the top.

The lightbulbs popped and went out, plunging us into darkness. I slammed into a wall and was soaked as water continued to rise. People were screaming and thrashing, and we kept getting tangled together. Someone's arm struck me across the face and snapped my neck back. *Ouch.* Seconds later I took a blow to my stomach. Nails scraped down my skin, and I had to disentangle myself from people who grabbed me as though I was a lifeboat. Trying to hold on to each other would only ensure we drowned quicker.

All the items in the container made the situation worse because it restricted movement. I struggled from behind a table only for another one to hit me and send me down.

My entire body was submerged. The container was filling up fast.

I broke through the surface. Gasped for air and clutched a table, trying to keep from going under again. Panic, fear, and anxiety rioted through me as terrified screams echoed off the metal walls. I didn't know what to do. I could yell for my friends, for Reshmi, but we were all in the same predicament.

How the hell had this happened? I gritted my teeth as I tried to pull myself further onto the table. Something heavy slammed into my legs and knocked me off and I went under again. My panic skyrocketed as I tried to find my way up, but the items in the water made it feel as though I were navigating an obstacle course designed for failure.

My lungs burned. Where was the surface, where was it! I was flailing my arms and legs, trying to move things out of the way, trying not to give in to the burn in my muscles as I started to tire.

Finally, my head broke through and I sucked in a deep breath. The screams and desperate cries for help felt like a physical assault against my skull.

I was paralyzed by the fear that this shipping container would soon be serving as our grave.

I couldn't tell how much water had filled it up, but it didn't matter. Once there was no longer a pocket of air, a surface we could break through, we would drown.

We would drown in a shipping container at the bottom of the river.

No. No. Oh no.

Survive. I had to survive. I had to do something to save all of us.

Vanish. I could Vanish the container!

But first, I had to touch it. And I could barely see my hand in front my face.

Move. Just move. I would eventually come to one of the sides if I kept moving.

But moving was damn near impossible and I kept getting pulled under. Water choked me and I was becoming more and more fatigued. I could barely control my movements so there was no telling if I was heading closer to the sides or moving in circles.

Don't stop, don't stop. I was terrified beyond belief, but if I didn't do something, we would die before anyone could save us. The only magic that could help was mine.

I could do it. I had to.

My throat felt choked, but this time it was with tears. I was once again draped over some large object, trying to kick my feet and move forward as water continued to push me every which way.

I couldn't save us from Elsewhere. Remi had done it by sacrificing himself.

I hadn't been able to save Vonuis from the criminals I'd Vanished without making a grave mistake that had taken Marrik from me.

When it came to being safe from the HC, I had to rely on Paluna's machinations.

This time *I* had to do it. I had to save myself and everyone else.

I pulled myself up, and when I raised my hand, it connected with something hard and cold. Something that was not yet wet.

The shipping container! I was sure there was little time left before the entire thing filled up and the air pocket was gone. I had to be quick.

I got my other arm out of the water and called up my magic. A gasp tore from my throat as my magic felt like lightning streaking through my body. I hadn't Vanished anything these past few weeks, so I hadn't had time to assess the strength of my magic.

I propelled myself up, arms above my head, palms spread wide. They slapped against the container and I pushed my magic into it.

I couldn't doubt my magic. I had Vanished a warehouse bigger than this when I'd practiced with Onyx. I was strong enough. I was—

The touch of metal under my palms disappeared. It Vanished!

But that meant the pocket of air also disappeared and water washed over me completely. I was pushed down amid people and items and couldn't get my bearings so I could swim to the surface.

I was so disoriented I couldn't tell which way was up.

Panic. Panic. The container was gone but if we couldn't make it to the surface—

Something brushed against me. Seconds later hands hooked under my armpits and I was pulled up. I suddenly found myself moving fast. All the debris in the water was still knocking into me, but whoever was holding me never wavered from the direction they were going. I got a sense of powerful kicks as my body, which was little more than dead weight since I could do nothing to assist, was held tight against them.

Finally, we broke through the surface. I gasped in air as I choked and sputtered. I felt close to death as I tried to keep breathing, to suck air into my lungs instead of water.

My vision was blurry as I turned my head, but I caught sight of dark skin covered in scales. It was Emricka, the Mutans Witch Rowan had called out to when we were walking past the river.

I would have collapsed in relief, but well, I was already collapsed in Emricka's arms. I was exhausted, half the river felt like it was inside me, and my emotions were spiraling through all the worst ones, though a thread of relief wound through.

Emricka reached the shore and got us out of the water and several feet away from it. I dropped onto the gravel but had to pull myself up so I could vomit. Emricka gently patted my back as I retched, my stomach clenching painfully as it tried to expel nasty river water.

"You're okay, you're gonna be okay," she kept saying. "You're Kitaine, right? I saw you on television yesterday."

I was shaking as I raised my head and looked around. Further relief edged in when I saw that other aquatic Mutans Witches had joined Emricka to rescue us. I saw Tau, Jeon, and Reshmi, as well as Aura and HC witches being pulled onto the bank. Once a Mutans Witch got someone to the shore, they dove back into the water for someone else.

We all need to make it out. Please, let us all make it out alive.

From the time I'd broken the surface of the water I'd heard sirens. Paramedics had arrived and were making their way to us.

"KIT!" Jiano's voice bellowed. "KIT! Where is my sister! I swear to God, you'd better let me through, I am getting in that fucking water! Kit!"

"Ji ..." But that was nothing more than a wheeze that would never reach Ji's ears. Thankfully, Emricka helped.

"Hey, Kit is over here, she's over here!" Emricka stood up and waved while I collapsed back to the ground. I had the distinct feeling I knew what a fish flopping on the shore felt like. Not quite dead and not quite alive.

It wasn't long before Jiano was on their knees at my side, pulling me into their arms.

"Oh, fucking hell, Kit!" Jiano clutched me against their chest. "When I heard a shipping container full of Vanish Witches fell into the river I almost slapped the person who said it for making up something so ridiculous."

"What the hell happened?" Rowan was with Jiano.

"Those of us who were in the water saw," Emricka said. "The barge the container was on blew up and the entire thing fell into the river!"

"Holy shit!" Ro exclaimed. "It was done on purpose; you can't tell me otherwise. Emricka, girl, thank you for saving Kit." She knelt next to Jiano. "We gotta let the paramedics look at her, Ji."

"Get one over here, please," Ji said. Rowan nodded and jogged away.

I sucked in a breath and used what strength I had left to push against Ji until they let me go enough so I could sit up.

"The barge ... blew up?" My voice was hoarse.

"I bet it was—"

"Hey, look over there!"

We looked where Emricka indicated and saw a boat pull up. The purple and cream colors identified it as belonging to the High Coven's marine task force who patrolled Vonuis' rivers.

The boat docked, and over half a dozen officers emerged. Each of them was holding a handcuffed person by the arm.

My eyes widened. The handcuffed people were the barge's crew.

"We saw some people on jet skis not too long before the barge exploded but didn't immediately make the connection," Emricka said. "I'm glad they were scooped up though."

"The barge's crew," I said, before pausing to cough. "It was a set up."

"I'm gonna conjure a shadow beast and tear them apart," Jiano growled. I started to feel Ji's magic rise and clamped a hand around their forearm, squeezing until it quelled.

The riverbank was crowded, so it wasn't easy to keep sight of the task force officers, but their captives weren't going quietly, and the shouts that rose above the melee made me feel like shards of ice had speared my heart.

"NORMIES FIRST! DEATH TO WITCHES!"

"THIS IS ONLY THE BEGINNING! WITCHES MUST BE STOPPED!"

"MORE MAGIC, MORE PROBLEMS!"

"NORMIES FIRST! NORMIES FIRST!"

"Fuck." It was bad enough an anti-witch group had just tried to kill a bunch of us, it was even worse that it was the group Marrik's family was a part of.

There was a small hospital in The Bramble and that was where the paramedics had been dispatched from. I'd been loaded into an ambulance and wrapped in a warming blanket. Jiano rode with me and called our parents. They already knew what happened, since cell phone pictures and videos had spread across social media. Because it was so chaotic, Jiano advised that it was better for them to stay put than try to barrel down here.

My mother hadn't agreed until Jiano switched to a video call so she could see that I was very much alive and had all my faculties. Standing beside her, scales had rippled across Dad's skin as he conveyed his distress that an anti-witch group had attacked us.

At the hospital I got out of my wet clothes and into dark gray sweats. I was given a Regen potion to drink, which expelled everything from my stomach. I threw up so much river water I was surprised there was any river left. My scrapes and bruises were treated, and after checking my lungs to make sure they were free of water and some other tests, I was allowed to leave. The hospital was in a frenzy. I wanted to check on my coven-mates but didn't want to impede the doctors and nurses.

But I could already tell that a lot of people hadn't fared as well as I had.

Jiano and I made our way back to Celestine. No one was there. Every single one of my coven-mates were in the hospital. At least, I hoped they were. I prayed no one had been left behind in the river. Prayed no one was heading for the morgue instead of a hospital bed.

I was unfathomably angry. We'd been the victims of a premeditated, coordinated attack by people who hadn't given a second thought about trying to drown us simply because we were witches. Today would have been a massive tragedy if I hadn't been able to Vanish the shipping container.

And that was the doubled edged sword witches always had to live with, wasn't it? There would always be people who feared and hated us because they didn't trust our magic, but without our magic we couldn't protect ourselves from them.

"Marrik still isn't answering," Jiano said, lowering their phone and glaring at it as though it had offended them. We were on the couch in the seating area, and I had a moment of déjà vu. The last time I'd sat here was when Namira had tracked me down and we'd had the tensest conversation of my life.

I couldn't call Marrik myself because my phone and bag belonged to the river now. Jiano had been calling and messaging him since they'd hung up from talking to our parents but had yet to receive a reply.

"He'd told me Namira wanted to drive out to rock gardens in the south and reception is spotty down there." My throat was sore from coughing. I was trying not to feel uneasy about Ji's inability to reach him. He was spending the day with his cousin, I'm sure he was fine. The lack of reception was probably the culprit or Marrik would have seen the incident on social media same as my parents did. He would have called me, and when he couldn't reach me, he would have tried Jiano.

"Rowan and Hye-Jin are grabbing us some food," Ji continued, reading texts. "Valentino and Arjun are coming over. Calla is assisting at the hospital."

I nodded. A lot of Regen Witches had medical training since their magic aligned with healing. Even if they didn't, they could take instructions about infusing magic into potions or healing small cuts or wounds. Calla had worked in the medical field for a few years before she'd joined the bordello.

"I hope everyone is okay," I whispered. I wanted to see my coven-mates walk through the door.

"Calla said so far four deaths have been confirmed," Jiano said sadly. Their hand, which was on my knee, gave a gentle squeeze. "But their names haven't been released yet."

"Oh gods, oh no. No, no, no." Ji pulled me into their arms. My body shook as I sobbed against their chest. I'd been holding on to the hope that every single one of us had made it out of the river alive, and now I had confirmation that we had not. It didn't matter who those four witches were; whether they were from Celestine or Aura, whether I was close to them or not, none of us should have died. Not a single one of us should have died today.

"This shouldn't have happened," I sobbed. "They dropped us in the river to die, like we were trash being tossed out. They were gonna kill dozens of witches and lose no sleep over it. Sick, evil, evil people!"

"They were caught at least." Ji's voice was warm with anger. "And I have more than half a mind to find those sons of bitches and make them choke on a shadow so they know what it feels like to drown."

"It was awful." The memory of the shipping container filling up with water would fuel my nightmares for a long time. "Dark. Everyone screaming. Water flooding in and the objects in there making it hard to move. I kept getting dragged down."

"You Vanished the container, right?"

"Yes. And it was almost too late, the water had almost reached the top, there would not have been any more air to breathe."

"Oh, Kit." I wasn't the only one shaking, a tremble was going through Jiano. "Why do I keep almost losing you?"

"I'm sorry."

"Hush. What do you need to be sorry for?"

I released a sigh that felt as though it had expelled my soul. I was so tired and not just physically.

"I feel like no matter what I do I keep fucking up in the worst ways." I swiped the heel of my palm under my eyes. Jiano reached for the box of tissues on the coffee table and I pulled a few out.

"I tried to Vanish criminals and I Vanished Mar," I continued. "I tried to save us from Elsewhere but my plan went awry and in the end Remi saved us and it cost him everything. And now I'm like a beacon shining in the face of the haters. Maybe they would have orchestrated that attack anyway, but I can't help but feel as though it was no coincidence that it happened when I was on the barge."

I sighed again and looked at Ji. "And I've brought trouble to the bordello too. The High Coven has their eye on you because I tried to Vanish Gladstone there."

Ji gave me a gentle smile. "My baby sis, you have a hero complex, did you know that? You want to save everyone but you wanna do it in the best way, the "right" way. You want to Vanish the bad guys then go home and flirt with Remi and hit the sheets with Marrik. You want this perfect situation where the outcome is always what you want it to be: the heroes win and the bad guys lose. But, Kit, you need to understand that while that will certainly be the case sometimes, it won't be the case all the time."

Fresh tears welled as the truth of their words sunk into me. Jiano had always been perceptive, and when it came to me they never shied away from telling me like it was.

"When you make a choice to do something like be a Vanish Witch vigilante, you have to accept that even your best laid plans may go left," they continued. "And you have to accept it because you *chose* the vigilante path. You put yourself in the position where you could do something great like removing a violent or corrupt person, but you could also get hurt or killed going after a mark, or you could Vanish the wrong person."

"Which I did."

"Yes. It was a consequence of your choices. Same as stopping underground fighters from being killed or people from being kidnapped and trafficked were good consequences of Vanishing certain people. And while your choices could bring trouble for others, you don't need to worry 'bout no eyes on my bordello. I will protect the Hexes come hell or highwater and you know there's nothing about this that I hold against you."

"I know, but—"

"It will always be a mixed bag: good consequences, and bad. You tend to focus on the bad. You *know* there's a lot of good. We take our wins and we weather our losses the best we can. One of your losses was reversed, wasn't it? You got Marrik back. And Remi will always be a hero in our eyes and never forgotten."

"Remi." I had left his amulet at home as the top I'd chosen wouldn't have hidden it very well. I was glad I had made that choice, as it could have gotten lost in the river.

Actions and consequences, like Ji had said.

"The visibility you gained off yesterday's press conference may help keep you safe from the High Coven, but maybe it also drew more danger to you and other witches," Ji said. "Mixed bag. Doubled-edged blade. You have to be prepared for a lot of things to be both good and bad, Kitten."

"But the bad is death, Ji." Another sob choked me. "Death. Witches died today!"

"I know." Ji gathered me into their arms and I started sobbing again. "And I am so sorry any of this happened. But do not blame yourself. The witch haters were bound to take things up a notch after realizing we all got a little stronger."

Stronger because the ley lines were back. Which was a consequence of my actions. How was I not supposed to feel guilty?

But I didn't say anything more; I couldn't. All I could do was let Jiano hold me as I cried. As I screamed and sobbed and wished I had the kind of magic that could undo this terrible, terrible day.

Chapter Eleven

I couldn't sleep.

Glancing at Marrik's phone on the bedside table, I saw that it was after two in the morning. Marrik was spooned around me, and his arm was a warm weight over me as we lay on my bed. His snores had been keeping me company for some time.

Jiano had finally gotten hold of him when he'd hit stable reception as Namira drove back from their excursion. We'd met up at my parents' rental house where Marrik had been churning with deep emotions over the fact that Normies First had carried out an attack that almost killed me and he hadn't been able to get to me sooner. Namira seemed shocked as well and said she didn't have intel on whether Marrik's family had been directly involved.

We'd spent a few hours there, having dinner and watching the news reports of the incident.

Seven witches had drowned. Three of them were from Celestine. One of them was Elliot. I had cried on and off for hours until I'd gotten a dehydration headache. I didn't even have a phone so I could check in with everyone, although I was certainly not the only one whose phone had met a watery grave. All I kept thinking was how this never should have happened. How I should have thought about Vanishing the container sooner. How if I had done so, the Mutans Witches would have been able to reach us quicker and no one would have drowned.

Guilt felt like it was shredding everything inside me to dust.

I knew what Jiano had said was right. I couldn't expect a bright sunny path through every problem. I had to accept that not everything would turn out perfectly and there were things I had no control over.

But I hated it. I wanted to save the day without losing anyone. I was likely the strongest witch in the entire world. And still, seven people had died today. My stronger magic hadn't been enough.

What if I could have used Vanish transference? Or if I hadn't needed to touch the container to Vanish it? Would it have bought us time? Made it so no one drowned?

Tears slipped down my cheeks. I wiped at them then gently moved Marrik's arm so I could get up. Being wrapped in his arms was comforting, but I was too restless and emotional to sleep.

And … I glanced at Marrik. There was a crease to his brow, as though he was having troubled dreams. Ever since I'd met Marrik and found out what his family was like there'd been a small voice lodged in the back of my mind:

How long could I be in a relationship with someone from a witch hating family?

It didn't matter how wonderful Marrik was. And he truly was. He'd drawn boundaries and put space between him and his family long before he'd met me. He made no excuses for them and made it clear that he would never take the side of hateful people over mine or any other witch. But we'd still had to keep a low profile, and now we couldn't even do that. I was known to everyone, his family knew I'd Vanished him, and there was no denying how much of a target I'd become.

I loved Marrik. I had missed him every single day I thought he was gone forever. I wanted to stay by his side, to support him through his transition back from Elsewhere, to continue to heal what was broken between us.

But, as I was learning more and more, I may not always get what I wanted. And I couldn't ignore the fear that had taken root that the circumstances of our lives might reach a point where we were cleaved into too many pieces to put back together.

I wiped my tears again then eased off the bed and left the room. I washed my face and headed to the kitchen for a glass of water, taking it to the living room and turning on a lamp.

I sat on the sofa and sipped.

"Savior of the Ley Lines." One of Paluna's merch T-shirts was on the coffee table.

"Failure of everything else." Self-pity wouldn't get me anywhere but the deaths of those seven witches was a ghost haunting every breath I took. Elliot had been my friend. It was impossible to reconcile the vivid memory of us chatting and walking from Celestine to the river with the knowledge that he was now a cold body in a morgue locker. That there were people who loved him who were torn apart by grief at his loss.

All because of prejudice. Of the made-up beliefs witch haters had about us that led them to feel as though eradicating us was the only way they could live peacefully. They didn't give two shits about *our* lives and *our* peace.

I was so angry. So grieved.

My eyes fell on something else on the coffee table. The suppression gloves the High Coven had oh-so-kindly gifted me. I picked one up, running my thumb over the fabric.

This was what the High Coven wanted for stronger witches. How were they any better than groups like Normies First? They lived in fear too, which was why they sought to implement measures of control. That was what led to the amulet experiments; it was all to make sure our witch leaders and their task force remained stronger than the rest of us.

"Actions and consequences," I whispered. They got their amulets and advanced magic-tech, but it came at the cost of witch lives. But while I sat here with intense emotional pain over what happened today, I was sure Linton Gladstone never lost sleep over his actions. Maybe some of the witches who were part of his deadly program did, but it didn't matter when they still bled witches dry.

I smoothed out the glove in my hand. Something like this could stop accidental Vanishing. There were witches who had issues controlling their magic. The same way my father spontaneously shapeshifted when he was jolted by deep emotions, there were scenarios like that for all the witch classes.

Health issues could cause magical mishaps too. There were studies on witches with sleep apnea that looked at the ways their magic manifested when they slept. They'd repel or magnetize something. Partially shapeshift. Kill or overgrow the plant on their windowsill. Vanish Witches would wake up with their blanket or pillows gone or an article of clothing.

Using our magic was like flexing a muscle. We were in control of it. But there were a lot of things that could affect our control.

With weaker magic, Vanishing your pillow or the ball you were playing with was the most that would happen. But now that we could use the ley lines to grow stronger ...

You could accidentally Vanish the partner sleeping next to you, or the friend you were playing with.

I ground my teeth together. I hated the idea of these gloves, but I couldn't act as though there wouldn't be benefits. But I'd be stupid to think they'd only be used on people who would agree to wear them because of their control issues.

I turned the glove over in my hand, straightening out the fingers. I slipped it on. I'm not sure why. I hated how these things felt. How would someone who had trouble controlling their magic fare wearing these for hours?

They'd have to work on how tight they were. Damn things would turn your hands cold and blue real quick.

And—

"*Kit.*"

I sucked in a gasp and held very, very still, my eyes growing wide and darting around the room.

"Remi?" Tears welled again. I was in a terrible place emotionally, had I imagined—

"*Kit ... Kit ...*"

No, I had definitely heard Remi's voice. But how?

I looked down at my hand inside the suppression glove. I'd dreamt of Remi when I'd fallen asleep with these gloves on. And now, I had one on and I'd heard Remi's voice.

But I was awake. Last time it had been a dream.

It had been a dream. So how was Remi …

"Remi, where are you?" His amulet was around my neck and I raised my hand to grasp it. There was a slight warmth to the amber stone embedded in it.

"Here," came his soft, strained voice.

"I … am … here …"

"Where, Remi, oh God, where are you? Please, are you truly not gone?"

I pricked my finger and fed the amulet a drop of blood. Nothing happened. Frustration lanced through me.

"Onyx did something, she did *something*. What did she do?" If I could hear Remi while I was awake then something was going on and I had to figure out what.

"Kit … Kit …"

I wanted Remi to say more, to explain. But it didn't seem as though he could talk much.

I chewed my lip as I looked at my gloved hand. If I wore the gloves and fell asleep, would I dream about Remi like last time?

I had to try. This was no coincidence, nor could I continue to believe that dream had just been a dream.

The gloves were tight, and I hated the way they made me feel as though my magic was nonexistent. But I could endure a few hours of wearing them to see if Remi appeared in my dreams again.

I reached for the other glove and pulled it on. But I didn't head back to my room. I curled up on the couch and kept my hand around Remi's amulet.

"Remi, if you are still with me, I will find you, I promise," I whispered.

"Kit …"

Every now and then Remi would say my name. Eventually, it lulled me to sleep.

I was once again in a dream carved out of darkness. But it was only seconds before I heard Remi whisper my name and turned to see him standing behind me.

My heart ached to see him like this. Withered, desiccated, his hair stringy and sparse, so transparent I was afraid I would blink and he'd disappear.

I moved forward and gently slid my hand around his wrist. He shuddered at my touch, a wheezing sound easing from his throat. His once vibrant, hazel eyes, now dull and sunken in, looked down at me.

"Remi, talk to me. I thought I had dreamed you a few days ago but just now I heard you calling me when I was awake. Are you—"

I was afraid to say it because I was scared of either answer. If he was gone, I had to live with his loss. If he was still with me but he was like this … a withered phantom … I could not bear it.

"Are you in the amulet?" I finished. "Did Onyx save you from Withering completely?"

Remi nodded, a slow movement of his head. I sucked in a breath as conflicting emotions spiraled through me. Sorrow, happiness, confusion, fear. The idea that Remi was still here was wonderful. But he was Withered. And if he was in the amulet, why hadn't he come out when I'd fed it blood?

"She … did not let me … Wither … completely." Remi's voice was like the faintest rustle of wind through dry leaves. I took a step closer, my hand tightening around his wrist.

"She took … what was left … and put it … back." He raised his hand and touched my chest, where the amulet lay. His hand slid over the dull, amber stone and his expression became even sadder.

"So that's what she did." I was having an impossible time getting my emotions to settle. I thought back to those final moments when there'd been nothing but noise, the ground had been shaking violently, and Elsewhere had been collapsing around us. Onyx had touched Remi and he'd dissipated into motes of light around her hand. Then she'd come back to me and touched the amulet.

A gift. May you one day know how to use it.

Was Remi the gift? I frowned. She'd also touched me, and I'd felt something pulse into me. Had she done something other than put what was left of Remi back into the amulet?

I had thought about that moment over and over again. Tried to discern if I felt any different but couldn't identify anything that felt off. But I could continue to puzzle that out some other time. Right now, the most important thing to focus on was Remi.

"Remi, have you been calling for me? All this time, have you—"

He nodded. "Did not think … you could hear me."

"I didn't until that last dream. And just now when I …" I looked at my hands. The suppression gloves weren't represented in the dream. I frowned.

"Both times involved wearing gloves that suppress my magic."

"Su … suppress?" Remi's eyes widened.

"New tech the High Coven has come up with. Wearing them cuts me off from my magic."

"Kit … are you … is there danger …"

"I'm fine," I said quickly. Trust Remi to be in the condition he was in and care more about me. "I don't know why my magic being suppressed allows me to hear you and brings me to you in my dreams but—"

"You … are strong," he whispered. "I … am weak."

I stared at him as I turned that over. Could the strength of my Vanish magic have something to do with it? Made it so I couldn't hear Remi?

"Shit." I ran my free hand through my hair. Here was another double-edged blade. I had stronger magic but it somehow made it so Remi couldn't get my attention from inside the amulet.

"But I've fed the amulet blood so many times. Why haven't you come out?"

"Weak," he said sadly, shaking his head. "Cannot ... do ... much." He looked around at the dark void. "Can only ... wait. I waited ... and hoped ... that you would ... hear me."

"Oh, Remi." I looked around as well. "When you're in the amulet, is this what it's like?"

He nodded. "In here ... there is nothing. But when I was with you ... it was everything."

His thin hand touched my face. "I miss you ... Kit."

I leaned into his trembling touch. "I miss you too, Remi, so much. I wanted you to come back, I wanted to find a way to give you something better than what you've had, trapped in this damn amulet."

"Will ... never have ... what I want."

His voice was so grieved. I felt crushed by how terrible things had been for Remi for so long. Centuries. He deserved better. I had to figure out how to help him.

"Onyx saved you from being destroyed but you're too weak to come out of the amulet and I can only hear you or dream of you when I have suppression gloves on." An uncomfortable feeling wormed through me. What if I'd never encountered these gloves? Remi would have been trapped in the amulet endlessly. Calling for me and I never would have heard him.

I shook my head. I couldn't dwell on what could have been, I had to focus on the variables at hand.

"Remi." I locked eyes with him. "I don't know how to get you out of the amulet if my blood isn't enough, but I will find out, I swear. I'll talk to Paluna, she's my best resource. She was looking into your bones and probably knows some Mortem Witches I can talk to."

I couldn't go inquiring at the Mortem Witch coven houses. Not when it came to a ghost amulet I wasn't supposed to be in possession of.

Remi's lips gave a faint twitch; he was trying to smile. He nodded.

"Believe … in you …"

"I won't fail you, I swear." I tried to put as much conviction in my tone as I could to make sure he understood. "One way or another I'll get answers on how to get you out and how to bring your ghost back from this state."

"Bring back." He sounded heartbroken.

I wished I could promise him life. But I would not offer him promises I couldn't keep. The only possibility was that he could become rejuvenated and remain a bound ghost. Or perhaps be free and at peace should Paluna's thoughts about a ritual that could unbind him from the amulet using his remains come to fruition.

But the first step was figuring out how to get him out of the amulet and become whole again.

"I'll bring you back however I can."

It was the safest promise I could make.

"And I'll come again. Every night. I don't really understand how we're able to interact like this but I'm glad. Maybe Onyx did something that allows my subconscious to meet you in the amulet."

I'd wear the suppression gloves if it meant I could be with Remi. And I would do whatever it took to help him.

"I'm here until I wake up." His hand was still cupping my cheek and he slowly moved his thumb across my skin. "Although it would be nice if we had better views. Remember when Onyx turned her dingy bar into a sunlit café? That'd be nice. If I could shape this dream the way Onyx shaped Elsewhere I could—"

A strange feeling suddenly came over me. It started as a pressure in my head, but it didn't feel the same as Memoria magic. It shivered down my body and made me gasp, my eyes going wide. Something about it very faintly reminded me of Onyx.

Seconds later, the landscape around us shifted. There was a rippling motion in the air and the darkness melted away, allowing a new scene to bleed through.

Remi made a sound of surprise. The darkness in our immediate vicinity had turned into a sunny café. It was very similar to the one Onyx had created with a cream and lavender color scheme and huge windows that looked out over a grassy expanse, beyond which was a sparkling lake.

"Whoa. Whoa." I kept looking around. The tables were laden with food and drink but empty of patrons. A gentle wind spiraled in from the open windows, its warmth easing over us. The strange sensation that had come over me tapered away.

"Beautiful," Remi said. "How did ... you do this?"

"Um ..." I frowned. "I guess my dream responded to what I'd said?" That was the most plausible explanation, though I had to admit it didn't quite feel right.

A gift. May you one day know how to use it.

Something about this kept tugging me back to Onyx. But whatever had happened, at least it wasn't a bad thing. This was much better than that unfathomable dark. Even if only lasted for the duration of my dream, at least Remi could have a different view for a while.

"Why don't we enjoy it while I catch you up." We walked toward the windows, stepping over the low sill onto the grass. It felt impossibly soft and real under my bare feet. The sun was warm on my shoulders and the breeze blowing off the water felt wonderful. Remi and I stood side by side and looked around. He squeezed my hand and turned to me.

"Tell me ... what has been ... going on ..."

I couldn't help the flinch those words produced, and Remi's brow wrinkled in concern. I released a sigh.

"It's been about three weeks since we came back from Elsewhere," I started. "And there's been quite a bit of trouble ..."

Chapter Twelve

My plan for Wednesday morning was to head to the bordello and ask Jiano to take me to Paluna so I could talk to her about Remi, but that plan was thwarted when Marrik and I were driving to Kiss and Hex and he got a text from Namira asking to meet up.

"She wants to talk about yesterday," Marrik said. He was in the passenger seat wearing a short-sleeved button down with a pattern of banana leaves that made me tease that he looked ready for a cruise. His excuse had been his lack of desire to paw through the tubs of clothes he'd brought from the storage unit. I'd emptied a couple drawers for him, putting my own stuff in tubs, but the majority of his clothes were still boxed.

I could only tease so much though, as the strain of his biceps against the sleeves, and the way it was fitted to the more muscular body he'd gained in Elsewhere was a welcome place to rest my eyes. The day was humid, and he'd stay cool in the light colors. I'd thrown on a floral romper and sandals, with my hair smoothed up into a puff.

"Does she have intel?" The events of yesterday weighed heavily on me. Jiano texted Marrik that they'd gotten me a new phone, so I'd soon be back in communication with my coven. I'd wanted to go to The Bramble today, but all witches were warned off heading there as the wreckage in the river was dealt with and the investigation continued. All the coven houses were going to be searched to ensure Normies First or other anti-witch groups hadn't targeted them with explosives or other nasties. The only thing I could be thankful for was that arrests had been made.

"I think so, she's being vague." When I glanced at Marrik before making a turn, I saw that he was frowning. "But I told her I want to stay close to you today."

"Have her come to Kiss and Hex," I suggested with a shrug. "We can talk, then I can head to Paluna."

"I hope she has resources that can help Remi." Marrik reached over and squeezed my thigh. Remi's amulet was tucked into the romper, and there was a knot of sadness wedged within me now that I knew he was in there and couldn't come out. I'd told Marrik everything this morning. He'd found me asleep on the couch with the suppression gloves on, so of course he'd had several questions. After I'd explained he was stunned, but supported my plan to talk to Paluna about what we could do for Remi.

"So much is going on," I said. "I barely have time to focus on one thing before something else comes along. I ... I almost died yesterday. I lost friends. Elliot ..."

I turned onto the bordello's block and pulled into a parking spot. Marrik unclipped his seat belt and leaned over, pulling me into his arms. I unbuckled so he could wrap his arms around me.

"I want to say so many things," Marrik whispered. "About how I wished I'd been able to save you. About how terrible I feel that it took so long for you to get hold of me. But I am so, so glad those Mutans Witches were in the water."

"I need to thank Emricka properly." I sniffled. There went those damn tears again. "Need to thank all of them."

Marrik pulled back and looked into my eyes, bringing his hands to either side of my face.

"I ..." He released a sigh, his eyes searching mine. "How can I sufficiently convey the path I have already traveled with losing you and the realization that I am still on that path even though you are right before my eyes?"

"Mar ..." Marrik's pain and my own twisted around my heart, my soul.

"When I was in Elsewhere you became a dream and a nightmare, Kit," he continued. "You were hope and you were a haunting. I wanted to be back in your arms even though they were the arms that had thrust me into Elsewhere. But I would have torn every single Blight apart if it would have gotten me back to you. And now we're reunited, and you almost died, and I was so far away, and it was the group my own family is—"

A frustrated sound released from him. His face contorted as he squeezed his eyes shut, his jaw clenching as he pressed his forehead against mine.

"The hateful fucking group my family is part of almost killed you and cost several witches their lives. How can I ... how can I begin to ..."

Marrik didn't know how to finish that sentence and I didn't know what to say in response. He was feeling the same things I was; our love for each other wrapped in shards that might shred us beyond repair.

"I love you, Kit." He raised his head, angling it to the side, his breath coming in short pants as his nose brushed mine. "God, I love you so much and I'm scared I will lose you. I'm scared all that's meant for me is the pain I felt every time I thought of you when I was in Elsewhere."

"Marrik." My eyes were swimming in tears. Marrik was echoing the thoughts that had been churning in my head. Of course he felt them too; Marrik wasn't the type to put his head in the sand to avoid the truth. He knew as much as I did how fractured the ground we stood on was. How easily it could crumble and bury our relationship.

It had been fractured before he'd Vanished. Our separation had only put distance between our issues but now they were back in our hands, along with so many new ones.

But I didn't want to think about that right now. Marrik's tongue slid across my bottom lip as he angled his head the other way. I felt the brush of his lashes as he inched closer. I let the heady attraction between us pull me into him. It was a wanting, a yearning to defy the odds stacked against us because we were both stubborn as hell and wouldn't give up without a bloody, all-consuming fight. Not after everything we'd been through.

"I love you too," I whispered. My name wrenched from his throat before he captured my lips. His tongue was a slow brush against my mouth and I opened to let him in. To fall into the pleasure and arousal kissing him always brought forth. To tune in to the firmness of his hold and the way his breath quickened, same as mine did, as though we were running and were out of breath. We kissed and heat built between us, the air warming in the confines of the car. A drunken sensation came over me as Marrik kissed me like it was the last time.

The kiss broke but we stayed closed, heads pressed together, our breathing loud in the quiet.

"I—"

The chirp of Marrik's phone jolted us. We moved back and he checked his messages.

"Namira said she'll be here in about fifteen minutes."

I nodded, then darted a kiss on his lips and got out of the car. Marrik and I were still full of cracks, but we wouldn't be healed by a make-out session. When things felt a little more settled, we'd need to start therapy.

We headed to the front door and were let in by Ji, who swept me into a tight hug before stepping back and making a flourish at the bar where a fantastic breakfast spread was set up.

"Come, come, eat up. I am under strict orders from our mother to make sure you eat until you burst." Ji greeted Mar and we headed to the bar.

"This looks great, thank you. I'll try not to disappoint, just be ready to clean up after I explode."

Ji chuckled, then whisked something from the pocket of their floral robe. They were bare-chested under it, wearing cotton shorts, fuzzy slippers, and a glittery turban.

"New phone, courtesy of Paluna," Ji said. "Same number, and she was able to get your contacts back even though your sim card is in your old phone. Don't ask me how, I continue to straddle being impressed and disgusted by her resourcefulness."

"I know the feeling," I replied. "I appreciate this, I'll thank her later." It was way nicer than my previous phone, which had been at least three years old. I was never one for upgrading every time a new model dropped. Plus, phones were expensive and I'd been on a tight budget.

Although it hadn't missed my notice that Paluna had dropped the rest of the money she said she was gonna pay me for Vanishing Gladstone. I was up a hundred thousand dollars, but I'd barely had time to wrap my head around that.

"You kept your stuff backed up, right?" Marrik asked as we picked up plates and started to fill them. There were jam-filled pastries, muffins, scones, fresh fruit, thick, crispy slabs of bacon, toast points, coffee, tea, and juice. Ji swished behind the bar and produced a bucket of ice with a bottle of champagne nestled in it. They popped it open and started to make mimosas.

"Yup." I turned the phone on and logged in to the cloud system that kept my phone backed up. It would take some time for everything to download so I shoved the phone into my purse.

"Where are the parentals?" I asked Ji, accepting the flute they offered and taking my plate to one of the round tables opposite the bar. The partially open louvers threw slants of light across the table and floor.

"Calla mentioned that the hospital in The Bramble could use extra assistance, so Ma went to help," Ji said. "Dad drove her down in the car they rented."

I nodded, feeling like a vice was around my heart. The events of yesterday were so visceral; that feeling of almost drowning, of how scared everyone had to have been, of the ones who hadn't made it. Marrik, who'd sat down opposite me, reached over to squeeze my hand.

"I'm glad she went." Ma had started a Regen Witch clinic before we were born and switched to part time after. She'd scaled her hours back even more in the last few years, spending more time teaching Regen Witch clinicians about healing magic than seeing patients. In Luneso, the northern witch territory she and Dad lived in, her salves and potions were highly sought after.

Hexes started moving through the bordello as people woke up. Everyone gave me hugs and expressed their gratitude that I was alive, their condolences for those who had died, and their anger at Normies First. Then they filled up a plate and snagged a mimosa. We ate and chatted until Marrik's phone chirped and he told me Namira was outside.

"Let's talk out back," I said, popping a mini corn muffin into my mouth. I didn't relish seeing Namira, but if she had intel on the attack yesterday it could help us stay ahead of another one. Because I had no doubt that this was only the beginning for Normies First and the other anti-witch groups. And I was very, very, aware that the target on my back was bigger than anyone else's.

Marrik agreed, so we headed through the front door where Namira was milling around on the sidewalk. She wore shorts and a graphic T-shirt with her braids in a plait over her shoulder.

"Hey." Namira gave Marrik a hug. When they pulled back, she looked at me and couldn't seem to settle her expression.

"I'm ... glad you're okay," she offered. She seemed tense, her arms crossed tightly over her chest. She wasn't exuding friendliness, but at least it wasn't outright malice.

"Thanks. Inside is a little busy, let's head to the back." I led the way down the side and into the yard. We sat on the long, wooden bench near the fence, which was covered in ivy and rustled in the morning wind.

"What have you heard?" Marrik asked. He was holding my hand and Namira kept glancing at it. But she didn't say anything, so I'd take that as progress that she was trying to respect what Marrik had said the other night at dinner.

"I spoke to Quinn," she replied. "She said our family has been zeroing in on Kit. She doesn't think they were part of what happened yesterday, but they—"

"Hold on." Marrik made the time-out sign with his hands. "You spoke to Quinn, and she offered this information to you? *Quinn?*"

He'd told me about Quinn. She was their younger cousin, and her parents ran a large chapter within Normies First in Yarachon. Marrik said Quinn was in as deep as her parents were.

"Why the hell would Quinn tell you anything?" Marrik continued.

"She's trying to change," Namira said. Marrik made a sound of disbelief.

"You know our aunt and uncle sheltered her, Mar," Namira said. "She had little choice but to grow up as hateful as them. They kept her in their sprawling house and acres of land and were able to make that the center of her universe. But she left for college, and I was able to spend more time with her once she wasn't under their thumb twenty-four-seven. She saw more of the world and understood the narrow-minded prejudice she'd been living and breathing wasn't right. But her parents don't know, and she plans to keep it that way. She's using her proximity to them to help. Like telling me they've got something planned for Kit."

Marrik's eyes narrowed, and a cold feeling spread through me.

"Just like that, Quinn is being helpful." The skepticism in his tone was strong. I understood his hesitancy to believe Quinn was on our side. People could change, even the most hateful of them, but for the things that had their claws hooked deep into Quinn as she grew up under Normies First parents, Marrik was right to question this change.

Namira made an impatient sound and rolled her eyes. "You broke away from the family and kept yourself far for years, Mar. I stayed close to whoever I could. I've seen Quinn's growth these past couple years. She's not a saint, but she's trying. And isn't it more important that we focus on the fact that our family is gunning for Kit?"

"Let me guess, trying to drown me and other witches in a shipping container didn't quite yield the results they wanted so they're gonna try again."

Marrik made a growling sound as his hand tightened around mine.

"Like I told you the other day, Aunt Fallon and Uncle Barrett are up in arms that Kit Vanished you, her magic is stronger, and you're still with her. Quinn said they watched that press conference with their jaws dropped the entire way through. Then she says there was *a lot* of yelling. They think you've been brainwashed or are suffering some kinda Stockholm syndrome. Quinn said they see it as their duty to save you from Kit and are mobilizing to do exactly that."

"The fuck they are," Marrik said vehemently. "What exactly are they planning, Namira?"

"If I knew I would have led with that," she replied. "Quinn didn't know about the incident yesterday beforehand, and she doesn't have specifics on what they might try next. She said their plans are super locked down and she can't get a lick of information from her parents. But you need to be careful. If you," she glanced at our entwined fingers again and her brow creased, "if you insist you want to be together, you're gonna have to deal with what might come of that."

"If we insist?" Marrik's voice was warm with anger. "Namira, I already told you I'm not going anywhere. You're mad if you think this is a moment that calls for me separating from Kit."

"Even if it would save her?" Namira countered. "If you left her, it might help. Our family is dead set on saving you from the powerful Vanish Witch who almost took you from us permanently, Mar. Your parents are on a warpath. So if you—"

"I'm not bowing to bigots!" Marrik stood up as he yelled and paced a few feet away, dragging his hand over his head. "Don't you dare put the burden of this on us, Namira. Hateful sons of bitches are after not just Kit, but all witches, and I should placate them by leaving her? Are you fucking kidding me?"

It twisted something in my heart to see him defend me like this. In both a good and bad way. The knot of emotions remained complicated between us but there was one thing I could say with certainty.

"It's not guaranteed to work." Now that Marrik wasn't between us I could see Namira better. "I'd still be a Vanish Witch who got a power boost and has now become the boogeyman under their beds, ready to grab their ankles and Vanish them when they lay down to sleep. Marrik could leave me and they would still come for me. The hate groups won't be placated unless witches are wiped out. I hope you don't expect us to buy that Marrik making a show of breaking up with me would make them back off."

Namira's jaw was clenched as she listened to me. When I finished, she looked away and released a sigh. "I know. I guess I felt bad I couldn't come here with better info, so I thought I'd suggest something, anything … to help."

"It's appreciated." Marrik's tone was gentler. "We'll watch our backs as best we can. I will stand between anyone who comes after Kit. Even my own family. If you hear anything that could give us a heads up, please let us know, Mira."

"I will, I promise."

I smiled at Marrik, at the determination in his voice to protect me, but it wasn't an entirely happy smile.

It shouldn't have to be like this. Being together shouldn't be this hard.

But it was, and I had no idea what to do to change these variables for the better.

"What should we—"

My phone started ringing, cutting me off. I fished it out and saw that Ji was calling.

"Ji?"

"Kitten, would you mind coming back inside, you have a visitor." The tightness in Ji's voice had me on alert.

"A visitor?" I stood up. Marrik came closer, looking concerned. "Who is it?"

"Linton Gladstone," Ji replied darkly. I felt like I'd been sucker punched into another universe. "And he would very much like to have a word with you."

Chapter Thirteen

Marrik, Namira, and I entered the bordello through the back door, which was opened for us by Arjun, and followed him down the hallway to the front. Every step I took wound up more fear and anxiety. The hallway was wide, so Marrik was by my side, holding my hand, while Namira walked behind us. Marrik's face was steely and the muscle in his jaw was having a dance party.

What the hell did Gladstone want? I was under no illusions that he was done with me, but I'd been hoping to have a bit more time before I had to deal with the High Coven again. Can't a girl get a week or two of peace after almost drowning for fuck's sake?

Ji hadn't mentioned that there were officers and I hadn't heard the rumble of armored tanks, so that was my only hope that he wasn't attempting to arrest me again as we entered the front room and I caught sight of the despicable man standing near the bar. And he wasn't alone. There was a Black woman standing next to him. She was a head shorter than Gladstone and looked to be in her thirties. The warm yellow color of her skirt-suit flattered her ebony skin tone, and her shoulder length hair was styled in sister-locs. A large handbag was slung over her shoulder, and she held the straps with both hands as though she needed to keep the bag as close to her body as possible. She had a calculating look as she gave me the once over.

The only others here were Jiano and Rowan, who were behind the bar looking at Gladstone as though they wished they could crumble him to dust. The breakfast spread was pretty much wiped out and Ji must have asked everyone to make themselves scarce.

Arjun walked over to the wall near the door and leaned against it, crossing his arms over his chest and adding a glare in Linton's direction. Marrik and I faced him, keeping several feet between us. Namira came up on Marrik's other side.

The room was silent as we assessed each other. Linton's eyes flicked over every face before they settled on me. He wore a brown suit, his hair was gelled back, and his hands were clasped in front of him. But as I looked him over, I noticed the rigidity to his posture, and a tightness to his expression that made me think his emotions were more geared toward anxiety than malice.

Interesting.

"What do you want?" I broke the silence so I could get this meeting over with and head to Paluna to talk about Remi. I couldn't go two thoughts without thinking about the fact that Remi's desiccated, weakened ghost was trapped inside the amulet.

"Ms. Neris, good morning," Linton said pleasantly. I could have gagged. The nerve of him to greet me as though he hadn't recently imprisoned me, suppressed my magic, tried to have a Memoria Witch read my mind against my will, and threatened me.

"What do you want?" I repeated. Marrik shifted and I tugged on his hand. I was sure he wanted to wail on Gladstone, but we needed less trouble with the High Coven, not more.

When Linton replied, he said the last thing I would have expected him to say.

"Your help."

Another stretch of silence fell. I exchanged startled looks with Marrik and the others before we returned our attention to Linton.

"And what exactly can I help you with, Mr. Gladstone?" I kept my tone as even as possible and reined in all the snarky suggestions I was gonna tack on to the end of my sentence. The man I'd tried to Vanish because he was killing witches for their magic was asking me for help. You really couldn't make this shit up.

Gladstone straightened his spine a bit more. "First, let me say that the details of your televised interview were deeply fascinating. Your travails in this parallel world and your meeting with one of the witches who drained the ley lines. The fact that you are the one responsible for their return. What an astounding revelation. As are the details of coming across people and items that were Vanished. It would be wonderfully insightful for the High Coven to further debrief you on your experiences." He glanced at Marrik.

"You Vanished this man," he said. "It is a grievous offence to Vanish people, as you should know." A snide smile curled his lips.

I released a bark of laughter. He really needed to be fucking for real.

"And it's a grievous offence to use Memoria magic on someone without their permission," I fired back. "And there are several other grievous offences I can list that you might be familiar with."

I raised an eyebrow challengingly. "If you came here to tally up misdeeds, I hope you're smart enough to know which one of us is gonna lose. Vanishing Marrik was an accident and he's the only one from Elsewhere who deserved to survive its collapse." And Remi, but that didn't need to reach Gladstone's ears.

Linton's expression darkened as I spoke. I was bowled over by the audacity he had to come to Kiss and Hex and confront me like this. We could bat around what laws I broke and who I Vanished or almost Vanished all day, but I had leverage on him that should maintain my freedom, so I needed him to get to the damn point about why he was here because I had enough on my plate.

"Sir." The woman cleared her throat and took a small step forward. "Perhaps we should—"

Gladstone raised a hand and she paused. He closed his eyes, and it seemed as though he was trying to reorient himself. It was a nugget of satisfaction that I could throw off someone who was used to dominating a conversation.

He opened his eyes and lowered his hand, giving me the full weight of his attention again.

"Ms. Neris, you are a polarizing entity and the layers between us will be addressed in due course. However," he cleared his throat as though hesitant to continue, "as I said, I am here because your help is required. There is a situation for which it has been concluded that you are the best resource."

"What issue?" I ventured. "What help of mine are you asking for?"

"You are aware of the floating islands Magnes Witches pulled down after the ley line surge, yes?"

"Yes." Ah. I had a feeling I knew where this was going.

"Let me be as succinct as possible," Linton said. "The situation with the floating island to the east, which records have identified as carrying the name Nimbisu, has become dire. The others that were pulled down were over bodies of water and a mountain range. Three of them have already collapsed, causing tidal waves and disruptions with coral reefs and aquatic life, but so far, no human lives have been affected. The High Coven has had Magnes and Repel Witch scientists working on a solution to either bring Nimbisu down safely or push it back into orbit. But there are more factors working against us than for us."

He paused and cleared his throat. I was *not* enjoying the way his words were making me feel. Here came more trouble for my plate.

"For one," he continued, "though the ley line surge boosted the magic of all witches, it has not been to the level of the witches who propelled those islands to the sky and kept them there safely centuries ago. It was the combined strength of hundreds of Magnes Witches at the time of the surge that brought the islands down. For individuals to achieve the magical power needed to affect the islands would require drawing on the ley lines and there is not enough time to do so. Magical strengthening is a slow and incremental process that stretches the majority of a witch's life. Furthermore, while we have records that explain the intricacies of how the islands were maintained using magic and the gravitational forces of Aulura and Cebis, our scientists are not well versed nor trained in the process of handling the sky islands."

Linton drew in a slow breath and let it out. "Cebis' orbit will release its hold on the island in two days. It has already been weakening, which has caused the island to start moving, and its trajectory has been predicted to bring it very close to Vonuis. When it is completely released from Cebis' hold, Nimbisu will fall, and we are out of ideas as to how to prevent the massive death and destruction it would cause."

Everyone in the room sucked in a shocked breath and we looked amongst ourselves again. As Gladstone spoke, my bad feeling increased. We'd all been aware that the sky islands were a threat, but I'd had so much going on I could hardly fit their collapse into my knot of things to be worried about.

"Therefore," Linton was saying.

"You want Kit to Vanish it." Ji cut in. They looked grim. Marrik's hand tightened around mine.

Linton looked like he'd bitten something sour. "Yes," he said through his teeth. "We have made every attempt at a solution, but with a narrow window before a major disaster strikes, we have decided to inquire if Ms. Neris could use her stronger Vanish magic against the island before it renders destruction upon Vonuis. After what was learned from that press conference it has been impressed upon me that you, Ms. Neris, are likely the strongest witch in the world. You are certainly the strongest Vanish Witch, and your magic is uniquely suited to addressing this problem."

I was the strongest witch in the world. The strongest Vanish Witch. Words that had crossed my mind but were still hard to accept as fact.

It felt like everyone was holding their breath as they waited for me to respond. With almost any other request Gladstone could have made I would have told him to go fuck himself and not let the door hit him on the way out. But he was asking for my help against something that could kill a lot of people, myself and everyone I cared about included.

But there were some bumps in the road with what he was asking me to do.

"I'm not opposed to helping because I understand how dire the situation is," I said. "However, I am not sure my magic is strong enough to Vanish something of that size. It is larger than anything I've used my magic on."

"And how exactly would you expect Kit to Vanish an island that's way up in the sky, moving, and crumbling bit by bit?" Marrik asked. "Kit would have to touch Nimbisu to Vanish it and I assume you'd want her to do it before it makes it to the ground."

"Indeed," Linton replied. "There is no safe way to get Ms. Neris onto the island so she can make physical contact with it and be safe once it disappears."

"So how —"

"A Vanish Tide." It was the woman who spoke, cutting Jiano off. She drew herself up as she focused on me. "My name is Saffron Lomillot. I am a Vanish Witch and work for the High Coven. We have determined that the best course of action against Nimbisu is to request that Ms. Neris use a Vanish Tide on it from a distance."

"A Vanish Tide?" I repeated. "Is that the ability where we can push our magic outward and Vanish something without physical contact?"

"Precisely," Saffron said. "The formal name is Evanescet Tide. With careful calculations and approximations, we can position you at a point where you can aim your magic at the island and —"

"Whoa, whoa, whoa, time out please." I let go of Marrik's hand and stepped forward. I was starting to feel extremely overwhelmed.

"I don't know how to do a Vanish Tide. That was not something Onyx was able to teach me when I was in Elsewhere. She was a Mutans Witch and said teaching me higher level Vanish magic was beyond her capabilities. And even if I somehow learn in the next twenty-four hours, there's still the issue of whether or not my magic is strong enough to affect the island. It is … quite large."

"One thing at a time, Ms. Neris," Linton said, holding his hand up again. "Ms. Lomillot is here because she can offer assistance with teaching you how to release a Vanish Tide." He made a motion with his hand and Saffron reached into her bag and pulled out a large, thick book that was bound in dark leather with metallic accents and designs stamped into the front and back covers.

"The High Coven is in possession of grimoires from our ancestors," Linton said. "Grimoires that contain a wealth of information regarding spell work across all the witch classes, as well as information on our higher magical abilities. Including those of your class: Evanescet Tides and Evanescet Transference. We offer you the chance to educate yourself on these abilities and in turn, use your strength to help us."

My eyes were glued to the book Saffron held. Grimoires of past witches. Full of knowledge and spells. Of course they would be in the possession of the High Coven without the rest of us being able to so much as touch the covers.

I shook my head. That wasn't what I needed to focus on right now. I looked between Saffron and Gladstone.

"This grimoire contains the knowledge on how to release a Tide," Saffron said. "And we have what is needed to practice as this is not a situation we can leave to chance. If you consent to helping us, Ms. Neris—"

"Thousands of people could die if you don't," Gladstone cut in. I wanted to roll my eyes at him. He didn't need to guilt trip me. I wanted nothing more than to be disentangled from the High Coven, but I wasn't petty enough to act like this was a situation where I needed to laugh in their faces about wanting my help.

I had a lot of doubts and reservations about if I was strong enough to Vanish Nimbisu, but there was no time to hem and haw over it. I had felt like a failure a lot recently, but maybe I could succeed at this. Elliot and six other witches had died yesterday because I hadn't been able to save everyone in time. Remi was in a terrible state because he'd stepped up to succeed in Elsewhere

where I had failed. Jiano and pretty much everyone acquainted with me was under scrutiny from the High Coven because of proximity.

I had already chosen the path where I used my Vanish magic to help. No matter how dangerous or law breaking it was. Like Ji said, I had to take the good with the bad. Linton Gladstone was the bad, but maybe in this situation I could do good.

I looked at Jiano. They looked anxious, their arms folded over their chest, but they met my gaze and gave me a nod. I turned to Marrik and the solemn expression on his face.

"I support you always," he said. Next to him, Namira's eyes were wide. I couldn't guess at what she was thinking but I saw her fear. The idea that a huge island might crash onto us was terrifying. Arjun and Rowan carried similar expressions, but both offered me nods of support.

"Ms. Neris," Gladstone said. I returned my attention to him. "Time is not on our side, would you consider—"

"I'll help," I cut in. I was nervous, scared, worried, anxious … but I was also determined.

"Teach me how to create a Vanish Tide and I will do my best to Vanish Nimbisu before it falls."

Chapter Fourteen

About an hour later I was following Saffron across a wide expanse of grass to a cottage that reminded me of the ones in The Bramble. It was two stories tall, made of dark gray brick covered in ivy with large, circular windows.

It was one of several cottages that sat in a large clearing in the middle of a forest. All of the houses were connected by stone pathways. The clearing was enclosed by tall trees with wide trunks, and the space was neatly planted with flowerbeds and flourishing plants.

"You doing okay?" Marrik asked. He was on my right, holding my hand, while Jiano was on my left. Namira was on Marrik's other side. I hadn't expected that she'd join us, but she had asked if she could come. Maybe she needed to see definitively that the High Coven's plan to have me Vanish the sky island would work. Linton had tried to dissuade the others from coming, but Marrik, Jiano, and I had made it clear that over our dead bodies would I go anywhere with any High Coven witch alone.

I believed they needed my help and that this wasn't some elaborate plan to ensnare me, but I wasn't gonna take any chances.

"I'm as okay as I can be," I replied. Saffron looked over her shoulder and gave an encouraging smile before turning back around. Gladstone wasn't with us. He'd entrusted this endeavor to Saffron and left her with the parting words that he expected to hear of its results in due course. The tension hadn't left Saffron since.

"I believe in you, Kitten," Jiano said. But there was a thread of anxiety in their tone. They were looking around. "This is an interesting spot. After the journey it took to get here, it's very much giving secret location."

"Yeah, seems like a restricted access sorta place." We'd gotten here after driving out of Vonuis, following Saffron's car down winding roads that took us through a couple small towns before we ended up in a forested area called Youne Wilds. We'd turned down a narrow road that I was sure I would have missed if I hadn't been following someone. The drive down that road had been long and more than once I'd been worried my car would scrape against the trees. We'd finally emerged into a huge clearing and been led toward these buildings.

"We're here." Saffron led us up to the dark blue door of the cottage, opened it with a key, and led us in. We entered a large, single room. To the right was the staircase that led upstairs. The floor was hardwood, and there was minimal furniture. A few armchairs sat near a small, low table on one side, while a couple sofas were positioned elsewhere. The middle of the space was empty save for a large, plush rug. What really drew the eye were the floor to ceiling bookcases that ran the length of one of the walls. There were a lot of books that looked similar to the grimoire Saffron had. Some shelves had an assortment of items instead of books.

On the wall directly in front of us were windows. A couple other cottages were visible through them. Beyond them, I could see hills and rock formations. Below the windows, narrow tables held books and knick-knacks.

"What is this place?" Namira muttered as she looked around.

"This area is called Moonglade," Saffron replied. "And this is a Vanish Witch learning center. All of these houses have endured from our past, when our magic was stronger and more witches were able to learn how to wield the higher abilities of their class."

"So they're coven-houses," Ji said. "Where you hoard grimoires full of knowledge the rest of us never get to see?"

Saffron gave a tight smile. "They are coven-houses, yes, but they are situated near a ley line well. Their proximity to the well made it a suitable place to study and learn, as well as regulate the well's use."

"A ley line well," I repeated. Veins of the ley lines ran across the entire world. But they could only be drawn from to strengthen our magic at a place where several of them crossed, which was known as a well. In Elsewhere, there were so many of them in a confined space that just about everywhere was likely a well. Here, mapping had been done centuries ago to discover where enough lines crossed to make a well, and their use was monitored by the High Coven, who assigned each witch class a phase of one of the moons when they could draw from them.

I hadn't had much time to think about ley line wells and where they might be, but it was cool to come to the place of one.

"The well here has been strengthened and in due time the High Coven will allow for its use," Saffron said.

"Those are all Vanish Witch grimoires?" I indicated the tightly packed bookcases.

"Grimoires and journals," she replied. "The covens had strict protocols regarding documentation of our magic. We have a wealth of technical knowledge such as how magical strength ties into the size of objects that can be Vanished with a Tide or Transferred, how close or far one needs to be to successfully release a Tide, and so on."

"*We* have a wealth of knowledge, huh?" I gave her a sidelong glance and she shifted uncomfortably. *We* certainly didn't have access to that kind of information. Our Guardians were very capable, but Reshmi had never told us technical details about higher Vanish Witch abilities. She didn't have access to tomes like these.

"What are those?" I walked over to one of the bookcases where random objects were neatly lined. Among them were chipped vases in antique styles, figurines made from metal, crystal, or stone, glass spheres in different hues, and clay plates with intricate designs around their circumference. My eyebrows rose when I noticed that there was also a human skull.

"These are relics," Saffron said as she came up next to me. Ji and Marrik were looking the shelves over with interest while Namira hung back, continuing to look as though she'd stepped into the gaping jaws of a whale meant to swallow her whole.

"I've heard of witch relics," Ji commented.

"They were vessels of power or something, right?" I tried to remember what I'd been taught. There were so many fascinating things about our abilities, spells, and magical items, but because so many things hadn't been relevant for so long it was easy to forget them entirely.

"Indeed," Saffron replied. "Relics were items that were buried deep in the ground as close to a ley line as possible. Over time, they would absorb power from the ley lines, and after they were dug up, they were sources of power for witches that provided an alternative to using the ley lines to boost their magic since there was risk of over drawing and incurring serious injury. Or worse."

"A lot of witches died because they weren't able to handle stronger magic," Marrik said.

"Yes, drawing on the lines always carried a risk, which was why many witches didn't bother to strengthen their magic past a certain point. Better to have medium strength and your life than try to max out and die." She swept a hand to indicate the items. "But with a relic, you could access stronger magic. For example, a witch whose magic may not be strong enough to do a Vanish Tide could execute one while holding a relic."

"Incredible," I said. "The magic eventually ran out, right?" I was absorbing this information like a sponge.

"It did," Saffron answered. "All of these relics have been null for decades. Relics were usually beneficial to the generation after the ones who'd buried them because they took years to absorb power from the ley lines. There was a lot of trial and error as well because not all substances absorbed magic well. You could bury something only to dig it up ten years later and find that it disintegrated under the ley lines' power. Glass, clay, rock, and certain metals proved to be the best choices."

"And bones?" Jiano pointed at the skull with an eyebrow raised.

Saffron cleared her throat and dipped her head. "Ah … yes, it was determined that bones were the strongest relic material. Both animal and human, but human was the strongest. Of course, um, there was a lot of controversy around creating relics using human remains. It was eventually outlawed, but people continued to use human bone relics in secret."

"I'm not surprised," I said. Relics were incredibly cool, but it gave me an icky feeling to think about using human or animal bones that way. "I bet there are still a lot of relics buried out there."

"Without a doubt," Saffron said. "So many relics were buried over so many centuries it's a given that many are still deep within the earth. We are sure to see them re-emerge in this new era."

"Very dope," Ji said. "Minus the bones."

"Thanks for the info," I said as we turned away from the shelves.

"Of course. Now, Ms. Neris—"

"Kit or Kitaine is fine, please," I cut in. Saffron nodded. She'd stopped in front of the large rug in the center of the room and pulled the grimoire out of her bag.

"We can get started with teaching you how to create an Evanescet Tide as well as how to do Evanescet Transference, an ability witches commonly called Shifts. While only the Tide is required for Nimbisu, Mr. Gladstone gave authorization to teach you Shifts as well. As a … a sign of good faith."

She stumbled over her words at the end. Good faith my ass. Not that I was gonna say no to learning both skills.

"So," Saffron continued. "If you are ready—"

"What if I said I wasn't and bolted?"

Saffron's eyes widened. I shook my head and stepped forward.

"Kidding. I know the situation is dire but I'm looking forward to learning how to do Tides and Shifts." I had wondered if I'd be able to learn them, but you could not have told me I'd come into the knowledge this way.

"If your entourage wouldn't mind giving us some space, you're welcome to have a seat."

"Entourage," Ji said with a chuckle.

"Well, I am the strongest witch in the world, apparently. I think that warrants some lackeys." I grinned. "How about one of you fetch me some bon bons while someone else fans me with a palm leaf?"

"I provided a lavish breakfast you cheeky brat, don't push your luck." Ji's tone was amused and they gave my arm a squeeze before breezing over to one of the sofas. The long, sheer robe, patterned with monstera leaves that they wore over jeans and a tank top, flounced behind them.

"You got this." Marrik pressed a kiss against my temple. His lips lingered there. "It's another difficult situation but if anyone can do it, you can."

"I'll do my best." I leaned into him for a moment and smiled when he pulled back and looked down at me. When I glanced past him I saw a dark expression on Namira's face. When she caught my eye she tried to smooth it but didn't quite manage. If Namira ever truly warmed up to me it would be the greatest miracle that ever occurred.

Namira offered no smooches or witty banter, just a curt nod as she followed Marrik to where Jiano was sitting. I lowered myself onto the rug next to Saffron.

Saffron opened the grimoire. As she turned the thick, hand pressed pages, I saw writing in various colors of ink. I could tell multiple people had written in the book. Grimoires could be solitary efforts or they could be communal. There were also sketches of things I couldn't identify, as well as drawings that looked like maps.

Saffron stopped somewhere in the middle. At the top of the page were the words Evanescet Tide Incantation.

"The ability to push your magic outside of yourself relies on a spell that has been tied to the Vanish Witch bloodlines longer than anyone can originate," Saffron explained. "The spell allows you to push your magic past the confines of your body, but you must be mentally strong as well. A lot of Vanish Witches practice meditation before they attempt to create a Tide. It requires clarity of the mind to achieve success."

"I think the only thing that could give me clarity of the mind is to scoop my brain out entirely."

Saffron's response was a wavering smile. I was anxious. The emotions that had clamped onto me when Gladstone had explained the situation prevailed. I was fighting not to be crushed under the weight of being the only person who stood a chance against the collapse of Nimbisu. That if I failed, a lot of people would die.

I took a few slow, deep breaths. Calm, I needed to be calm. I wouldn't get a chance to help if I didn't find the headspace I needed to be in.

"An edible would have been quite an assist, wouldn't it?" Jiano called. I turned and flashed a smile.

"Perhaps." It would have relaxed me, at the very least. But I had to do this edible-free, alas.

"This is the spell." What Saffron pointed to were more like symbols than words. Some of them were minimal while others were complex. There were curves and angles, intersecting lines, and dot-work.

"I think it's safe to say ... I can't read this." I tentatively touched the page below the spell, feeling a bit awestruck. I'd never seen a Vanish Witch spell before. Never knew the language our spells were written in.

"I am versed in the old spell languages; I will teach you." She pointed at the words, moving her finger as she pronounced each one.

"*Ae huo monsi clurett meor wrentu och tivaru ae zumnaf dreemalo ilzum qi voudamkh.*" She spoke slowly and with clear enunciation.

I sucked in a breath as a shiver went through me, raising goosebumps. My magic stirred, like a faucet being turned on. Just hearing the incantation had an effect.

"Wow," I whispered.

"Spells are powerful," she said. "I'll read it a few more times, then you can practice until you've got the pronunciation right."

"Okay." I did my best to relax. I cracked my neck, stopped balling my hands into fists, stretched my back, and tried to even my breathing. I pushed the anxiety down and focused on the more upbeat emotions in my grasp, the ones that were excited to learn a high level Vanish ability.

Saffron read the incantation several more times, then led me through saying it. It was harder than I expected. There were times when I had to pitch my voice lower or higher over a word or syllable. Saffron made me stop and start over every time I got something wrong. Dozens of times.

"You got it!" I was startled when Saffron said that. We'd been sitting here so long I was starting to feel sore.

"Really?" I wouldn't admit how disgruntled I was feeling over how challenging learning the incantation was, but I was relieved that I'd finally nailed it.

Saffron nodded. I turned to Marrik and the others and gave a thumbs up. Marrik clapped and Ji whistled. Namira sat with her arms and legs crossed and gave another nod. I turned back to Saffron.

"We will need to make our way outside to practice Tides," she said. "But before that, I shall teach you how to do Vanish Shifts."

"Does this one involve an incantation too?"

"No, but it does involve blood."

My eyebrows rose as she drew her bag closer and retrieved something from it. It was a small bottle, about the length of my index finger, made of clear glass, with a round stopper.

"This bottle is hundreds of years old and the knowledge on how to make them was not well preserved, so they are not plentiful," Saffron said. "It can contain magic without being affected by it."

"Wow." I took the bottle from her. The spell work woven into it felt like a soft prickle against my skin as I held it between my fingers.

"If you release your magic into the bottle, it won't Vanish," Saffron said. "Shifts are a two-part process and involve a blood and magic anchor. You must mix your magic and blood in this bottle. You would then leave it somewhere, and anything you wanted to Shift would move to where the anchor is. But the second component is extremely important. In order for it to be a Shift, you must Vanish something with both magic and blood."

My brow furrowed. "You're saying I have to bleed on the thing I want to Vanish in order for it to Shift to the anchor."

"Precisely. But it won't be a lot of blood needed and the amount is not dependent on the size of what you are trying to Shift."

"Good to know."

"We can practice Shifts as well." She retrieved a few other things from her bag. A small dagger, antiseptic wipes, bandages, and a small container.

"A Regen salve." She wiggled the container before setting it down. "It will heal the cut quickly." She offered me the dagger by its hilt. "Cut across your palm and bleed into the bottle. Then add your magic."

"Got it." I hesitated before accepting the dagger in my right hand and turning the palm of my left hand up.

"Do my eyes deceive me or pray tell is that a dagger?" Jiano called out.

"Kit?" Marrik sounded as concerned as Ji.

"It's okay," I told them. "A bit of blood is required for Vanish Shifts."

"Let's make sure it's only a bit," Ji said.

"I'll avoid cutting anything essential, promise." I took a steadying breath and brought the dagger closer to my palm. I wasn't a wuss, but it wasn't like I went around slicing my hand open on purpose all the time.

Better to do it quick than linger about it. I swiftly moved the blade across my palm. It was *sharp*; I didn't need to apply a lot of pressure. A line of blood welled up. Saffron handed me the open vial and I poured my blood in, filling it almost halfway. She then helped me clean the wound, apply the healing salve, and bandage it. It was already feeling much better before she put the bandage on; the Regen salve worked fast.

"Now, add some magic."

I awakened my magic, enjoying the way it felt like a wind was billowing inside my body. Plumes of dark blue smoke wafted around my hands. True to what Saffron said, the vial didn't Vanish when my magic touched it.

"Now ... uh ... put it ..."

I glanced at Saffron. She looked nervous and had very subtly leaned away from me.

Strongest witch. Strongest Vanish Witch.

She might be here to help me, but she also had a fear of me.

But there was no point in assuring her I had no intention of Vanishing her. It stung though, to see this kind of reaction from a fellow Vanish Witch. I understood, but it stung. Same as it was a dagger in my soul that there was so much fear against me and other witches that people saw murder as their only recourse.

The cold, dark, drowning depths of the shipping container reared in my memories. I closed my eyes and breathed past it.

Stay in the moment, I told myself. I had to focus on making sure the sky island didn't fall on our heads.

I opened my eyes and brought my hand over the mouth of the bottle. My magic drifted into it, stopping against the barrier of blood.

"That's enough." Saffron's voice was a bit shaky.

I quieted my magic, and when I moved my hand, Saffron put the stopper back on then instructed me to give it a shake. My magic and blood mingled, reminding me of a lava lamp.

"This is ... cool." I was at a loss for better words to articulate looking at an anchor of my blood and magic that would allow me to transfer things instead of Vanishing them. Could I set anchors up in prison cells? Vanish criminals right into a jail sentence?

A thought for another day.

"Let's practice Shifts then we can practice Tides." Saffron repacked her bag and we stood up. "Leave the anchor near your friends then we'll have you Shift something over to it."

I jogged to where the others sat. Ji and Marrik looked curious while Namira looked cautious. I showed them the anchor and explained Shifts and Tides.

"Amazing," Ji said, taking the vial from me. "So much more used to be possible with stronger magic, huh?"

Marrik leaned to get a better look at the anchor. "It's a bit concerning that Shifts always have to involve blood though."

"Saffron said the amount of blood needed isn't dependent on the size of what I'm tryna Shift, so that's good at least." I took the vial from Ji and placed it on the ground in front of them. "Time to see if it works."

I headed back to Saffron, who was at one of the tables under the windows. There was an open box in front of her and she pulled out several items: a small book, a figurine of a cherub, a baseball, and a cracked plant pot. She handed me the dagger again.

"Prick your finger and touch them after you call up your magic." She laid the items side by side then stepped away. "They should then Shift to the anchor."

I was excited, I couldn't deny that. To tap into another Vanish ability was tremendous regardless of the circumstances that got me to this point. I pricked my finger and a bead of blood rose. I awakened my magic and touched my finger to the book.

It Vanished. Seconds later, Jiano made a whooping sound and I turned to see them holding the book over their head and waving it. Marrik was clapping. Namira was looking at the book with wide eyes.

"It worked!" Ji called out. "You Shifted it over here!"

I grinned and fist pumped.

"I've got a few more items, hold on!" Several drops of blood later, the ball, plant pot and figurine had been transferred across the room.

"Incredible, Kit!" Marrik called. He was on his feet, giving an enthusiastic round of applause. I put a hand to my chest and gave a sweeping bow. Jiano whistled. Namira was also standing and clapped once, then hesitated, as though she wasn't sure how to react.

"Wonderful." I turned to Saffron, who was smiling. "You may keep the anchor you created. It will serve as the receiving point to anything you Vanish with blood." She handed me a couple other bottles.

"I've been authorized to give you two more anchor bottles."

Buttering me up so I would help them wasn't necessary, but it was ironic after I'd just been a target of their ire. I smiled and took the bottles.

"Thank you. I'm astounded that I've been able to learn so much."

"Yes, and now we must practice Tides."

Right. Because a sky island was en-route to crash onto us. My face sobered and I squared my shoulders. "I'm ready. What will I be trying to Vanish with a Tide?"

Chapter Fifteen

My Vanish Tide practice was going to involve one of the small hills I'd seen from the windows.

We were following Saffron across the grass in their direction. The Vanish anchor and the other two bottles were tucked into my bag, and the dagger pricks on my fingers were healed thanks to the salve. We walked far enough that the cottages were way behind us, as well as the tree line, then stopped. We were about half a mile from where a rocky hill towered about a hundred feet up. It was probably a couple hundred feet in length.

"You could practice a Tide on items like the ones you Shifted, but that won't give us a solid answer on whether or not your magic is strong enough to use against Nimbisu," Saffron said. "So we would like you to practice on these rocks. They are smaller than the sky island but have similar mass, according to calculations that have been done. As you know, the capabilities of Vanish magic aren't only about size, they're about mass. It is why you are strong enough to Vanish a living person, while someone else could only Vanish a cardboard cut-out of that person. They might be the same size, but the mass is different. If you are able to Vanish these rocks, you should be able to Vanish Nimbisu."

"As it catapults toward my head," I muttered. Every time I thought about this thing I'd been asked to do I wanted to scream.

But screaming wouldn't save anyone. My magic could.

"We will all step back and give you space and silence to ground yourself," Saffron said. "Settle your mind as much as possible. Then awaken your magic and repeat the incantation. Give your magic a mental push. I know that sounds nebulous but instinctually you will understand. Think of your magic as a muscle and push it outward. The spell will make it easier. Make sure you are facing the rocks so your Tide follows the path it needs to. Take as much time as you need."

But not too much because the sky was literally falling.

"Got it." Ji and Marrik offered words of encouragement. Namira had a skeptical look on her face. I couldn't blame her. Vanish Tides were not something that had been a part of witch life for several generations. A flowing wave of Vanish magic meant to make a monumental structure disappear was something that had to be seen to be believed.

Here went nothing.

I took a few steps forward. It was not easy trying to relax when I was here for anxiety inducing reasons, but I tried.

I took deep breaths.

I relaxed my shoulders.

I kept my hands loose.

I closed my eyes and tried to quiet my thoughts.

Water, darkness, screams, something knocked into me and dragged me down …

My eyes flew open on a gasp. My body tensed up again. Trying to settle my mind had raised memories of my brush with death.

God, that had only been yesterday. It had been one fucking day since I'd almost died and I couldn't even try to process the trauma of what had happened and the lives that had been lost.

Tears came to my eyes.

"Are you okay?" Saffron called. I lifted my hand and gave a wave, then wiped at my cheeks before I lowered my hand.

"I don't think I can do this," I whispered. How was I supposed to find a calm headspace so this would work? Not a single thing in my life was peaceful. There was so much pain.

Pain. An image of Remi, Withered, floated before my mind's eye. I lifted my hand and touched the amulet. Remi was trapped, he had deteriorated, he had not been able to escape pain for hundreds of years. He had been calling me and I hadn't heard him. He was a phantom lost in a void and I was the only one who could help him.

I was not the only one with troubles, with pain that felt like it would break them.

I had been through a lot, but I hadn't broken. And if I kept telling myself I couldn't do this, well, I damn well wouldn't.

You have a hero complex, did you know that? Ji's words came back to me.

Yeah, I did know that. I wanted to save people. Wanted to save myself. Wanted to save those I loved and people I would never meet.

I closed my eyes and concentrated on taking even breaths. Remi's face loomed in my mind, but this time I pictured him the way he was; handsome, with flowing waves of brown hair, mischievous eyes, and a roguish grin. I wanted to save him.

I felt myself start to relax. Determination filled me instead of fear.

I pictured my parents. The way their arms had held me when I arrived from Tsunsama. The way they cried on me. Ma had said she didn't want to live if I was gone. I had kept her at a distance after Marrik Vanished and she didn't hold it against me. My father had been under a constant partial shapeshift which meant his emotions continued to be deep. For the first time in my life I had seen him cry and it had been for me. And Jiano, a protective, insightful, understanding sibling I was lucky to have. We had always been close and nothing would change that.

My family. I wanted to save them.

I pictured Marrik. The man I had fallen so in love with. The man who was still by my side despite having plausible reasons to stay away from me. There were so many places where we were fragmented, but I wanted the time to heal them. I wanted to save us.

I pictured my favorite places in Vonuis. The bordello, my dingy office, The Bramble, the huge library downtown, my favorite places to eat, the park that showed movies on a big projector screen every weekend, the bridge that was an architectural masterpiece and spanned the river dividing uptown and downtown.

I wanted to save the city I lived in.

Calm. I felt calm. I could do this. I would do this. Because I was the only one who could.

I was the strongest witch in the world.

I awakened my magic and raised my arms, stretching them out in front of me with my fingers splayed. Smoky, blue magic drifted around my hands and forearms.

An incantation and a mental push.

One more deep breath and …

"Ae huo monsi clurett meor wrentu och tivaru ae zumnaf dreemalo ilzum qi voudamkh."

Something sparked, no, ignited within me. I felt like I was being filled up with magic, like a star was pouring its fire into me. But I wasn't a large enough vessel to handle it. I would overflow, I would burst, I would choke …

Push.

I pushed. I didn't know how to explain it, but I pushed my magic while I continued to whisper the incantation. And …

My magic flowed away from me.

My mouth fell open. Dark blue plumes of magic streamed from my hands, carried on the wind currents. The cloud of magic grew steadily until it was something similar to that Memoria cloud that had engulfed Remi and I in Elsewhere, though not quite as large.

But it was wondrous.

Behind me I heard shocked and impressed sounds, but I didn't dare turn around. I didn't want to do anything that might break my concentration.

The Vanish Tide raced toward the looming mass of rocks.

How would it happen? Would a lot of it have to wrap around the rocks? Should I start to walk closer? Would it—

My magic billowed against the rocks and it Vanished.

One moment it was there, and in the blink of an eye it was gone.

My mouth was gaping open as I stared at the spot the hill had been.

Holy shit. I had done it!

I quieted my magic and lowered my hands. When I turned around there were wide eyes and open mouths all around.

Jiano shook their head as though coming out of a trance. Then they put two fingers in their mouth and whistled.

"Amazing! Stupendous! Magnifique!" they shouted. Marrik dashed over, grabbed me around the waist and picked me up, spinning me around.

"You are absolutely incredible!" He landed me on my feet and pressed a hard kiss against my mouth. "Not that I didn't already know that, but … wow! You did it. You really did it!"

"Vanish Tides, Vanish Shifts, I bow to you, baby sis." Jiano gave a dramatic bow with their arms out before pulling me in for a hug. When they released me, Saffron came forward with a smile and a round of applause. Namira held back, her expression shifting between fear and awe. It probably wasn't comfortable for her to see how strong my magic was, but this particular ability was needed for a task that would save a lot of lives, so hopefully it didn't deepen the dark feelings she had about me.

"That was perfect," Saffron said. "You are quite something, Kitaine. In one afternoon you have mastered two high level Vanish abilities. Mr. Gladstone will be very, very pleased to hear how things transpired."

Hearing Gladstone's name was like a sour twist in my gut, but thinking of his high forehead and beady eyes wouldn't dampen my mood.

I had stronger magic, a lot of support, and I had determination. For a while, that was all I was gonna let myself focus on.

Chapter Sixteen

Turns out, creating Vanish Tides and doing Shifts leads to extreme exhaustion.

I'd been feeling it as we wrapped up with Saffron and headed back to my car. I'd asked Marrik to drive because I was starting to feel weary. At some point I had fallen asleep. When I woke up, I was in my bed with Marrik snoring beside me. I'd had no idea how long I'd been knocked out, but I was still exhausted so I'd fallen right back to sleep.

When I woke up in the morning, I felt rejuvenated, but I also felt a pang of guilt because I hadn't been able to wear the suppression gloves while I slept so I could meet Remi. I hadn't dreamt of him, which confirmed that the suppression gloves played a role in us being able to connect. I guess it really had to do with how strong my magic was and how weak he was.

There were two things on my to-do list today: make progress on how to help Remi and Vanish Nimbisu.

I was set to Vanish the sky island tonight. Evacuation precautions were being taken, which included Umbra Witches creating anchored shadows across the city to get people out should the worst happen. I was nervous about facing a falling land mass, but I had seen with my own eyes that my magic was strong enough to Vanish it.

I wondered what would come of the dance Gladstone and I were doing after this was done. Guess I'd find out.

After breakfast, I freshened up and threw on white shorts and a mint, eyelet blouse, then Marrik and I parted ways for a few hours. He wanted to head to the storage unit to bring a few more things back to my apartment. So far he'd mostly brought clothes, but he wanted to retrieve some of his art supplies and overall remind himself of what he owned since he'd been gone for so long. I was glad that he seemed to be moving toward his art. Even if he didn't get back into paid gigs, working on art could be therapeutic.

I dropped him off at the storage unit then headed to the bordello where I caught my parents up on my new Vanish abilities. The news and social media made it clear that everyone in Vonuis was scared about the pending collapse of Nimbisu, but my face had been alongside every post and report. It was being spread far and wide that Kitaine Neris, Savior of the Ley Lines, would soon be Vanishing the sky island and saving everyone.

My media presence today was propelled by the High Coven, and it was amusing to know that it played right into Paluna's plan to keep me in the public eye in a positive way.

I continued to thread nervous and anxious feelings as I thought about what I had to do, but I kept picturing the rocky hill I'd Vanished yesterday, and amid the nervousness was a kernel of confidence that I could do what needed to be done with Nimbisu. My parents were nervous too, but were impressed with my new abilities. I'd practiced transference by Shifting the paperweight on Jiano's desk. I'd left the anchor at home, so when I got back to my apartment I'd text them a picture to show that it'd worked.

Ji took me through the anchored shadow in their office bathroom then headed back. The slap of my sandals echoed off the stone as I walked across Paluna's spy cavern. Paluna looked up from where she was leaning over someone's shoulder as they pointed to something on a monitor. She gave me a smile as I came closer. Her hair was done in neat, two stranded twists that she'd pulled up into a bun, and she was wearing trouser jeans and a white blouse.

"I feel as though we have a lot to catch up on," I said when I reached her. We stepped aside to talk near an empty desk. As usual, the place was full of her people doing what they did to keep her operation running smoothly. I noted that many monitors were zeroed in on Nimbisu.

"Many things I already know," she replied. "You met with my husband yesterday and learned some new things."

"I was thrown for a loop when I saw Gladstone standing in the bordello. Could not have expected that he would ask for my help."

"He was left with no other recourse, but I'm sure he tried to come up with a solution that did not involve you. He expressed a desire to address the issue himself, being that he is a Magnes Witch, but he lacks the magical strength and the knowledge, though he was loathe to admit it."

"I'm not surprised he wanted to be the hero. I could tell he wasn't happy to come to me with this. But this situation isn't about our personal issues. A sky island falling is a problem for everyone."

"It is," she said gravely. "I had hoped the High Coven would have figured out how to manage the land masses the way they were in the past, but we need much more time to become capable at handling them. You are meant to Vanish it tonight?"

I nodded. "There's a mountain they want me to do it from about an hour and a half outside the city. Based on the island's trajectory it will be the best place to release a Vanish Tide."

"I will have eyes on you. I trust and believe in your strength, Kit. I know it has not been an easy few days for you." Her face showed concern. "My operatives did not come across the Normies First plan to target the shipping container. I regret that I could not have helped avoid that situation. I was not yet at The Bramble when the attack occurred."

"You do a lot, Paluna, and I'm grateful for your help. My heart is heavy, and I'd be lying if I said I was past the incident but," I took in a shaky breath, "Marrik's family is targeting me specifically. His cousin said they are on a mission to remove me from Marrik's life. And clearly, they don't just mean to break us up. I'm worried about what they might do."

"I'll do all I can to help you," Paluna said. "Normies First is a vast network and they are very good at planning their attacks. I'll keep a close eye on Marrik's people."

"I appreciate it." I felt some ease having Paluna as an ally. Without her network and resources I knew I would be far worse off right now. And every time the little voice in my head told me that I wouldn't be in this situation at all if I hadn't agreed to work with her, I reminded that little voice that I also wouldn't have gotten Marrik back nor returned strength to the ley lines.

Mixed bag. Doubled-edged sword. Story of my life.

"No way!" The shout of someone across the room drew our attention. "How stupid can people be?" I recognized the person who spoke, Titan, the man who'd been monitoring Nimbisu the last time I was here.

"What has occurred, Titan?" Paluna queried. We walked over.

"Our drones circling the sky island have picked up three people who parachuted onto it," Titan said. My eyes widened when I looked at the screen and saw exactly that. The drone was high up in the air, but Titan typed on the keyboard and the camera zoomed in. We were able to make out three people with colorful parachutes dragging behind them looking every which way as they walked across the uneven surface of Nimbisu.

My heart felt like it'd clattered through my ribcage and into my stomach.

"More people pulled this stunt?" I said. "I mean I'm not really surprised but come on!"

"They're a group of daredevils with a large social media following." A woman with short hair dyed purple came up on Paluna's other side and tilted the tablet she was holding so Paluna could see the screen. "They'd been hinting at a big stunt for the past few days. Guess we know what the stunt was."

"Oh, for fuck's sake." I smacked my forehead. "The sky island that's moving, crumbling, and about to be released from the gravitational hold of one of the moons keeping it afloat has idiots traipsing across it for social media likes. And I'm supposed to Vanish it tonight."

Paluna shook her head and released a sigh. "This should have been anticipated, since others did the same a few days ago, but it is a very alarming development at this point. There is little time left for Kit to Vanish Nimbisu."

"I'm hearing that the High Coven is aware of the stunt and are taking measures to get them off the island." This from someone else who'd come over and appeared to be listening to an earpiece. "There's no telling when they will decide to jump off so there's no time to wait them out."

"So dumb," I muttered. "I've half a mind to Vanish the damn thing with them on it."

Paluna chuckled. "I do not begrudge you those dark feelings. However, let us hope good sense prevails and they leave quickly." She turned to Titan. "Keep the drones on them and let me know of any updates."

"Yes, ma'am," Titan replied. He shook his head at the screen, muttering under his breath about how stupid those people were. I sincerely hoped those fools got out of there soon.

Paluna indicated for me to follow her and led me to where a wide table was set up with various items.

"Very troublesome issues of islands in the sky aside for the moment, there is something I want to talk to you about," she said.

"Me too. I was going to come yesterday but Gladstone changed the way I thought my day was gonna go. But I really need to talk to you about Remi."

Paluna's eyes widened. "Well, it seems this conversation will be well aligned. Because it is Remi I wish to speak about as well."

"Really?"

"My team found his bones." She gestured to a box on the table. It was made of dark green metal with plenty of rust. It was about four feet long, and though I could tell an attempt to clean it off had been made, there was still quite a bit of dirt caked onto it.

"Remi ..." I tentatively reached my hand out. This old, rusty box contained all that was physically left of Remi. Something inside me ached terribly.

"I never called off the search," Paluna continued. "And my team finally came across one of Ziyelle's spell rooms. She hid them quite well; this one was deep within a cave on Xislao."

Xislao was one of the smaller Tropical islands and was very remote. It was accessible only by boat.

"And you're sure this is Remi?" I didn't doubt Paluna's search, but I knew Remi wasn't the only ghost Ziyelle had bound.

Paluna pointed to a spot on the box and I leaned closer.

"Oh." A rectangle of metal was affixed to the box with bronze nails. There were two words etched onto it: Remington Glace.

I placed my palm on the rough surface of the box. "Remi."

"The bones are inside, I had it verified at the site and I also took the liberty of having a look once the box arrived. One of my Mortem Witches confirmed that every single one of Remi's bones are there. There is a small piece of one of his knuckle bones missing, and that must be the piece fused to the amulet."

I nodded. Fusing a piece of the ghost's bones to the amulet helped keep them bound to it.

"I know that we'd spoken about a roundabout way to unbind Remi from the amulet so he could cross over," Paluna said. "But it was unforeseen what happened in Elsewhere. I still continued to search because I felt at the very least your family could put his bones to rest with dignity."

A sad smile twitched my lips as a tear rolled down my cheek. I looked up from the box. "That brings me to why I wanted to talk to you about him." I reached into the neckline of my blouse and drew the amulet out.

"Remi isn't completely gone." Paluna's eyes widened. "Onyx saved him at the very last moment, right before he would have Withered like she did, like Elsewhere did. She saved what was left of him and put him back into the amulet."

"Really? Are you sure?"

I nodded, then spent the next few minutes explaining how I'd been able to connect with Remi in my dreams, and that the suppression gloves played a role. When I was done, Paluna was holding her chin in a thoughtful manner, her brow creased.

"Fascinating. And interesting and concerning and hopeful." She reached up and gently touched the amulet.

"My blood hasn't been able to draw him out, he's too weak." I couldn't keep the sadness from my tone. "I was hoping you might be able to find information on how we can get him out. But I don't want him to exist as a bound, desiccated ghost. He seems like he is in so much pain. I want to help him. Even if …" I glanced at the box that contained his bones. "Even if that means doing the ritual to free him to the Afterlife. But not unless we can rejuvenate his ghost."

I couldn't fathom sending Remi to an eternity on the other side in the state he was in.

"This problem has many layers." Paluna tapped her chin then lowered her hand. "I will look into how we might be able to get him out of the amulet. It will likely involve strengthening his ghost while he's in there."

"How would we do that?" I wanted to feel hopeful, but hope was a dangerous thing. I needed something sure.

"I don't know. But I will have my team on it, specifically the Mortem Witches. Ziyelle herself might be a source of help." She indicated some of the other items on the table. There were several books, some of which looked like grimoires with old, leather covers with gems embedded in them or stamped patterns.

"Her spell room was so well hidden it was never looted. We took everything. All her journals, grimoires, and books. They rightfully belong to your family, of course, but I hope you will allow us to analyze and catalogue them before turning them over. Many of them require some restoration as well. And I would like to make digital copies."

"Yeah, of course, that's no problem."

"I actually found one that you might find useful regarding the Memoria Witches in Jiano's care," she said. "The one who recreated your Elsewhere memories at the press conference in particular."

"Milene's magic is stronger than we knew. She can make someone's memories visible to others and can do the same with dreams." I frowned. "And you found something helpful for her among Ziyelle's tomes? But she was a Mortem Witch."

"There are connections between the witch classes that we might not think possible," Paluna replied. "Perusing Ziyelle's journals made me aware of ties between Memoria and Mortem magic that once led to powerful spell work. Thus, Ziyelle has written extensively about Memoria abilities."

"Memory and death magic, huh? What could be done by mixing those?"

"I read of an interesting practice that involved ensconcing a ghost within a memory, usually drawn from the deceased's loved one," she replied. "It was a way to help restless ghosts that resisted the Afterlife and remained manifested here. Temporarily sustaining the ghost within a soothing memory helped them cross over. With the weaker magic we've had for the last few centuries, Memoria Witches haven't been able to continue the practice. Restless ghosts are forced over by Mortem Witches where they've no choice but to spend their Afterlife with those unsettled emotions."

"That's incredibly sad." It continued to be deeply fascinating to learn about what we used to be able to do with magic. Valentino always said moving ghosts to the Afterlife was his least favorite bit of coven-work and I could understand why when it involved moving spirits who couldn't be soothed first.

"Someone on my team who has been reading Ziyelle's journals mentioned practices fusing ghosts to recreated memories," Paluna continued. "Recreations are something Milene is capable of, so this will be helpful information. That journal needs a bit of restoration, then I will turn it over to you."

"Thanks, I'm looking forward to reading it."

"There's a chance we will also find useful information on how to help Remi."

"If her writings can help us figure out how to strengthen him enough so he can get out of the amulet, that would be great. I never want him to be trapped inside this damn thing again. I want him to be free."

That was a half-truth. I wanted him to be free, but I also wanted him to stay with me. But that was selfish. To continue wanting the company of a ghost who was burdened by centuries of pain.

"Free."

Something about the way Paluna said that made me look at her questioningly.

"You've thought of something that could help Remi?"

"Perhaps." She said the word very slowly. "We already have layers to peel back with helping him, but I cannot help but think that finding his bones and him not being gone could mean there is another route we can take once we replenish him and get him out of the amulet."

"What do you mean?"

"Let me show you something." I followed her to another table. There were metal boxes on it similar to the one Remi's bones were in, but these were in much better condition.

Paluna opened a dark gray box and I made a disconcerted sound when the contents were revealed.

The bones of a small animal were neatly arranged on a black, velvet pillow.

"A cat," Paluna offered.

"Er ..." I looked at the other boxes. Some were small, some were larger than the one she'd opened. "Are all of these animal bones? And why do you—"

"I am a Regressa Witch. One of the abilities of my magic is being able to revert something to a previous state. Before the ley line surge, I could do little with my magic as Regressa has long been one of the weakest witch classes and would have been the next one to die out. The day of the surge, I reverted a bottle at the bordello back into its components of sand and limestone. We've all been testing the new limits of our magic, right? Even with the coven assessment, I wanted to see how much stronger I'd gotten."

"I see." I looked from the cat bones to her. "So these bones ..."

"Watch." She looked down at the box and held her palms over it. Seconds later I felt her magic rise. I hadn't met a lot of Regressa Witches, so I wasn't too familiar with the feel of their magic. It was a twisty kind of feeling, like when someone grabs your forearm and twists your skin in opposite directions. It wasn't a harsh feeling, though. Paluna's Regressa magic was a shimmery, soft, yellow color that reminded me of early sunrise. It pulsed over the box, easing over the cat's bones.

And I witnessed a magical transformation I had never seen before.

Under Paluna's magic, the bones rearranged themselves into a proper skeleton. And then the cat … stopped being a skeleton. I was equally parts awestruck and disgusted as I watched the cat's body build back from bones to flesh. Muscle and sinew rippled over the gleaming bones, organs appeared, veins and arteries flowed, pinkish flesh covered all of it, and finally, glistening black fur rippled over the animal.

"Oh my God." My mouth was open in shock. Paluna quieted her magic and lowered her hands. I stared at her. "Whoa. Oh wow. Um … amazing. You … wait." I turned back to the cat. It was on its side, eyes closed. I leaned closer.

"It is still quite dead," Paluna said. I straightened up.

"Oh."

"My magic does not restore life, alas, even at its strongest. It can, however, revert a skeleton to its previous state of being. A state of being when it was a complete body."

"Oh. Oh!" My head whipped over to the table where Remi's bones were. "That's why you wanted to show me this." I turned back to her. "Because you could … you're saying you could revert Remi's bones back to his body?" I was getting excited and hopeful and I tried to curb it. Paluna could revert his body, but she couldn't restore life.

"Yes, I probably could. However, the limits of my magic seem to be here." She gestured at the cat. "I have reverted the bones of mice, cats, and small dogs. Larger dogs I am unable to. So I am not yet strong enough to revert the bones of a human. Were I to strengthen my magic on the ley lines, then perhaps."

"And that's possible now." I was still trying to temper my excitement, but it was hard. We weren't on a free and clear path to resurrecting Remi, but the fact that we had this many variables going meant something could come of this. It meant that maybe … *maybe* … Remi could get what he wanted. Life, a beating heart, breath in his lungs.

Holy shit.

"There was a ley line well where I went yesterday to learn Tides and Shifts," I said. "A place called Moonglade. You could strengthen your magic at a well. I could teach you what Onyx taught me."

"That well will not be the best one since it is under the control of the High Coven, but I have uncovered old maps that indicate where many others are. I will be paying attention to when the covens will be allowed to start drawing from wells, but I suspect it might take some time. Us witches must venture into this new era with caution. The ley lines are only partially back and have not been drawn on for centuries. It is an education that we have lost, though much of the process was written down. To actually practice it – under the guidance of witches who do not know any more than we do, will be a slow endeavor."

That sobered me. I had to pump the brakes on this trajectory because even if Paluna could revert his bones tomorrow we still had no idea how to bring him back to life. Onyx had said resurrection was the kind of ability they'd reached for when they drained the ley lines and obliterated themselves. I couldn't be foolish enough to believe that we could ask a Regen Witch to whip up a life-giving potion or something. And we first had to see about healing his ghost before we could figure out how to put him back into his reverted body.

So many unknowns, so many steps. But this was *something*. I could tell Remi; I could give him some hope. And I'd do my damned best not to fail him.

"I don't want to make false promises." Paluna said. "We could not even hope to resurrect a person and not have to deal with the moral or legal implications of it, but—"

"But I don't care," I cut in. "Ethics, jail time, moral implications, people beating on our door to resurrect someone for them if we truly figure this out. I don't care. I'll lose sleep over that later. Please, let's figure out how we can help Remi. We can put reverting his body on the back burner since your magic isn't strong enough. But I really want to get him out of the amulet."

Paluna nodded. "I'll do all I can to figure something out, I promise."

"Thank you." I was a tumult of emotions. I knew we had a long road ahead, but this path that had opened up was welcomed. If we could really figure out a way to bring Remi back to life—

My phone started ringing. I fished it out of my bag, thinking Marrik was calling, but it was Jiano. I couldn't wait to tell them and my parents about this.

"Hey, Ji, I—"

"Kit, I need your help." Ji sounded frantic, snapping me to attention. "Milene wandered off. She has her phone and it's pinging that she's closer to you than she is to me. I went on an errand with the parentals so I'm not at the bordello, but I'm heading back now. Can you—"

"Share her location with me, I'll go get her." I'd have to leave through Paluna's office, so I started toward the door that led up to it. Paluna fell into step with me.

"How the hell did she get all the way over here?" The bordello was about thirty minutes away on the other side of the river.

"She's been walking," Ji replied. "Phinra says they were both napping, then she woke up and left Milene asleep. She was in the laundry room helping out and when she went back up to their room about an hour later Milene was gone. I don't know where she's going or what headspace she's in. Please—"

"I'll find her, Ji, promise." Paluna opened the door and let me lead the way, running up the stone steps to the paneling that opened into her office.

A lot was going on with Milene but so much was going on with me we'd barely been able to pay attention to her needs. And now she'd wandered away. Guilt latched onto me. As I ran out of

Paluna's office I prayed I found Milene before someone who might mean her harm did.

Chapter Seventeen

My panic was short lived as I followed the location tracker Jiano sent me and found Milene on the bridge that connected uptown and downtown.

The bridge had a lower level for vehicles, and an upper one for pedestrians. Thankfully, Milene was on the upper level.

"Milene!" I pushed through people, ignoring the recognition I triggered and shouts for an autograph or photo. I had forgotten how visible I'd become, but this wasn't the time to play into the 'public's darling' ploy Paluna had enacted.

After running halfway down the bridge, I finally came to Milene, who was walking slowly and looking around as though inspecting every mote of dust that flitted past her eyes. When she caught sight of me, she waved. I gave her a quick look over. She wore a pair of cotton shorts and a slouchy T-shirt with a smiley face graphic. Her hair was tousled, and she seemed oblivious to the hot concrete under her bare feet. Her phone was in her hand.

I braked several feet away and grabbed the railing to catch my breath. I'd been running since I'd left Paluna's office about eight blocks away. Paluna had offered to send a couple of her people with me, but I had declined since we were trying to keep our acquaintance low key and we could never be sure when the High

Coven did or didn't have eyes on me. The last thing I wanted was for them to see highly trained people helping me track a witch they'd twice tried to kidnap. Though if it had seemed like Milene was in greater trouble, I would have accepted the help.

"Milene?" I got enough of my stamina back and straightened up, taking a step toward her and placing my hands on her shoulders. "Are you okay?"

"Yes." Her gaze swept over my face and a jarring feeling went through me. I almost dropped my hands and stepped away but managed not to. I was here to help her, yet that unsettling jolt was because I'd expected her to use her Memoria magic on me again.

The strength of Milene's Memoria magic scared me, and I wondered if we would ever truly be able to help her handle it. Especially because her magical strength was wrapped around years of being mentally and physically abused. But we had to do something to help her and Phinra, and we had to figure out what that something was quick.

"Let's head back to the bordello." I took Milene's hand and tried to walk, but she resisted. "Phinra is waiting for you. She's worried. Why don't we head back so she can see you're okay?"

"My sister," she whispered. "There are things she did not tell me."

"What things?"

Milene shook her head and released a little sigh. "I must make it right."

"Milene—"

"I'm tired."

"Uh … Okay. Let's go back to the bordello so you can rest."

Milene gave me a dreamy smile but didn't resist when I tugged on her hand again. We started walking off the bridge. I used my free hand to update Jiano that I'd found her and she was okay, then opened a ride-share app and called a car. We could have gone to Paluna's office and through an anchored shadow back to Kiss and Hex, but again, I didn't want to draw too much attention to my movements there.

I bought Milene a pair of dollar store flip flops, a bottle of water, and a chocolate bar while we waited for the car. Once we were on our way, I released a sigh. Retrieving Milene had gone as smoothly as it could have, and I was thankful for that.

"Milene." She was chewing her treat and staring out the window. We were back on the bridge, this time on the lower level. "Where were you going?" She was prone to wandering off, but did she ever have a destination in mind? I'm not sure anyone had ever asked.

Milene turned to me with a smile on her lips.

"Home," she whispered.

"Home?" Did she mean the place she lived with her abusive foster family?

"Phinra is at home waiting for you."

Her smile widened. "Yes. I have to help my sister."

"Help her how?" Between the two of them, Phinra was doing better, so I'd say Milene was the one that needed help. Then again, she could be referring to something I knew nothing about.

"How do you have to help Phinra?" I prompted.

"Someday," was all she said. She lowered the hand holding the chocolate bar and laid her head on my shoulder. Her body relaxed against me.

"Someday," she said again. I wanted to press her for answers but decided not to.

A short time later, she fell asleep.

Once we arrived at the bordello, I roused Milene and we headed inside where Phinra embraced and fussed over her. I'd kept texting Ji while in the car, so everyone was as up to date on the situation as I was. None of us understood what Milene meant when she said she was going home and had to help Phinra. But a pin was put in asking her more questions when it was clear she was very tired.

"Get her freshened up and put to bed," Jiano said to Calla. "I'll have food sent up."

Calla nodded, and she and Phinra headed upstairs with Milene. After they were gone, I slumped forward on the bar. Several Hexes were around, including Rowan and Arjun. My parents were also here. Dad gave me a gentle pat on the back as I lay flopped like a dead fish.

"We really gotta figure something out with Milene," Rowan said. She had shifted her wings, as well as a fantastic, feathered outfit with a scattering of feathers covering her breasts and a short, feathery skirt swishing around her hips. It was the fullest skirt I'd ever seen her make with her magic.

"She slipped out right under our noses," Ro continued. "There were a lot of us here, how didn't we realize she was gone?"

"Would hate to make them feel like they're trapped here but we may have to see how we can better monitor them," Arjun said. His long, dark hair was in a fishtail braid over his shoulder; Ma's handiwork. He wore a loose tank and spandex shorts, so he was probably gonna work out in the basement gym before the bordello opened.

"For real," Ro replied.

"We haven't been pressing the issue of Milene starting therapy since she's been resistant, but we may have to," Ji said. They were dressed in harem pants over a pink bodysuit with a plunging neckline and a pattern of hibiscus flowers. It seemed to be another hat day for Ji and Ma given the two ribbon adorned hats at the end of the bar. Ma's day dress had a pattern of olive oil bottles. I always had to give Ma props for finding the kitschiest clothes in existence. Dad's attire was jeans and a short sleeved, striped button-down.

"When we tried to get her to talk to a therapist she screamed for twenty minutes," Ro said. "She doesn't seem to want anyone encouraging her to probe at what's inside her head."

"I remember," Ji said. "But something's gotta give. We'll figure it out. Getting Milene help is a top priority but I honestly don't know who could help her control her magic. She is likely to be stronger than any Memoria Witch we approach."

A sobering truth.

"Still gotta try," Arjun said.

"I'm gonna talk to Paluna about it," Ji said. "She's gotta know someone we can get in touch with as a starting point. Jamari Zhao or someone else."

"She might already be ahead on getting us a resource for Milene." I told them that Paluna had found Remi's bones as well as a trove of items from one of Ziyelle's spell rooms, including journals and grimoires. I'd already told Jiano and my parents about my connection with Remi through my dreams and that the remnants of his ghost were still in the amulet, but I held back from leading the conversation toward what could be done to restore both his ghost and his body. I wanted more solid information before I said anything.

"Paluna told me one of Ziyelle's grimoires might be helpful. Even though Ziyelle was a Mortem Witch there are apparently correlations between Memoria and Mortem magic, and Ziyelle's notes might be helpful for Milene. Once she does some restoration and cataloguing of the grimoire she'll hand it over."

"That would be wonderful," Ma commented. "And I must let her know how grateful we are that she located Remi's bones. We can finally treat his remains with the respect he deserves."

Maybe we can do more than that, I thought. Hoped.

We chatted about Milene a bit more, then Arjun and Rowan headed to the stage. Ro would be performing tonight, to Arjun's guitar, so they were gonna practice. Several Hexes were lounging on the chairs in front of the stage, so they had a test audience ready.

"Did you eat, Kit?" Ma queried. She'd moved behind the bar with Jiano and was taking directions on mixing a drink. My mother was the kind of person who would follow instructions halfway then do her own thing, so she could either produce a unique drink that was pleasing to the palate, or something that would burn a hole through all your organs.

"No. Not since breakfast. What time is it even?" I fished my phone out as Dad answered to tell me it was after three.

"You have to eat before you do your Vanish Tide later," Ma said resolutely. "See how it exhausted you yesterday?"

"Yes, Ma, I will eat. Please fill me up."

"I ordered food while you were heading back," Jiano said. "The best our favorite Indian restaurant has to offer is on its way."

"Yum." I was ready to devour some naan and curry. It would be good fuel for Vanishing falling land masses.

"Where's Marrik?" Dad asked, looking into the glass Ma slid in front of him with suspicion. Her eye had been drawn to the colorful mixes, so she'd made something that had grenadine, blue curacao, and crème de menthe, as well as rum and peach schnapps. I'm pretty sure Jiano had been trying to show her how to make a Cosmopolitan.

"He texted while I was in the taxi that Namira called and said she has solid intel on Normies First's next move against me," I replied. Ji and I were staring Dad down as he lifted the glass and took a sip. He did a full body flinch, his face contorting in a comical grimace as he put the drink down, but he gave Ma a thumbs up, which pleased her.

"Say the word and I'll get an ambulance here, Dad," Ji said in a loud whisper. Ma swatted at them before she looked at me, her face sobering.

"Did Marrik say what they're going to do?" Ma asked.

"He said Namira wants to tell him in person because she's worried her phone could be tapped since they know she's been around him. They're gonna meet up at a park then he'll come by and give me an update."

Dad placed his hand over mine and squeezed. "Won't let nothing happen to you. Too much has almost taken you from us. It's difficult not to … not to want to stay with you at all times. I'm getting old, maybe I can't do much, but I will always try to protect my family."

That brought tears to my eyes. "Dad, please, my tear ducts have been working overtime."

"I know what you mean." He looked from me, to Ji, to Ma. "When I was told you Vanished, I cried because I felt helpless. And because I wanted to reach for hope that wasn't there for me to reach."

"Dad," I whispered.

"All I have ever wanted to do is protect my family." My throat grew tight when I saw tears shining in his eyes. "That is who I am. That is the nature of my creature, my magic. I'm a tracker and a protecter. And when I met your mother and we had children, protecting you was my focus. Remi too. It was why we never gave his amulet up. No one could have protected him better than us."

Ma passed Dad a cocktail napkin, but he just squeezed his hand around it. A tear slipped down his cheek.

"I always thought I did good raising my children. I stepped in when I needed to help or defend you. Was always there for you to come to. I didn't think there was anything I could not save my children and my wife from. And then you Vanished, Kit. And I thought, what could I have done to protect you?"

"Dad, there was nothing—"

"Protecting those you love isn't always about fighting," he said. "I can use my fists and claws, I can take up a weapon, I can charge ahead against anyone who lifts a hand against the three of you, but that isn't all there is to it." He released a sigh as he adjusted his glasses.

"What if I'd been closer, what if I'd called more, what if I'd known you were Vanishing bad people? Could I have advised you, would you have told me about the agreement you made to Vanish Gladstone? Was there anything I could have done to make a difference?"

He shook his head. "I failed to protect you. And I had no ability to protect Jiano and your mother from their grief. But we got our miracle; you are back, so I want to say to my family that I will not fail you again. I will protect what is closest to my heart."

"Dad." I was too choked up to say more. Jiano and Ma were dabbing at their eyes. I threw my arms around my father and hugged him tightly. He had always been the quiet but strong canopy over our family. He needed to know that he was in no way a failure in the face of everything that had happened. But maybe we'd need some family therapy to work that out.

"With my words, with my claws, I got you," Dad said when we pulled apart.

"I appreciate that more than I can say," I said.

"I would fight too, you know," Ma huffed, putting her hands on her hips. "I know a thing or two about potent potions. We Regens haven't been strong enough to cultivate a lot of the flora that pack a real punch, but some things may be possible now that the ley lines are stronger." She winked. "If anyone hurts my family their ancestors will regret ever starting their family line."

I chuckled. Truth be told, she was probably the one someone with bad intentions would have to be more afraid of. Dad might finish someone quick, but Ma and her knowledge of the darker aspects of Regen magic would make them suffer.

"Our little hellcat mother," Ji said, patting her on the head, which caused her to make a face at Ji. Or maybe it was because Ji had pried the bottle of rum from her so she wouldn't pour it into the tumbler she'd already poured orange liqueur, vodka, kaluha, and triple sec into.

"By the way, thanks for helping out at the hospital, Ma. I'm glad that everyone is recovering. I'm just so mad and so sad that happened. No one should have died."

Ma patted my hand. "I am glad I was able to help. There were a lot of injuries that needed tending. Many wounds got infected from bacteria in the river and we almost lost someone to sepsis but were able to save him."

I nodded. My heart hadn't stopped feeling heavy about the events of that day and the people who'd enacted it. Elliot and the other witches had friends and families grieving their loss while Normies First was still targeting us. One way or another this had to end.

Darkly, I wondered if I could use myself as bait, gather them together, and release a Vanish Tide to take them out. Using myself as bait in Elsewhere had gone completely wrong, but maybe I could do it right this time.

I shook my head, staring down at the surface of the bar. That wasn't gonna be the way I took care of Normies First, there were too many ways it could go wrong for everyone involved. And despite Marrik's divide from his family, Vanishing his parents and other family members would be a big issue. Marrik had a lot of anger and frustration toward his people, but he also had sadness and longing. I knew he wished that things could be different and was constantly under the stab of pain that it never would be.

So I couldn't Vanish my man's family. But I also couldn't fall victim to them. Namira could pass on intel about their next attack and we could avoid it, but then what? I had to keep dodging them for the rest of my life? Some people had been arrested after the drowning attempt but there were more out there, planning to come after witches again. I wouldn't have any measure of safety unless every witch hater was locked up and their prejudiced groups ground to dust.

I made a sound of frustration and only realized I'd banged on the bar when Dad covered my tightly closed fist with his hand.

"Kitten?" Ji queried.

"Sorry, I was spiraling on thoughts of how to get the witch haters off all our asses. I'm frustrated that our lives are in danger just for being witches."

"Humanity will never get off this hamster wheel, I'm afraid," Jiano said. "As long as there are differences among groups of people, there will be fear, misunderstandings, violence, and attempts at eradication and suppression. What could actually change that? I'm not sure the deities who shaped our world and allowed for some of us to have magic even know."

"You're right," I said softly. "I still hate it."

"As we all do," Ji replied.

"Drink something, honey, it will help relax you." Ma slid a glass in front of me that smelled so strongly of alcohol and was such a mix of acidic colors, I recoiled, bringing my hand up to cover my mouth and nose.

"Forget the witch haters, it's gonna be my own mother that takes me out."

"Well, I never." Ma kissed her teeth. Ji and Dad laughed.

"I'll try it, Tia Nolla." Valentino came up to the bar next to me, leaning on his forearms and looking into the glass. He was bare chested as usual, wearing one of his signature short-shorts. Hye-Jin was on his other side, wearing a curve hugging crochet dress over a bandeau bra and matching boy shorts.

"Knock yourself out. Literally." I slid Val the glass and he picked it up and tossed it back. I gasped. He downed the thing in one gulp! He slammed the glass down and made a sound like he was a corpse that had been jolted back to life.

"That will put hair on your chest and everywhere else!" Val said. Ma preened and tittered.

"I am both impressed and thoroughly repulsed, Val," Ji said, shaking their head.

"Dear God, Val, does being a Mortem Witch mean you're dead inside?" Hye-Jin stared at the empty glass with a wrinkled nose. "That thing smelled foul." She glanced up at Ma. "No offense, Auntie Nolla."

"I'm a good drink-maker, see!" Ma put her hands on her hips and tossed her head.

"No, Valentino is dead inside, that's gotta be it," I said. Ma swatted at my forearm. Val was grinning.

"Alright, our food should be here soon," Ji said. "Let me save you from Ma's chaotic mixes."

"You haven't even tried one!" Ma protested as Ji shooed her from behind the bar. "And Eldrick you only took one sip, I saw you."

"One was … quite enough." Dad coughed into his fist as though his throat was still burning.

"Hmph." Ma fake pouted as she perched on the stool next to Dad. I took her place behind the bar and helped Ji mix up some drinks. The food arrived, enough for the entire bordello, so the front room was soon crowded with Hexes digging into delicious Indian food. Some took their plates to eat elsewhere while others hung around. Ma seemed mollified to pass drinks around and identify them with outrageous, made-up names that made the recipient laugh.

As I returned from the bathroom and sat back down to finish my food, taking a sip of a wonderfully made Cosmopolitan, I realized that for the first time in a while I felt some measure of peace. All was not right in my life, but being surrounded by my friends and family, laughing, and sharing a meal, reminded me that amid the bad there was good. That analogy kept being relevant. I'd have to keep reminding myself to not only pay attention to my failures, grief, or problems, but take the time to live in the good moments and cherish them.

"Kitten, when do you need to head out to deal with the sky island?" Ji asked. I checked my phone and saw that it was after four.

"Soon. Saffron said they'll be sending a car for me at four-thirty."

"Alright, well—"

Ji was cut off by a deafening explosion that shook the building. I fell off my stool and people started screaming. Before I could try to get my bearings, another thunderous sound rang out, and the front door was blasted in.

"Kit!" Dad was reaching down to help me up. He'd been jolted into a partial shapeshift, so it was a scaled and clawed forearm that pulled me to my feet.

"Kit! Ji! Eldrick!" Ma's frantic voice. I heard Jiano yelling as well, heard screams from the Hexes who'd been in the front room with us. But I could barely see them because greenish smoke was rapidly billowing into the room. The screams and shouts cut off and were replaced by the sounds of bodies hitting the ground.

Shit. The smoke was some kind of knock out agent. It stung my eyes and clogged my throat. I staggered into Dad and we fell to the ground, both of us wheezing.

"Kit …"

"Da … Dad!" My eyes watered, and my brain felt foggy. I tried to pull myself up on a stool but couldn't manage.

We were under attack. Without a doubt it was a hate group.

The louvers shattered and fiery projectiles streamed in. Scorching heat washed over me. The room was quickly engulfed in flames and thick, black smoke.

The bordello was on fire.

They were going to burn us alive.

Chapter Eighteen

I couldn't see anything or anyone. All I heard was the roar of fire and screams turning to gasps and chokes. A high pitch wail from Ma clenched my heart before it abruptly cut off. Any time I tried to call for someone I wheezed and coughed instead.

I was on my hands and knees, barely able to breathe, feeling the heat of fire all around me. Flames were eating up the bordello's front room. My body was weakening as though my bones were dissolving.

I collapsed.

No. No. Get up. I had to get up. Had to get everyone out of here. My family. My friends.

Panic, fear, and horrific terror spiraled through me at the realization that this attack had been so meticulously planned there was no way to survive it. By compromising our senses first, they made sure we could not move to exits, or shadow travel, or use any form of magic to get out.

I wanted to cry out for my family. Wanted to tell them I was sorry I had brought this upon them. We were all witches and would always be the target of hate and violence, but the target on my back was bigger since it'd been announced to the world that I was the reason strength had returned to the ley lines. Witches becoming stronger was at the festering, putrid core of the anti-witch groups' fear.

This was my fault … my fault …

I had to save them. How could I save them?

Please … let me save everyone …

Something pulsed inside me. Like a flare had burst to life in the darkness of my mind. A strange, indescribable feeling shook my body. It was unlike anything I had ever felt, though something about it was vaguely familiar.

Had I felt this before?

The sensation, which felt magical, continued to ripple through me and impossibly, I felt strength flow through my limbs. It was still hot, stifling, and dark, but my senses were starting to feel less compromised.

What was happening? Where was this sudden strength and clarity coming from?

Questions for later.

I crawled forward and my hand landed on something thick and scaled.

Dad's arm!

I tugged, but he didn't move. He was unconscious. God, I prayed he was just unconscious.

Panic continued to course through me. I seemed to have regained some stamina but there was no way I could carry everyone out. Plus, there were people upstairs, including Calla, Phinra, and Milene. If only I could get everyone out quickly.

Realization was like a strike of lightning in my skull.

I could do Vanish Shifts! The anchor of blood and magic was at my apartment. All I had to do was Vanish them with a touch of blood and they would be transferred somewhere safe.

I groped around until my hands curled around a bottle. I smashed it then dragged the jagged edge across my palms. I didn't even take a moment to acknowledge the pain. Time was running out. I didn't know why I was able to resist being knocked out, but I had to take advantage of it as long as I could.

I channeled magic into my hands then touched my father. He Vanished.

My heart felt like it had been sliced in two as my panic surged. What if it hadn't worked? I'd seen with my own eyes that I could successfully do Vanish Shifts, but I had only learned this technique yesterday. What if I had Vanished …

I shook my head. It was not the time to entertain the worst kind of thoughts. This was the only way everyone had a chance of being saved so I couldn't stop. I moved forward and soon came to another person. I could tell it was Ma. I touched her with blood and magic and she disappeared. Then I kept moving.

Jiano had been behind the bar. I backtracked, using my familiarity with the bordello's layout to make it around the bar. I felt strong enough to stand, but standing up in a room that was on fire was a bad idea. I soon brushed up against Ji and used my magic to Shift them. Then I quickly moved from behind the bar to find everyone else.

The fire had eaten up the walls. Debris was falling everywhere. A large piece of wood from the ceiling fell across my back and I cried out as I slammed to the ground. I pushed myself up and got the smoldering wood off me, gritting my teeth against the pain. I kept going.

Smoke was filling my lungs and it wouldn't be long until the entire room was engulfed in flames. But somehow my stamina held. Had the knockout stuff burned out? Maybe that was it. But it didn't feel like that was the only reason. There was still a strange feeling resonating throughout my body. Something was slithering in my mind that felt ancient and unreachable and as bright as all the stars in the sky. I didn't understand it, and I was still terrified, but I didn't stop moving.

I thought back to everyone who'd been in the front room. Four people had been eating at the tables behind the bar. Including Val and Hye-Jin. I reached for their fallen bodies and counted as I Shifted them.

One. Two. Three. Four.

Good. Who else?

Arjun and Ro on the stage. Five people on the chairs in front of it. I crawled there, unable to see anything but smoke and fire. I felt around frantically, and soon came to the first person. My hands were screaming in pain from the wounds and from my journey across the scorching, splintered floor, but I stayed focused on what I had to do.

One. Two. Three. Four. Five.

I Shifted the Hexes who'd been sitting by the stage. Then I crawled onto the stage and found Ro and Arjun and Shifted them as well.

I got everyone. The relief was staggering but this wasn't over yet. I was close to the hallway so I crawled to it and made my way down. The fire had almost reached it and the smoke certainly had. My lungs burned and I moved with my eyes squeezed shut and my head down. When I came to the staircase, I headed up.

It was smoky here but not as much as the front room or hallway, so about halfway up I stood and broke into a run. I hit the second floor and started shouting as I flung open the door to every room. Thankfully, they were empty. There were several Umbra Witches among the Hexes, and they all had anchored shadows in various places throughout the bordello. It was likely they'd gotten everyone on the second and third floors out, but I had to check to make sure.

I ran up to the third floor. The sounds I heard coming from downstairs were heartbreaking as fire ate up the bordello. But at least my people were safe. I had Shifted them to my apartment. They were safe.

Loud, horrendous, gut-wrenching screams were coming from Milene and Phinra's room. I ran through the door and saw the twins and Calla, looking petrified. Milene was the one screaming. Her arms were tight against her chest, her hands balled, her head thrown back. Phinra had her arms around her but couldn't seem to soothe her. Calla was holding both girls.

"Kit!" Calla turned wide, tear-filled eyes to me.

"Everyone else ... who was up here ..." I was soaked in sweat and barely able to breathe. I doubled over, slapping my bloody hands to my thighs as I tried to keep myself upright. I couldn't collapse yet.

"We are the only ones left," Calla replied. "But Milene … we have been unable to move her. Someone was coming back to take us through the shadows but—"

The fire must have triggered something traumatic for her. There was no time to try and calm her and we had no escape routes from up here. I straightened up and stumbled over to them.

"What's happened?" Calla asked. "Fire? Is everyone—"

"Trust me," I gasped. "I will … see you … soon." I called up my magic and quickly touched the three of them. They Shifted.

I almost collapsed onto one of the beds, but I turned and stumbled back to the door and staircase. But when I got to the second floor, I realized that was the furthest I could go. The fire was spreading fast.

I had no idea if I could Shift myself and now wasn't the time to try. I backed up and headed into one of the second-floor rooms. Whatever stamina I'd tapped into was draining. If I didn't make it out, I would be burned alive. The witch haters may have been aiming to kill a building full of witches, but they would be satisfied even if it was only my death they could claim.

I had no time to think through another plan. I couldn't go downstairs, wasn't gonna try to Shift myself, and couldn't travel through any of the anchored shadows alone. There was only one way out and it was gonna hurt like a son of a bitch, but hopefully I'd survive.

I opened one of the windows and threw myself out.

I opened my eyes to blurry vision and a heavy feeling, like an elephant was lying on top of me. Like I wasn't human anymore but a slab of stone that was being compressed by other slabs of stone. There was soreness at various points in my body, most significantly my back, but I did note that there wasn't any excruciating pain. I suspected the heaviness in my limbs and the cloudy feeling in my head had something to do with that. Pain meds.

Which meant …

I blinked a few times to settle my vision and a hospital room came into view. I tried to turn my head and groaned at the protest my neckbones gave. I heard someone take a sharp breath and my eyes soon landed on Marrik.

I tried to smile but it was probably more of a grimace. Marrik was to my right, in a chair pulled close to the bed. He was leaning forward with his elbows on his thighs. His hands were covering the lower part of his face.

"Hey." The croak in my voice would make a frog proud. But the sound of my voice made Marrik flinch, and that made me frown. I swept my eyes over him. He was tense, his shoulders hunched, his hands shaking from how tightly they were clasped. His brow was deeply creased, and his eyes looked …

God, they looked like there was indescribable pain eating away at him. He had to have been worried about me, but I was okay … wasn't I?

"Am I … dying or something?" I rasped. "I don't feel great but is it … that bad?"

A sob wrenched from him. He dropped his head and made an anguished sound. One of his legs started to bounce restlessly. I felt like I couldn't breathe unless Marrik spoke. What had him so on edge?

He raised his head. "You … you aren't dying."

That was a relief. But I still didn't understand why Marrik was like this.

"You were treated for smoke inhalation, and you fractured your forearm. Lots of cuts and bruises, a concussion …"

I looked at my body. My left forearm was in a cast, and I had bandages on both arms. I could tell there was one on my forehead as well.

"I was prepared to break something, I'm glad a fracture seems to be the worst of it." I returned my attention to Marrik. "Hey, what's with you? Did something—" Panic gripped me as I thought about all the people I'd Shifted. It had worked, right?

"Marrik, is everyone okay? The only way I could save them was to Shift them. The anchor was in my apartment—"

Another sob wrenched from him. He dropped his head again. His leg continued to bob. His body was so coiled with tension I was afraid he might jump up from the chair and start screaming.

"Marrik. Talk to me, please. What is it?"

"I shouldn't be here," he whispered. "I shouldn't be here, it's because of my … But there was no one else who could … I …"

"Marrik!" He brought his gaze back to me. His eyes were wet with tears.

"Did my family get Shifted to my apartment? Did the Hexes? Tell me. Please."

If he said no. If he said no …

Seconds that felt like an eternity passed.

Marrik shook his head.

I screamed. Loud, long, wordless. I threw my head back and screamed.

"Kit, wait, Kit!"

The door opened and people ran inside. But I didn't pay attention to them. Marrik got up and I heard him talking but I barely followed what he was saying. A short time later the door opened and closed again.

I kept screaming. Sobs shook me. Tears poured from my eyes.

"Kit, I'm sorry, let me explain properly, let me talk! They didn't Vanish!"

I almost choked on the breath I'd sucked in so I could scream again. I brought my head down and blinked through the tears so I could see Marrik. He was gripping my forearm, his teeth clenched, streaks of tears on his cheeks.

"What. Happened." Those were the only words I could get out.

"It was … it was Normies First who set the bordello on fire."

"I know that." My patience was wearing thin. If they hadn't Shifted to my apartment but hadn't Vanished, then I needed

Marrik to explain what the fuck it was that had him acting like this.

"But it … it wasn't just about … Oh God." Marrik brought the heels of his palms to his forehead and kept speaking without looking at me. "After you were brought to the hospital I went back to your apartment to pack a bag for you. But when I got there, the door was open; someone had broken in. The apartment wasn't ransacked and there didn't seem to be anything taken, but the break-in had to have been for a reason. I contacted Paluna and she ran through the surveillance she'd been keeping on your building."

He dropped his hands so he could reach for his phone in his back pocket. He pulled something up on the screen and laid it on my lap as I sat up a bit more. A video. He tapped the screen to play it.

"Paluna says there was some interference with her surveillance which was why she didn't see this happening in real time," Marrik whispered.

I sucked in a breath that felt like it sent jagged, broken glass straight into my lungs.

The footage was from one of the drones Paluna used to keep an eye on my building and surrounding area. It showed Namira entering my building as someone exited.

"Namira … broke into … my apartment?"

"She … she kept asking me where I was staying and I ended up telling her." Marrik sounded so anguished, but I felt as though I was sliding into a cold, hollow, numb space. Like frost was creeping over my heart.

"Paluna told me to search the apartment carefully because there had to be something she was there for," Marrik continued. "So I did … and that's when I saw that …"

"The anchor." I felt like I was being cleaved into pieces.

"You'd left it on the nightstand." Marrik's voice was a hoarse whisper. "And it was gone."

I stared at Marrik. My mouth open, my eyes wide, my brain unable to comprehend what was happening.

"That happened yesterday morning, not too long after we'd left," Marrik said. He looked like he would rather throw himself into a grave and suffocate in its depths than keep talking but I needed to hear what he had to say next.

"Marrik, where is Namira? You were supposed to meet up with her, weren't you? Where is the anchor?"

"She never showed up," Marrik said through clenched teeth. "I think she wanted to lure me away so I wouldn't be at the bordello when the attack happened. She never had intel for us because she … she's been working with my family all along."

The revelation hit me like a ton of bricks and I don't know why. It wasn't like I was under any illusions that Namira liked me. From our first meeting it was clear that she held a deep grudge. Her dislike was warranted, but I had thought … hoped, that because she hadn't been part of the witch haters in the family, she was actually making an effort to get to know me and accept that Marrik and I were staying together.

But that had all been a lie. A ruse to stay close to me and gather intel that she could funnel to them.

Like my new abilities and what I could do with them.

So when they set the bordello on fire, they were prepared for the possibility that I would use Shifts to save everyone.

"Marrik." I reached out and clawed my hand around his forearm. I was a riot of the worst emotions possible. I touched Marrik and felt a fracture explode between us so dark and deep I was no longer sure we could drag our relationship out of it. We were cracked in so many places. Too many places.

But I could deal with that later. Right now I needed to know where the fuck my people were.

"Where did Namira take the anchor?" Oh God, I could have Shifted everyone into a Normies First base where they would have been quickly gutted. My breaths were coming in short, fast bursts. I was gonna hyperventilate.

"Paluna figured it out." His voice was low and strained. "Her team saw. Oh God, Kit I am so, so sorry."

"Marrik."

"There was a trio of people who parachuted onto Nimbisu yesterday afternoon."

I made a sound of shock.

"I saw them when I was at Paluna's base. They're a stunt group."

Marrik nodded. "With a Normie's First member who got the anchor from Namira and took it up there. And that is where Paluna's drones later saw everyone from the bordello that you Shifted."

"My parents," I hissed. "Jiano. Ro, Arjun, Val, Hye-Jin, Calla, Milene, Phinra. Several other Hexes. You're telling me that they are all on a sky island that is about to collapse? A sky island I am supposed to Vanish?" I sat up straighter. "Holy shit, how much time is left before—"

"Hours," Marrik whispered. "You've spent the night here. It's Friday morning. Nimbisu will be completely released from Cebis' hold and make its way to the ground in about three hours. Paluna has been tapped into the High Coven's team that's working on the sky island and she said there is no way to get them off. Nimbisu is moving faster and faster in a trajectory that will crash into Vonuis. The city is trying to evacuate, but they are still counting on you to Vanish it."

"But if I use a Vanish Tide …" I felt as though I was choking on the words. "If I use a Tide everyone on Nimbisu will Vanish as well."

Marrik dropped his face into his hands and made a terrible sound that felt as though it echoed off my bones.

"This is what they fucking wanted! To put you in an impossible position. To make you the one responsible for wiping out over a dozen witches, including your own family." He sounded raw with anger and sorrow.

"I've been so fucking stupid thinking Namira was on our side! This entire time," he raised his head, his anguished eyes locking with mine, "this entire time she's been working with my family to tear us apart and take down as many witches close to you as possible. It was all a lie, everything she said about Quinn helping us, it was a fucking lie. Kit, I am so sorry."

"Sorry won't save them!" I screamed. Marrik's face contorted in distress. I felt detached, numb, weightless. I felt like I was floating in outer space with no air to breathe and no heartbeat but my own rapidly dwindling one.

I was in an impossible position. If I did nothing, Nimbisu would crash, my friends and family would perish, and so would a lot of people in Vonuis.

If I used a Vanish Tide, Vonuis would be saved, but I would lose my family and my friends. I would once again Vanish people I loved.

I was the strongest Vanish Witch. The witch with the strongest magic in the entire world.

And it still wasn't enough to save the people I loved.

Chapter Nineteen

I'd been taken to the hospital in The Bramble. After I was examined, I was released, although I strongly suspected I would have been made to stay longer if the entire city hadn't been counting on me to address the sky island. A nurse helped me freshen up and change into clothes Marrik had brought, trouser jeans and a sleeveless lemon-yellow blouse. I noticed that he'd brought my favorite pair of low tops and that made a sharp, sizzling ache go through me.

But I shied away from examining the fractures between Marrik and I. There was nothing else I could think about until I got my family and friends to safety.

There had to be a way to save them and save the city. There *had* to.

But what the fuck could I come up with in less than three hours?

Vanishing Nimbisu while everyone was on it was out of the question. I would never recover from saving the city only to wipe out my family and so many Hexes in the process. I might as well die immediately after.

I was so angry, so frustrated, so fucking pissed off that I couldn't seem to do anything right. Couldn't save the day without having to weigh the wins and losses. Ji had been right that I couldn't expect every single situation to wrap up perfectly, but couldn't it happen *sometimes*? At least once? Couldn't I save the people I cared about and the city?

Was it always having to take the bad with the good?

I emerged from the room. Marrik was waiting in the hallway and took the packed bag as we headed to the elevators. I received a lot of uneasy, even grieved looks. No one was in the dark about what was going on. Every single person in Vonuis knew that terrible things were coming, but they weren't more terrible for anyone but me.

Downstairs, a contingent of anxious High Coven witches awaited us. I recognized only Saffron, but it was clear all the people with her were from the HC. Saffron jolted when she saw me, paused for a moment, then rushed forward.

"Kitaine, I'm so glad you're okay. But, um … there isn't a lot of time. Vanish Tide—"

"What is the plan to save them?" My voice was hoarse from all the smoke I'd sucked in. My pain was being kept in check by Regen meds, but I still felt unstable on my feet, and pangs of hunger clenched my stomach. But I had to hold myself together. There'd be time to collapse after this was over.

Saffron hesitated. She looked over her shoulder at the other witches and there was hesitation among all of them. Marrik was next to me, silent and tense.

The realization hit me so hard I almost fell flat.

They had no ideas. No plan, no hope to offer me. They came here only so I could Vanish Nimbisu. They couldn't save the people on it and would do nothing but count them as an unfortunate loss.

I drew breath to speak and a sob rattled out of me.

"Kitaine, I'm so sorry—"

"Don't you fucking dare!" I snapped. Everyone in the vicinity flinched. Marrik edged closer.

"Don't you dare open your mouth to tell me you expect me to do a Tide while my family and friends are on that fucking island. I will rip your heart right out."

Saffron gasped and took several steps back.

"Kitaine, the situation is … is very dire. If you don't Vanish Nimbisu, the city will—"

"And what about my family!" My hands fisted and I stepped forward. Marrik grabbed my arm but I pulled away. It was all I could do not to unleash my rage on him for the role he played in things reaching this terrible, terrible place.

"You want me to be a hero, to step up, to save the city, but who will save me from who I will be on the other side of Vanishing people I love?"

I couldn't picture it. Couldn't fathom it. Would not think I was at a point where I would be without my parents and sibling. Jiano and the Hexes had to come back and repair the bordello. Knowing Ji, they'd make it even better than before and throw a lavish re-opening. My mother needed to come back and pester me to eat, steal treats out of Dad's hand, and wear dresses with tacky prints. Dad needed to come back so we could keep doing our weekly crosswords, so he could offer to repair anything we needed, could hold my forearm the way he did when we shared a joke and he was laughing so hard his whole body shook.

I wanted to see Rowan learn how to fly. Arjun and I were supposed to get new tattoos together, we'd planned it over a month ago. Calla was healing and embracing intimacy among her friends again. Phinra and Milene were only seventeen, they deserved to grow up, to heal, to find mentors who could help them with their magic.

"Or," I growled, "maybe the better question is who will save all of you from who I will become."

Saffron and the other witches had wide eyes and fearful expressions.

"If you try to tell me my only choice is to Vanish that island with my people on it, I will make sure all of you are next."

I was beyond reasonable thought at this point. I didn't give a damn that I was threatening High Coven Witches. I meant every word.

"What is the use of having stronger magic, the ability to do Tides and Shifts if—" I paused, my eyes widening. I took a few moments to think something through, then brought my gaze back to Saffron, who was looking at me like I was a wild animal that had escaped its cage.

"Shifts and Tides," I whispered. I took a step closer to her. "Is it possible to use a Vanish Tide to do a Shift? If I release a Tide using blood, will it Shift the island to where I establish an anchor instead of Vanishing it?"

Saffron was so still it was like she'd petrified. She wasn't even blinking.

"Saffron!"

She jolted and dropped her gaze from mine.

"It … it should not be possible—"

"Should not? Has it ever been done? We have two hours left, Saffron. Talk."

"There is one documented instance of something like that but the witch who performed a Shifting Tide was incredibly strong and executed it on something that was maybe a hundred feet away. It … it was so taxing on him that he almost died."

A ray of hope erupted inside me. "That's what I'll do then."

"But it has only been done once!" Saffron stressed. "By a stronger Vanish Witch, a shorter distance, and a smaller object. If you try, you might not survive!"

My bag had made it all the way through the fire and its aftermath as it'd been slung across my chest. Marrik had left it in the room with me. I opened it and fished out one of the empty anchor bottles Saffron had given me.

"Here's what we're gonna do." I gave Saffron a focused stare. Behind her, the other witches had fallen silent. My voice was cold steel.

"I'm going to create another anchor," I continued. "And I will position it somewhere safe for Nimbisu to Shift to. Then you will take me to the nearest ley line well and I will strengthen my magic. There has to be one closer than Moonglade; we don't have enough time to get out there. Then you will take me to the highest elevation in Nimbisu's trajectory and I will release a Shifting Tide. It will work."

It had to. *It had to.*

"But—"

"No fucking buts!" I yelled. "Because your plan is no plan! You came here to round me up and have me Vanish the island with everyone on it. Unless you have any other plausible ideas on how to rescue them, shut the fuck up. This has a chance of saving them and the city too. So." I took another step closer. "This. Is. What. We. Are. Going. To. Do. Do you understand?"

"Y—yes," she stammered. "There … there is a ley line well at the High Coven's headquarters uptown."

Of course there was. It was unsurprising that they had built their skyscraper on top of a well, even if it hadn't been one they could have drawn from.

"And um … the High Coven's building is in line with Nimbisu's trajectory and is the tallest structure in the city, so you could go up to the roof to … to try to …"

"Good. Let's go." I strode forward. The sea of High Coven witches parted like giant hands had moved them to the side. It was a moment where I could have felt powerful, having HC witches looking at me in fear and awe, but I couldn't feel anything other than overwhelming anxiety until I was on the other side of this plan and knew it had worked.

I heard Marrik following me but I didn't look at him. Didn't ask what he thought about the plan. I was going to fall apart over the situation with Marrik soon, but I had to keep holding it together for now.

"Wait, the anchor!" Saffron caught up to me. "Where are you going to place the anchor?"

Outside I paused, looking around. Not too far away I could see several coven houses.

"I have an idea and I will need the help of an aquatic Mutans Witch," I said. "If one by the name of Emricka is available, I need her now."

The first place we checked was a Mutans Witch coven-house. Emricka and Rowan were in the same one, so I knew which to head to. Lucky for us, Emricka was there, and like every single witch we encountered as we walked through The Bramble, she was stricken by what was happening. A lot of people had called out to me while others stared with looks on their faces that made it feel like a fist was squeezing my heart.

"Why aren't you guys evacuating?" I asked Emricka after we'd hugged. We stood outside the doors of her coven-house. Marrik, Saffron, and the other HC witches hung back.

"The Umbras have anchored shadows ready for us," she replied. "A lot of us are still trying to convince family members it's in their best interest to leave, get them here, and take them through a shadow. There are a series of anchored shadows that will take everyone into the safe zones the HC has mapped out. I just got my grandparents through."

"The stubbornness of humanity." I shook my head. There would always be people who would hunker down and refuse to leave through hurricanes, tornadoes, and land masses careening down on them.

"I hope everyone mobilizes," I continued. "I plan to Vanish the island, but you can't be too safe in a situation like this."

"You're gonna Vanish it?" Emricka's eyes grew wide. "But Rowan and your family—"

"I have a plan to save them and I wanted to ask if you would help me."

"If there's anything I can do I absolutely will. What do you need me for?"

"Gimme a sec." I fished the anchor bottle out, along with a small dagger one of the HC witches gave me. Even though my left forearm was in a cast, my hand was usable, so I was able to re-open the cut I'd slashed during the fire and squeeze my blood into the bottle. I was so focused on the countdown clock over all our heads that I barely registered the stinging pain. After I'd filled the bottle halfway with blood, I awakened my magic and directed it into the bottle. Blue tendrils of smoke flowed in, after which I closed the bottle and gave it a shake to mix the blood and magic.

"This bottle is key to saving everyone," I said to Emricka. She handed me a napkin she'd fished out of her bag and I closed my fist around it to absorb the blood from the wound.

"I would like you to take this anchor out into the water," I explained. "My plan is to use a Vanish Witch ability called Shifts to redirect Nimbisu from the sky to the location of this bottle, which will act as an anchor to draw it in. So you have to take it out into open water with nothing else nearby. If you can tie it to something that will keep it safe and relatively in place that would be helpful."

Because what wouldn't be helpful was the bottle breaking or getting carried off by a seagull or being swept away to a location that couldn't accommodate Nimbisu.

"We have buoys in the coven-house," Emricka said. Her face settled into a look of determination. "I can place the anchor inside one so it will be safe from breaking, and the buoy will keep it in place. Will that work?"

"Perfectly." I handed her the anchor. "Can you do it right now?"

"Yes." Electric green Mutans magic sparked over her. Pink and gold scales rippled over her brown skin and gills appeared at the sides of her neck. "I'll go change into a swimsuit and follow the river out into the bay. I'll swim a few miles and leave the buoy in open water."

"Thanks, Emricka. This is a big ask but—"

"But I'm glad you came to me, and I am happy to do it. To help save everyone. I won't let you down." She gave me a nod then ran back into her coven-house.

I trusted her, but I wanted to see this part of the plan through, so I waited for her to come back out, then we jogged to the river. My breath caught and I stumbled back when the river came into view.

Cold. Dark. Screams. Almost no more air to breathe.

"Kit." Marrik's voice was soft and his touch on my elbow tentative, as though he expected me to flinch away from him. My stomach lurched as uncomfortable feelings roiled through me at the memory of the shipping container incident, but I pulled in a deep breath and straightened up.

I had to be strong right now. I had people to save. I could fall apart later.

"I'm okay." I strode forward without looking at Marrik, who didn't say anything more as he trailed behind me. Another Mutans Witch had offered to swim out with Emricka. I remembered seeing him the day of the assessment when we'd observed the Mutans Witches in the water. He was the witch whose forearms had shifted into what looked like crab claws. There were hard, gleaming patches of shell on his skin, and two long, slender antennae curved from his forehead. Fully shifted, he'd be a formidable sea creature. His name was Robin.

Emricka carried a small buoy that the anchor had been placed into. A thick cord was attached to it and slung over her chest.

"Thank you both," I said. "Text me when you're out of the water." I'd exchanged numbers with her.

"Will do," Emricka said. Robin nodded, and they dove into the water. I allowed myself a moment to be impressed by their fluid motions, then I checked the time and turned to my entourage, settling my gaze on Saffron.

"Step one is done. Now for step two. Take me to the ley line well."

Chapter Twenty

Confidence warring with anxiety and uncertainty about a dangerous situation was a feeling I hoped I would not have to get used to. But I had a sneaking suspicion I was gonna be out of luck in that regard.

I was standing near the location of the ley line well within the High Coven's skyscraper. Truth be told, I'd never been inside this building before. It was a hundred floors and housed the vast number of witches who supported the High Coven. I might have been hard pressed to determine what one organization needed a hundred floors for, but this building was their main hub on the entire continent, so it made sense that it was robust.

We'd entered into a fairly typical lobby with a reception desk, plush carpeting, and a seating area. Saffron spoke to the witch behind the reception desk then beckoned to me and led me past it, through a set of glass doors. Beyond it was an open space with unstained wood floors, a multitude of flourishing plant life, and cozy seating areas that would fit in better at our coven-houses than a skyscraper. Off to one side was a waterscape where clear water climbed up and cascaded down gray rocks.

The space reminded me of those houses that were built around an inner courtyard. The middle of the building was hollow; I could look up straight to the ceiling. The floors wrapped around, each one barred by glass. In the center of the ground floor, a square of packed dirt was left bare.

That was where the ley line well was.

"Kit." I stopped and glanced at Marrik. "Are you sure about this?"

"About saving my family from the danger yours put them in? Yes, I am."

Marrik flinched. I didn't regret the words or the tone. I wasn't gonna hide how incredibly fucked up this situation was and all the variables that had gotten us here. Deep in my heart I knew … *I knew* that the ground below our relationship had been crumbling, eroding, was being swept out to sea by tempestuous waves.

But we still couldn't address it. Not yet.

"Kit …" Marrik looked pained. He had not meant for any of this to happen, but still …

I turned away and shoved our relationship woes back into a box, then stepped up beside Saffron, who was shifting from foot to foot and kept looking at the time on her phone.

"Nimbisu is descending toward Vonuis faster and faster," she said. "It will crash in about half an hour."

"No, it won't," I said resolutely. I looked around. The witches who'd been with Saffron were still hovering.

"Where's Gladstone?" I inquired. "I would have expected to see him right about now."

"I've been in communication with him, he is needed elsewhere as the city evacuates, but he is aware of your plan."

I didn't ask if he conveyed to her what he thought of it. I truly didn't give a fuck. Saffron hadn't shown up with a plan to save my people because Gladstone and the other council members hadn't tried to come up with one. All they wanted was for me to Vanish Nimbisu regardless of anything.

"I see." Better that he wasn't here anyway. I knelt down in front of the dirt patch and pressed my hands against the ground. My breath caught as power thrummed into me. The feel of the ley lines wasn't as strong as they'd been in Elsewhere, but it was still far stronger than anything I'd ever felt in this world.

I thought about my crash course lesson with Onyx. Anxiety twisted in my stomach at the thought that it wasn't possible to know your limits until you reached them. I'd already grown my magic a lot in Elsewhere, what if that was as strong as I could get?

I could use a Vanish Tide against a large mass, that had already been proven. But to do a Shifting Tide, I needed to be stronger.

So I had no choice but to test my limits.

And if I died … well I guess I'd soon reunite with my family on the other side.

No. I didn't want to go into this with dark thoughts. Instinctively, my hand reached up and touched my chest where Remi's amulet was hidden. Marrik had taken it off me and kept it safe. I had put it back on at the hospital.

I'm about to do something reckless, Remi, I thought. This would be the moment where you berate me but come along for the adventure.

I lowered my hand and placed it against the dirt. Then I closed my eyes and settled myself as much as I could as I thought back to what Onyx had taught me.

You must let the ley lines in so they can latch on to your magic and nurture it.

They want to make magic stronger, but they are all or nothing.

Take only a sip. Then break the connection.

Connect, sip, break. Drop the anchor in and reel it back. Close the door before too much floods in.

I awakened my magic and sent it into the earth. I recalled the memory of when I'd first done this. Onyx looking speculative in front of me, Remi hovering nervously next to me.

My magic dropped into the veins of magic tangled deep below my palms. I felt a frizzle travel into me like an electric shock. As my magic touched the ley lines, it was fed by them. The best analogy was that it felt like I'd been holding something light that was progressively getting heavier. The tug of it drew me forward but I kept my balance. Sweat beaded my forehead and my muscles strained as I worked to keep myself still and maintain my focus.

Enough. I'd taken enough. I recalled my magic, but the tremendous power within the ley lines rushed back with it. I wouldn't truly be stronger unless I consumed the power my magic had picked up, so I kept myself open as my magic rushed back into me.

It was heady, like a rush of wind howling through me. Like powerful waves were crashing over me. That sensation made me grit my teeth against being distracted by thoughts of my near drowning. I couldn't lose focus now. If I didn't stay in control the power of the ley lines would tear me apart.

I'd drawn in enough. I shut my magic down and fell onto my forearms, gasping. Marrik worriedly called out to me.

"I'm okay," I rasped, pushing myself up. I was feverish and coated in sweat. When I straightened up, I met Saffron's wide, awe-struck eyes, but also realized my audience had grown.

Dozens of witches stood around me, gawking like I was some fantastical being. No one had strengthened their magic on the ley lines for centuries. Despite a well being right here, it was likely that drawing from it hadn't yet been allowed.

But now, they had witnessed someone draw on them with no guidance but my memories. Their awe was understandable, but it wasn't the time to gawk. Time was running out.

"I am going to do this one more time, then that should be enough."

I hoped, prayed, it would be enough.

"Then, I am going to use a Shifting Tide against Nimbisu."

And save everyone.

Everyone.

I felt alive in a way I'd never felt before as I stepped off the elevator and onto the roof of the HC's skyscraper, the hilt of a small dagger tight in my grasp. Saffron and Marrik were the only ones with me, by my request. It had not made the other witches happy, but I didn't care. I was certain the High Coven wished to record and analyze my Shifting Tide, but they could get the details from Saffron. This was a situation where I had no guarantee of the outcome because all of this shit was happening too fast.

I'd just learned how to do Tides and Shifts. And an hour ago I'd learned they could be combined. And even though I had strengthened my magic and felt like I was bursting out of my skin with power, there was no telling if I was strong enough to do this until I tried.

And if I failed, I died. Marrik died. Saffron died. Countless people in Vonuis died if their stubborn asses refused to leave. My family and friends died.

Remi's amulet might survive. But there would be no one left to help him.

I had myriad reasons why this had to work. But it was daunting and overwhelming, and my emotions were all over the place. I felt so strong magically, yet I was riddled with the crippling fear that nothing I did would be enough.

"You have everything you need."

For some reason, Onyx's words came to mind as I stood in the middle of the roof and stared up. Nimbisu was huge and looming and descending. Chunks of it fell as it moved, raining debris that I hoped wouldn't cause too much damage. Our only saving grace was that Aulura's gravitational hold kept it from dropping like a weight. If both moons had released it there would not have been a chance to Vanish it; it would have fallen in the blink of an eye and decimated whatever it landed on.

There was a morbid fascination with watching a giant land mass slowly crumble and fall. It was like staring down your death and being unable to do a single thing to avoid it.

Except that I could. I rallied my confidence as I walked forward.

"Kit." I turned at Marrik's call. He walked up to me, his face solemn, eyes searching mine. "This may not mean much to you anymore, but I believe in you. You can do this."

My throat grew tight. *This may not mean much to you anymore.* Marrik wasn't in denial about our cracks and splinters. He'd already anticipated that we were about to shatter. It brought me nothing but pain to know how much we'd broken. The pressure that had been on our relationship since it began had become too much for us to fight against.

"Thank you," I whispered. I turned to Saffron to see if she had anything she wanted to say. She was looking at her phone.

"Five … five minutes," she said nervously. She looked like a slight wind might knock her over. I felt bad for her. I didn't know exactly what her role was within the High Coven, but no matter what she was a person like anyone else, standing at ground zero for a catastrophic event instead of running away from it because she'd been commanded to be here.

"You two step back, please." Saffron scuttled back but Marrik hesitated. I gave him a tight smile and nodded. I could guess that he wished to stand by my side in support, but I would feel better if I wasn't crowded while I released a Tide. I didn't want to take chances on what it might touch.

Marrik stepped back. I walked to the center of the roof, sweeping my eyes around. It was a nice rooftop; the ground was smooth, dark gray concrete, there were shaded seating areas, and even a bar. It was surrounded by a wall that was about chest height, and on top of the wall was metallic caging that curved inward at the top.

I stared Nimbisu down. My mother was up there. She was probably doing a lot of screaming. I was sure Dad had his arms around her and hadn't let go since they'd found themselves there. Jiano and Rowan would have enjoyed being up there had the situation not been so terrible. All of the Hexes had already been through a lot of trauma. I hated that this was happening to them.

I wondered if they were hoping someone would save them. Or if they'd lost hope. They knew I was supposed to Vanish the island, would they think I'd go through with it with them on it?

"Th ... three minutes," Saffron called. Her voice shook with fear.

I cut my left palm with the dagger, then cut my right. The pain was sharp, and I prayed I wasn't doing permanent damage to my hands with the number of times I'd cut them recently. Bright slashes of blood appeared. I awakened my magic, watching clouds of blue billow around my hands. My magic looked thicker, darker. Felt stronger.

I prayed with everything I had that it was strong enough.

I would either save everyone or lose everything.

I lifted my hands, palms spread wide. Drops of blood hit the ground. I was facing Nimbisu directly. I closed my eyes and pushed past my roiling emotions, clearing an empty space in my mind aggressively. There was no time for breathing exercises and meditation.

I relaxed. Took a deep breath.

I started to recite the incantation that helped unleash Tides.

"Ae huo monsi clurett meor wrentu och tivaru ae zumnaf dreemalo ilzum qi voudamkh."

I repeated it. Made sure my pronunciation was on point and my voice was strong and clear.

I focused on my magic and *pushed*.

It felt like I was pushing my soul out of my body. The power of my magic releasing was stronger than when I'd practiced at Moonglade. Saffron had said the only person documented to have done a Shifting Tide almost died. It certainly felt like death was encroaching on me. I was sweating, my muscles ached, and my bones felt like someone was beating them with a hammer. Magic erupted from me so strongly I was pushed back and almost lost my footing. I heard Marrik make a sound and prayed he stayed where he was.

Another sensation frizzled over me, tearing a gasp from my throat. It was that same feeling I'd experienced when the bordello was on fire and I'd somehow been able to keep myself from passing out. It felt like a cord was twisted around my body, over and under my skin. A cord made of starlight that burned with cool fire. It was alien yet familiar and I felt it course through my Vanish magic.

My body bucked at the pressure, but I managed to keep my footing. I still had no idea what this new feeling was, but it seemed to be helping.

A huge wave of Vanish magic streamed from my hands, filling the air and racing in the direction of Nimbisu like a blowing wind. The wounds on my hands pulsed as my magic mingled with my blood. I kept my eyes on the Tide, seeing Nimbisu beyond it. The sky island was close, so close, less than a mile away. Hours had turned to minutes had turned to seconds.

Any moment now, Nimbisu would—

The Shifting Tide reached it. And in the blink of an eye, Nimbisu Vanished.

I sucked in a gasp. I was breathing like I'd been running as fast as I could for an hour. My body was shaking. I'd gone from feeling overheated to feeling cold. I hadn't been at a hundred percent having walked out of a hospital a couple hours ago, and now I felt ready to go back. My stomach roiled with nausea and I had the distinct feeling I was going to black out.

I quieted my magic. It dissipated from the air, leaving the view unobscured. The view of a now empty sky.

I lowered my hands and stared at my palms. Bloody, trembling. When I took a step forward I stumbled and fell, crying out when my palms slapped the ground.

"Kit!" Marrik rushed forward and knelt at my side, holding my shoulders. He gently pulled me up. Saffron came up on my other side.

"Oh! Oh!" That seemed to be all she was capable of saying.

Black spots danced in front of my vision. I felt so weak. If death was the price of doing a Shifting Tide of this magnitude, I guess I had no choice but to pay it. But not before I found out if it worked. Not before I found out if my family—

My phone started ringing. I quickly reached for it. My hands were shaking so badly Marrik had to help me get it out of my bag.

Emricka. I answered on speaker.

"IT WORKED! IT WORKED!" Emricka screamed as soon as the call connected. "Nimbisu Shifted to where the anchor is, Kit! IT WORKED!"

The relief that clenched me was so strong I wondered if this would be what killed me instead of the magical strain. Tears poured down my cheeks. I wanted to speak, wanted to form words, wanted to talk to Emricka, but all I could do was sob.

"Me and some others are gonna swim out and get confirmation that everyone is there," Emricka was saying excitedly. "We'll get some boats to bring them in. I'll call you again and let you talk to them." The call ended and I still hadn't been able to get a word out.

But I hadn't needed to say anything. Emricka had said enough to make my heart and soul soar, to bring me the confirmation that this one time, everything had worked perfectly.

It worked. I had Shifted Nimbisu instead of Vanishing it.

I had saved Vonuis and my family and friends.

I wanted to think so much more, wanted to talk to Marrik and Saffron and get back down to The Bramble. But I had no strength left.

I collapsed into Marrik's arms and passed out.

Chapter Twenty-One

I didn't wake up for five days.

When I did, I almost passed out again, but it would have been out of joy because the first thing I saw was my mother, father, and Jiano leaning over me. Afterward they told me that once I'd started showing signs that I was waking up they'd gathered around to make sure they were the first thing I saw.

I'd then had several days in the hospital as they removed the feeding tube, made sure my vitals were stable, and ran a gamut of tests to ensure my body was recovering well. My mother had been allowed to bring me food and it was her sole mission to make sure I ate three meals a day plus the treats Jiano snuck in that she pretended not to see. This time I didn't fuss at Ma because I had lost some weight while I'd been laid up.

Four days after I woke up, I was discharged.

Well, I did stop by my apartment, where the broken in door had been repaired thanks to Marrik, but I had been spending most of my time at the rental house my parents were staying in, which was three blocks away from Kiss and Hex. Jiano was staying here as well, since the bordello would not be livable for some time. Ji was already in full swing sorting things out with insurance and scouting contractors. The fire had been put out before it could destroy Ji's office, which was at the end of the hall on the first floor, so while there'd been some damage, mainly in the form of grimy soot that coated the walls, the important business documents Ji kept there had been spared.

Calla, Phinra, and Milene were staying at the house as well. It was one story, but had four bedrooms and a finished basement, so there was enough room for everyone. A lot of the Hexes had family or friends they could stay with, and for everyone else, Jiano had rented another house five blocks over. My first night out of the hospital I'd walked into the Hex House, as they'd nicknamed it, and been swept into a huge celebration as everyone expressed their gratitude for figuring out how to save them. I had cried a lot of happy tears and been wrapped in tight hugs almost non-stop. Emricka had been there too and there hadn't been strong enough words to express how grateful I was for her help. She'd been instrumental in saving me twice now. One day I'd find a way to sufficiently thank her.

"Have another sandwich, Kit baby." Ma placed three tea sandwiches on my plate that still had one sandwich and two pastries on it.

"Ma, I am stuffed, you saw me clear two plates already." I was back to complaining. I was pretty much back to normal, though. Thanks to Regen magic, the fracture in my forearm was healed so I no longer needed a cast. The aches and pains from the fire were gone, and I was fully recovered from the magical exhaustion of unleashing the Shifting Tide.

"Don't force her," Dad said, patting Ma's thigh. We were in the living room around the coffee table, which had been set with finger sandwiches, assorted pastries, and fresh raspberry lemonade from a nearby café. They had been all too pleased to put together an order for the 'Savior of the Ley Lines and Vonuis,' and had loaded our order with extras.

My parents were on the floral loveseat adjacent to the sectional Jiano, Calla, and I were on. Phinra and Milene were on floor cushions on either side of the coffee table, having their fill of the treats. Milene was eating anything that had chocolate in it.

"Well, eat more later," Ma said sternly. I then saw a shiver go through her and she rubbed her forearms. Dad's brow creased and he put an arm around her.

"Phantom shivers is all," Ma said. "It was so cold up there. My body still remembers."

"Ma …"

"Cold, hard to breathe, terrifying beyond all measure." I turned to Ji, who was shaking their head, making their beaded earrings jangle. They were dressed similarly to me in denim shorts and a T-shirt.

"Darling, I think I know now what Elsewhere must have been like. A barren place with no hope. Finding ourselves on that sky island was horrendous."

"I hate how scared you must have been." I picked at the flaky pastry of a cream puff. "I thought I'd Shifted all of you to my apartment. When I found out what really happened … I can't even describe that feeling."

"We tried to rally," came Calla's soft voice from Ji's other side. "But it was difficult."

"It was so confusing when we realized where we were!" I turned back to Ma. Her eyes were wide, and Dad was still holding her. "The last thing any of us remembered was chaos breaking out at the bordello. Then all of a sudden we were on Nimbisu!"

"There were a lot of empty buildings," Dad said in his low, even tone. "All in bad condition but good enough for some kind of shelter. But the air was too thin, many people could not stay conscious."

Something felt like it was twisting in my gut. I'd heard all about their time on Nimbisu, but my horrified reaction would remain no matter how many times we talked about it.

"But you saved us." This from Phinra, who was looking up at me with a shy smile. "Um … it was very scary, but Madame and Calla kept telling us it would be okay. I don't know if … well maybe I didn't fully believe them, but I am glad everyone tried to comfort us even though they were scared too. Rowan, um … she said that if she could fly she could carry us down one by one. And Valentino said they could keep working on back exercises right then and there and she could have a go at flying us off and … um we laughed a little bit at that. So … I did cry a lot, but I do remember that I laughed too."

She ducked her head and bit into a pastry, her cheeks flushing. Milene had been staring at her as she spoke, a gentle expression on her face. I felt a surge of protectiveness for the twins. They had been through so much already. Now they could add terrifying sky adventure to the list.

"Phinra is brave," Milene whispered. "Always protects me. I will help my sister too."

Help my sister. That's what she'd said when I'd found her wandering. We still weren't sure what she meant by that.

Phinra looked up at her and smiled. Milene held out her chocolate croissant and Phinra took a bite.

"Too big," Milene said when she drew her hand back and saw how little of her pastry was left. She frowned and Phinra beamed at her.

"I kept thinking, Kit won't Vanish this island while we're on it," Ji said. "I knew you wouldn't do it, but the damn thing was falling and our only options were Vanish or crash. I cannot tell you what it feels like to see your end coming and be unable to do a thing about it."

"Unfortunately, we all know what that feels like now," I said softly.

"Rowan couldn't fly us off, and there were no anchored shadows I could take everyone through. Arjun couldn't use Magnes magic to keep it up. None of our magic could help us. But all I could think was that Kit would find a way to save us."

Ji turned to me and tightened their hand around my forearm. "I didn't want to give anyone false hope, but I couldn't stop believing in you. And maybe that was an unfair burden to place on your shoulders, but you came back from Vanishing so maybe I thought you knew a thing or two about pulling off the impossible."

Ji was smiling, but there were tears in their eyes. Same as mine.

"And you did it," Ji continued. "You pulled off the impossible. You're my hero."

"Our hero," Dad said. "We believed in you."

"I was so scared, but I didn't lose hope, Kit baby," Ma said. "I knew you would try your best to save us."

"There was no way I would have Vanished Nimbisu with you on it. I refused to think that was the only option." I wiped an arm across my eyes as Ji pulled me in and hugged me. Over her shoulder, Calla was looking on with a smile. Behind me, I heard my parents sniffle.

"When do we get to stop having tearful reunions after harrowing life and death events," I said when we pulled back. Phinra offered us napkins to dab at our eyes.

"I hope this is it for a very long time," Ji said. "We have earned the right to live without worrying that death is lurking around the corner."

"I hope you aren't bothered because you are so strong, Kit," Calla said.

"They're calling you Savior of the Ley Lines and Hero of Vonuis," Ji said. I cringed.

"I've been avoiding the news and social media but yeah, I've seen a bit of what's being said. I mean, I'm happy to help if we end up in more danger of massive things falling on our heads, but I want the time to try and work through everything that's happened and see what rhythm I can get back into with my life. I know it won't ever be the same as it was before I ended up in Elsewhere, but I need," a heavy sigh clattered out of my chest, "I need rest. I need to not be needed for a while."

"And rest you shall have, Kitten." Ji patted my knee. "For I shall conjure a shadow beast and claw apart anyone who tries to will it otherwise."

"Best big sib ever." I flashed a smile. "The High Coven is still circling. Saffron made it clear the council wants to meet with me to debrief, but I've been avoiding her calls. Frankly, I thought Gladstone would have shown his face by now, but I'm glad he hasn't. I don't want to deal with the issues between us yet. I'd be stupid to think he's let go of the fact that I tried to Vanish him."

"He is number one on the list for shadow beast mauling, to be clear," Ji said.

"Duly noted," I replied. "Though I hope I won't have to murder or vanish all my problems."

My phone, which was on the coffee table, started to ring.

"Speaking of problems," Ji commented.

"Marrik." Complicated feelings twisted inside me as I picked up the phone and excused myself, taking a few steps away. I answered, and the deep tones of Marrik's voice telling me he'd be here in a few minutes made tears come to my eyes.

What else could you do but cry when your love was collapsing?

I hung up and turned back to the people who were pretending they weren't paying attention. "Marrik will be here soon. I told him to head around back. I'll go talk to him there."

"Take all the time you need," Ma said, giving me a sympathetic look. Dad nodded supportively.

"Perhaps I wouldn't maul him completely but if you want him a little roughed up …"

I flashed Ji a smile. "I'll keep that in mind." Then I shoved my phone into a pocket on my shorts and headed to the back door.

I stepped out into thick, humid air and the sound of insects chirping in the bushes. It was early evening, though the sky wasn't completely dark yet thanks to the longer summer days. Aulura and Cebis shone in their soft, colorful hues on either side of a setting sun that painted the sky a fiery watercolor. There'd been a thunderstorm this morning and the back yard was askew with leaves, branches, and a few potted plants that had toppled over. Calla said she'd tend to them tonight. She sometimes had a hard time sleeping and enjoyed doing garden work under the moonlight.

The house had a small porch set up with wicker furniture, so I took a seat as I waited for Marrik. My palms were tightly clasped together and they were cold. My leg kept bouncing in the same nervous gesture Marrik had been doing in the hospital when he was waiting for me to wake up so he could tell me the worst news.

Heartache was a terrible, terrible thing. But so many of us yearned to love and be loved in return. We took our fragile selves and gave them to other people and the only protection we had against shattering was something as effervescent as *hope.*

We *hoped* we could make it. *Hoped* we would endure through trials and tribulations. *Hoped* the love we built with someone would always be respected and nurtured and kept safe and whole.

And it worked for some. Through many years where there may have been rough waters, but the ship never sank. For others, we sank, time and time again. Our fragile selves broke, reformed, were given to someone else, and broke again. We marched through our lives yearning for love and hoping it worked once we found it.

But sometimes it just could not work, no matter how much you refused to let that hope go.

Tears were slipping down my cheeks by the time Marrik rounded the back of the house. He wore a graphic T-shirt and jeans and had a fresh haircut and clean-shaven face. The fading light from the sun threw patterns over him as he walked under a tree. I trailed my eyes over him, taking note of the way his hands were balled into fists. The watch he wore was the first birthday gift I'd given him three years ago.

Forever ago, it felt like.

"Hey." He came up onto the porch and stopped a few feet away. His eyes swept over me. "You … look nice."

I smiled at him as I wiped my eyes. My shorts and T-shirt were nothing fancy, but Marrik always took me however I came. Ma had cornrowed my hair in one of her more complex styles.

"Thanks," I replied. "You too." I patted the cushion next to me. "Sit. Please."

Marrik walked over and lowered himself down, angling his body toward me.

"Are you settled in?" I asked.

"Pretty much. Still a lot of boxes to unpack but I've gotten everything out of the storage unit."

"That's good." Sadness tightened around my heart like barbed wire. Marrik had visited me a good deal while I was in the hospital, but he'd also been able to secure himself an apartment several neighborhoods over from mine.

That he had done so on his own meant he understood what we were careening toward.

"How … how is everyone?" Marrik asked. This beat of awkwardness between us made tears come to my eyes again. This wasn't how we were supposed to be.

But maybe there'd been no other ending for us from the start.

"Doing as best they can. Ma still gets phantom chills; it shakes her entire body. It was so cold up there, so hard to breathe. All the Hexes check in and everyone is coping. Many of them are working through it with their therapists. Milene hasn't wandered off again, thankfully."

"Glad to hear. I'll um … say hello before I go, maybe …"

"Yeah, of course." We stared at each other. I counted the seconds as they passed.

Marrik broke eye contact and stared at the ground. "They arrested the people who started the fire. There was a lot of surveillance around the bordello that picked them up."

"I saw." I swallowed past the thick feeling in my throat. We were finally wading into the rough waters that were sinking our ship. "But the people they arrested are only part of the network responsible for orchestrating what happened."

Marrik nodded, his face solemn. His body was rigid with tension. "I know. I've been following up with the task force and they claim they are investigating Normies First so they can flush out everyone. The people who parachuted onto Nimbisu with the anchor are in custody. I also gave them … I gave them my family's information. My parents, Quinn, Namira …"

"Marrik." It pained me to hear him say that, even though his family was directly responsible for trying to kill me and mine.

"I—"

"You don't have to say anything," he cut in. "Please. This is on my shoulders, not yours."

"But it hurts, and I hate to see you hurt."

Marrik turned his head and our eyes locked. Anguish was etched into his expression.

"Even now, after everything that happened, you wish to comfort me." He shook his head. "I don't deserve that."

"If I didn't love you maybe it would be easier not to care. But love makes things so complicated, doesn't it? It turns things that should be black and white into every shade of gray." I sighed.

"Don't get me wrong, I'm angry," I continued. "So angry at every single witch hater, but especially the people who did this. Angry at Namira for lying to us and using her closeness to you to help them execute their attack. When I think about the fact that they so callously decided to burn us alive and had a contingency plan in case it didn't work —" I stopped because my voice cracked.

"It is rage I cannot describe, Marrik. I am angry that people want to kill me, kill witches, simply because we have magic. This is my reality as a witch. I will always be susceptible to prejudiced violence I may not always see coming. Knifed in an alley, burned to death in my sleep, shot while I'm walking to my coven-house."

I looked up at the darkening sky. "I am forever at the crossroads of magic and death. And three years ago we met and we dated and we fell in love. And I knew, all along, that you came from people who would shun me and enact violence against me because they feared me. I can't say there's no merit to the fear of magic; look what I alone have done with mine."

I lowered my head, looking at the ground instead of Marrik.

"When I saw Namira's pain, it was understandable because I could see how much she cared about you. Of course she would hate me. Of course just seeing me touch your arm would set her off, thinking my magic could take you from her again. But I underestimated the rest of your people. I fell into the belief that because you were estranged from them it meant they didn't give a fuck about you or what you did. I figured you'd cut yourself free and closed the door.

"But there was a reason you removed yourself so thoroughly. A reason you didn't answer your parents' calls. A reason you were so careful about which family members you talked to and what you told them. A reason you didn't tell even Namira that you were dating a witch. It wasn't because they wouldn't care," I lifted my eyes to him, "it was because they *would* care. They would care very much. And they would make sure to do something about it."

"Kit." His eyes were shiny with tears. He looked broken and haunted.

"Am I wrong?" I whispered. "Tell me I'm wrong."

A sob escaped him. He shook his head.

"I knew." I laid my hand on his thigh. He stared at it like it was the most precious thing in the world.

"I always knew but I let myself deny it. Because I fell so in love with you that I wanted it to work as long as it could work. I hid parts of myself for that exact reason. So you wouldn't know how strong my magic was, so it wouldn't become a burden to what you were already hiding.

"So that information wouldn't find its way to the worst ones to hear it. We both hid parts of ourselves from each other, didn't we? Because I could see how much it hurt you every time you had to ignore a call. And I hated that reality for you. That you were such a wonderful person born into such a hateful family. That you couldn't have loving parents like mine who would be the last ones to ever hurt you. You deserved so much better than that, Mar."

"God." Another sob escaped him. He placed his hand over mine and squeezed.

"We had problems we ignored long before I Vanished you," I said. "We talked about them a bit in Elsewhere, remember? And then we made it home, back into our reality where our old problems were waiting for us."

"And new problems," Marrik whispered, "that were born from them."

"Yes." Another tear slipped down my cheek. "We haven't even had a chance to reckon with the fact that I Vanished you. And now ... your family tried to kill mine."

Marrik's expression twisted in pain. I hated having to say these words, but they had to be said.

"I'm not perfect," I continued. "You know that better than anyone else. Maybe we were doomed from day one, but I would have pretended not to see that doom coming. There are a number of things I'd have remained in denial about so long as it kept us together. But not … not this." I finished on a hoarse breath. It felt like a physical pain to say those words. "I can't be in denial about this."

Marrik nodded, a slow drop and rise of his head.

"This is something you can't forgive," came his soft voice.

"It's something I can't accept." I was so very, very sad. I wished there was magic that could fix every single broken part of us. But magic couldn't fix the fractures on the fragile selves we'd given to each other.

Marrik's eyes searched my face for a while. The grief I saw in them was my own. I wanted to believe we could stand against anything. But I couldn't.

"Can I ever redeem myself?" His voice was so low I almost didn't hear him. "Will there ever be something I could do that would place me back in your heart?"

More tears fell. "You will never leave my heart, know that. And I do not lay the actions of your family on your shoulders. But the proximity, Marrik … the information that made it from you, to Namira, to them …"

"I understand." He raised my hand and turned it so he could kiss my palm. Heat washed through me at the brush of his lips. He pressed my palm to his cheek.

"I don't want to give up on us." He lowered my hand but didn't let go. "I don't want to be gone from your side. I want to tell you that I will protect you from anything that comes your way. I don't want to be without you, Kit."

My eyes were blurry with tears.

"The terrible ache I have felt every single day is my love for you and the way I feel it being ripped away, but I can't let it go." His eyes were locked on mine. "I know this is what we need right now but maybe some—"

"Oh, Marrik, don't talk about 'someday' yet, please." Because I would give in. I would say 'okay, this is just for now, just for a while'. That's all I wanted it to be: a break, not an ending. But how could we get past something as terrible as this?

"I have to figure out my life." He was looking down at our entwined hands. "Figure out who I am on the other side of

Elsewhere. And I will. But I would be stupid to think the threats are over, I know they aren't." His hand tightened around mine. "My family will never touch you again, Kit. Not you, not your family, not your friends or any other witch. It is my mission to make them pay for what they've done."

"Mar, I know I walked the vigilante path, but you don't have to. I don't believe in the High Coven much, especially because their intel couldn't anticipate and stop the attacks, but I do believe they will ferret a lot of them out. The fire and the shipping container incident were highly visible. The hate groups can continue to make moves against witches, but more and more of them will be rounded up. I am certain the HC will use Memoria magic on the ones they have in custody to help find everyone else."

"But I can't rest with things this way." He shook his head. "I always chose you, Kit. I still choose you. I won't ask you to promise me anything, but I … I won't give up on us having a future. And I will make sure it's a future where you will be safe with me."

"I don't know if that's possible." God, I wanted it to be possible. So much.

Marrik raised my hand and kissed it again. He closed his eyes and took a shuddering breath. "You did the impossible, so why can't I?"

My eyes widened. His words were an echo of what Ji had said. "Mar …"

"Don't be a stranger, please," he whispered. "I know you need some time, but I will be close. If I can ever be of help to you …"

"I'll call." So much of this felt heartbreakingly wrong, yet I knew it was what we needed. As for the future … I would need a lot of time before I could think about the future.

"I love you, Kit." Marrik stood up and drew me with him. He pulled me in and we wrapped our arms around each other. I pressed myself against his chest, breathed him in, wet his shirt with my tears as I sunk into the reality that these would no longer be my arms to be wrapped in.

"I love you too." We pulled back and I looked up at him. Shared heartbreak. Marrik lowered his head and kissed me. A soft, tenuous kiss. A kiss that held the most fragile thing in the world between it. A fragile thing that fell and shattered into shards as plentiful as the stars above when the kiss broke.

Marrik hugged me for a long, long time. Then he stepped away, gave my hand one last squeeze, and walked off the porch and back around the house.

My love vanished from me.

Chapter Twenty-Two

I had become the main ingredient in a family sandwich. I was on the sectional, wedged between Jiano and Ma, with Dad on Ma's other side, his arm stretched around her so he could reach me. I was hugging a pillow to my stomach and there were crumpled tissues in my hand. Calla had taken Phinra and Milene down to the basement to watch movies and give me a little space.

Well, space was relative seeing as I was being smothered by my family, but I had no complaints. I had felt so hollow and empty when Marrik's arms had dropped away and I'd been left with the knowledge that I may not ever be within them again. Walking into the house had felt like I was moving through a fevered dream; so much of me wanted to reject that conversation, run back to Marrik, and tell him that we could work this out.

But I kept walking until I came back to the living room and collapsed into my family's arms. Whether there would ever be any hope of reconciliation with Marrik wasn't a question I would be able to answer for a while. The truth was painful, but it had to prevail. We needed to be apart right now.

We needed to break.

My family hadn't peppered me with questions or tried to rally positive vibes. They'd just wrapped me in their arms and let me cry and put pastries on my plate for me to nibble on. I nestled into their comfort and was glad that at a moment where I was falling to pieces, I had a soft place to land. If I hadn't been able to save them from Nimbisu I don't know how I could have handled all the shards on the road I had to walk.

My hand had been fiddling with Remi's amulet for a while. Because of the bruises and healing cuts on my hands, I hadn't been able to wear the suppression gloves so I could meet him in my dreams. When I tried to put them on the pain was unbearable.

But I had to make sure I focused on helping him. Paluna had checked in shortly after I came home from the hospital, but there hadn't been much communication with her since. I figured she was keeping her distance since the High Coven was still trying to deal with me in the aftermath of the Shifting Tide. But I wanted to follow up with her soon on how we could help strengthen Remi's ghost and get him out of the amulet. Then we could talk about what could be done with his bones.

I was thinking about finally getting up for a bathroom run when I felt a familiar, blooming pressure in my head. A headache quickly came on, and I sucked in a sharp breath as Memoria magic shivered over me. Seconds later, a memory formed directly in my line of sight, on the other side of the coffee table.

"Whoa!" Ji said. I started forward, my hands gripping the couch cushions, while my parents made sounds of surprise.

"Remi," I whispered.

"Oh dear," Ma said.

"Dance with me, oh lovely Kit." It was the memory of when Remi had asked me to dance in the bordello's front room a few weeks ago. The memory recreation included part of the bordello and everything I had taken in from my point of view: Rowan, Calla, and Arjun practicing on the stage, Jiano next to me behind the bar.

"Don't be a brat, dance with the man," Memory-Ji said.

Soon, Remi and I were dancing. Because the memory was from my perspective, all I saw was Remi as he held me.

"Milene." Jiano stood up and I turned to see Milene peering around the corner of the hallway that led to the basement. She jumped, then edged further in, keeping herself pressed against the wall.

"Kit was thinking about him and she was sad," she whispered. "I wanted to help."

"Now Milene, what did I tell you about—"

"It's okay," I cut Ji off. I looked at Milene. "I appreciate the gesture. It's nice to see Remi like this." Knowing what he was actually like within the amulet was tortuous. I wanted him to be like this again. I wanted to see if something could be done about having to remain a bound ghost.

Milene gave a shy smile.

"Oh, Remington," Ma said.

I moved from behind the coffee table and walked closer to the memory, watching Remi and I banter as we danced to Arjun's guitar playing and Calla's singing. Remi's glossy, dark brown hair moved as he tilted his head and teased me to relax. He'd been such an amazing dancer in life; something Ziyelle had exploited when he was a ghost, making him perform for profit. But whatever bad memories that had left him with, he'd never shied away from dancing with anyone. Calla used to love the way he'd twirl her across the floor.

I noticed that she and Phinra were now standing with Milene. Calla's hand was covering her mouth and I could see the sorrow in her eyes.

"Remi." I moved toward the memory and reached out to him, and was shocked when my hand connected. Remi's movements brought him closer to me and I stumbled as his swept-out arm bumped into me.

I kept my footing but something else happened: the amulet swung forward and connected with Memory-Remi. Something that felt like an electric shock sparked, stinging my skin. I wrenched back but the amulet seemed fused to the memory and the chain snapped off my neck. The memory had frozen, and I watched with wide, confused eyes as white wisps streamed up from the amulet and wrapped around the memory.

Remi's desiccated, skeletal ghost appeared. I saw his mouth and eyes wide open in shock at whatever was happening. Then the ghostly wisps and his decayed form disappeared.

Into the memory version of himself.

I sucked in a stunned, shocked, breath.

The amulet clattered to the ground.

The memory of Remi rippled like it was made of water. His body shifted in and out of focus for several moments. It finally stopped and Remi fell to the ground.

He groaned and shifted onto his back.

My jaw dropped because this wasn't something that had occurred when we were dancing.

I edged forward. What in the entire fuck had happened?

Everyone in the room was silent but we were all inching forward, closing in on the man on the ground.

"Remi?"

Remi opened his eyes and stared up at me. Our eyes locked and his mouth fell open. He slowly moved his head and took in Ji, Ma, and Dad, who were next to me. He propped up on his elbows and looked around the room, catching sight of Calla and the twins. Then he turned back to me.

"Remi?" Disbelief and unfathomable hope had a death-grip on me. I reached out a trembling hand to him. He stared at it for a moment, then took my hand. I helped him to his feet. He wasn't wearing what Memory-Remi had been wearing; his clothes had shifted into what he'd been wearing in Elsewhere before he Withered; a fitted T-shirt and camouflage pants.

"I'm still a ghost," he whispered. His hand was pressed against his chest as though feeling for a heartbeat. "But I'm … I'm …" He glanced at the amulet on the ground, then looked at me again with a beatific smile on his face.

"I'm whole."

"Holy shit," I breathed.

There were a zillion questions that had to be answered. But answers could wait. I threw myself into Remi's arms and hugged him tightly.

"Oh my God, Remi! You're back, you're back!"

I was crying again, but this time for much happier reasons.

"Kit. My Kit." Remi's arm wrapped around my waist. His other hand pressed against the back of my head. "I knew you would save me from that wretched amulet."

"You're back … You're out … You …" Out of all the shocking things that had happened recently, this was the very best one.

"I am with you again," he whispered, his face in the crook of my neck. "I do not know which deity granted this miracle, but it is one I fully embrace. However you did this, Kit—"

I pulled back. "It wasn't me." I looked over his shoulder at Milene, who stood between Calla and Phinra, her hands twisting in front of her, her gaze cast down.

"Hello, Calla, my sweet," Remi said. Calla was smiling and I could see tears in her eyes.

"Hello, Remi," she called.

"My Madame of shadows, hello again." Remi bowed to Jiano. "The most benevolent of all my amulet's owners, it has been a while. How lovely to see you." He tilted his head at my parents.

I stepped back and let everyone greet Remi. He had once been the only one Calla had allowed to touch her after her torture, and she pressed herself into his arms. She'd been gradually coming back to touching others, but this was the first time I'd seen her hug someone like this in a while.

"You rascally ghost!" Ma exclaimed.

Dad clasped him on the shoulder. "Good to see you again, Remington."

Ji gave him a crushing hug. "Welcome back, you rogue!"

"How did you do this?" I'd drifted over to the twins, who'd hung back. Milene was still looking down. Phinra looked nervous.

"We knew you could recreate memories other people could see, but how is it possible that the amulet touching a memory of Remi brought him out of it and restored his ghost?"

Milene raised her head and looked at me with wide eyes. "Do not know," she whispered. "I was not trying to."

No, she hadn't been, had she? She'd recreated a memory to try and make me feel better, but the amulet connecting with it had happened by accident.

I had no idea how to feel. I was elated, of course, but what kind of Memoria ability was this that could pull Remi's Withered ghost from the amulet and restore him by fusing his ghost to a memory of him? I frowned as I thought back to my conversation with Paluna. She had mentioned some kind of Mortem/Memoria connection involving ghosts and memories. Something along those lines was definitely what had just happened.

My goodness, Memoria magic was powerful. Milene … was powerful. And we really needed to work on helping her understand her magic. We all needed to understand it.

"Kit." I turned at Remi's call and saw him giving me a look I was very familiar with. "I am hearing there have been some dire straits lately. Would you care to regale me of your dealings with witch haters, the bordello fire, and islands falling from the sky?" One of his eyebrows rose.

"Wow, you guys covered a lot in a few minutes." I gave Calla and my family flat looks before I shook my head. "I'll tell you everything, but there are some other things I think you'd wanna hear first." I shifted my gaze to Jiano. "I wanna talk to Paluna, do you think we could pay her a visit? She'd mentioned that one of Ziyelle's grimoires could be helpful regarding Milene's magic, and that there was a connection between Memoria and Mortem magic. I have a feeling it could shed light on what happened with Remi."

"Good idea." Jiano was giving Milene a speculative look. "I am in disbelief that the memory of Remi she pulled from your mind was able to re-establish his ghost. Hopefully our disgraceful ancestor's writings can prove insightful."

Milene ducked her head and Phinra put her arm around her.

"That's what happened?" Remi asked. He was pressing his hand against his chest again. "And am I solid because of it, or because of the stronger ley lines?"

"The lines, I suspect," Ji answered. "The one that runs under the bordello also runs under this house. We're only a few blocks away from Kiss and Hex."

"Ah. Well, I hope there will be more places I can retain a solid form after our harrowing adventures in Elsewhere brought some of them back."

"We might be able to do better than that," I said. Remi's eyebrows rose, but I held back on telling him about his bones and the potential for Paluna's magic to Regress them back to a physical body. I wanted him to see his bones for himself, plus what could be done with them was part of a much longer story for which we had a lot of questions and few answers.

"Can we go see Paluna now?" Even if she wasn't in the bunker, some of her people were always there and would contact her.

"Yes. Kit, myself, and Remi will go," Ji said. "You darlings stay here and surprise us with something lovely for dinner, hm?"

"I'm in the mood for fried chicken," Ma said. "With a big chocolate cake for dessert. What say you, Phinra and Milene?"

We left the house to an enthusiastic agreement for fried, greasy goodness for dinner. At the mention of chocolate cake, Milene smiled.

The bordello was still smoky, but it had aired out a lot since the fire. Though much of that airing out was due to the fact that the entire front wall had collapsed. It had been tarped over, and it was a sad sight to see the state of the front room. But despite the left my Vanish Shift had taken, I was glad I had been able to get everyone out.

Ji was eager to rebuild, saying it was good because it would further shift the bordello from the days of its former Madame. I was so glad Encilla Tuvrou had Withered to dust during the collapse of Elsewhere.

We'd entered through the back door and made the short walk down the soot-blackened hallway to Ji's office. Since it hadn't suffered a lot of fire damage, the anchored shadow in the bathroom hadn't been disturbed.

"Oh my." Remi was peering out the door toward the front. "What a terrible ordeal transpired here."

"Technically, you were here for it," I said. "You just didn't know what was happening."

"It was a cruel precedent of the amulet that I could sense nothing of the outside world while I was within it. I regret my inability to be of assistance during such a dangerous time." He came over to where we stood near the bathroom door. "Though I will say that the lovely café setting did provide some alleviation."

I raised an eyebrow. "Wait, the café remained even after I woke up?"

"It did," Remi replied. "Which was quite a pleasant surprise even if I had no company but my own."

"But how?" I thought about how the landscape around us had changed off my words. The more I thought, the more I remembered that the strange sensation I'd felt when it happened was the same as what I'd felt during the fire when I'd avoided passing out and had the stamina to crawl through the bordello and save everyone. And more recently, I'd felt it when I'd unleashed the Shifting Tide.

And now that I could really think it through, it reminded me of Onyx's magic. The feel of it was nowhere near as strong as hers but it *did* echo of her power.

A gift. May you one day know how to use it.

A gift.

"Kit?" Ji came over and peered into my face. "Earth to Kit, what's up?"

I gave myself a little shake as I looked at Ji and Remi, who was also looking at me questioningly.

"I'm trying to figure out if a particular thread is straightening out or becoming more tangled," I said. "There's something going on that I think links back to my final moment with Onyx, but I'll expound on it later, let's go see Paluna."

Ji raised an eyebrow. "Very well. But I do expect to hear more of this."

"Does this thread have to do with our connection in the amulet?" Remi asked.

"It does. And maybe some other things too. And Remi, in case it needs to be said, you never have to go back into that amulet again."

"That's one thing I hope is never revived now that the ley lines are stronger," Ji said. "Binding ghosts. Any Mortem Witch I find out is doing it is getting a shadow stuffed down their throat."

"My knight in shining lipstick," Remi said in a swoony voice. Ji grinned. They were wearing a bold, pink lip stain today.

We followed Ji into the bathroom as they called their magic up. Inky black shadows flowed over their hands and forearms like gloves cut from the night sky. They touched the armoire's shadow to activate it.

"You are the first members of the family who kept me outside the amulet more than within it," Remi said. "When I found out your parents bought a house that ran on a ley line strong enough to make me solid it was such a salve to my heart."

There had been very few times I could remember Remi having to go into the amulet when I lived at home. He'd had his own room in the basement, and if people came over my parents trusted him to stay hidden and never tried to force him to get in the amulet. Thus, I'd been surprised when he'd said he wanted to come when Jiano and I moved to Sollunara. He was always out of the amulet at my apartment, office, and the bordello, but that was far more limiting than my parents' property, which had a few acres of land and was far enough from neighbors that no one would spot a ghost lounging under a tree in the back yard.

I now understood that Remi had wanted to stay close to me, and that was tremendous. He'd chosen proximity to me over staying where he would never have to be inside the amulet.

"The parentals were determined to do as best they could by you," Ji said. "Now hold on to me and let's go."

Remi and I took hold of Ji's hands and we stepped through the anchored shadow. The topsy-turvy, stomach lurching sensation came and went, then we emerged from the shadow cast by the large monitor.

"By the way, Kit, where is your dashing Marrik?"

My face faltered at the mention of Marrik. I looked away and cleared my throat.

"Ah," Remi said softly. "A tale for later, perhaps?"

I nodded.

We walked from behind the monitor and stopped dead in our tracks. Jiano and I sucked in sharp breaths.

There was no one here.

There was almost nothing here.

"What?" I took a few quick steps forward, looking left, right, up, and down as though this was some elaborate game of hide and seek and I would catch sight of someone peering from the shadows.

"Where is everyone?" Ji breathed. They came up next to me. Remi was looking around, frowning.

"Everyone and everything is gone." I was in a state of disbelief. All the gadgets, weapons, and gear were gone. All the laptops, computers, and tablets were gone. Only bare tables and a few larger pieces of equipment were left, like the monitor whose anchored shadow we'd used. My heart felt stricken when I looked over at the table Paluna had taken me to and saw that there was not a single item on it. Remi's bones, everything else that had been taken from Ziyelle's spell room. Gone. The boxes of animal bones she'd been practicing her magic on were gone too.

A terrible feeling crashed over me. "What happened? Where's Paluna? Where are her people?"

"She isn't answering." Jiano lowered the phone from their ear. "I tried the lines she gave me to contact her. Nothing."

"What could have happened?" Remi queried.

"What indeed."

We turned to the sound of that voice. The fortified door that led up to Paluna's office had been open a crack and it was pushed further open.

Linton Gladstone, wearing a crisp, black suit, stepped through.

We all gasped.

"So nice of you to finally stop by," he said smoothly. There was a cunning, devious look on his face.

"I've kept this place monitored, wondering if you might."

He'd seen us arrive on some camera he'd hidden here. And probably had an Umbra Witch bring him over.

"Where's—"

"My wife? My dear wife." He threw his head back and had a roaring laugh. "Oh, I am a smart man but I am also a fool, aren't I? My own wife was working against me all this time! A little nobody who caught my eye years ago, who kept my bed warm when my wife wasn't in it, who I blessed with marriage and a comfortable life when that dear woman died. To think of what she was capable of against me!"

I hated the sound of his laughter. The urge to lurch forward and Vanish him, finish what Paluna and I started, was strong, but I held back.

He finally stopped his ugly cackling and looked at us.

"She put you up to Vanishing me." His voice was low and steely. "She campaigned to make public my experiments if I didn't release you. She orchestrated the press conference that turned you into the darling of all witches. And I did not know! I did not know! Until very recently."

A nasty, cruel smile curled his thin lips.

"How did you find out," Ji growled. On my other side, Remi had edged closer. Linton flicked his eyes over Remi. I had no idea if he knew Remi was a ghost, but being in Gladstone's line of sight was exposure I'd never wanted for Remi.

"I have you to thank." His eyes were directly on me. "Several days ago, analytics on the suppression gloves you were given came in. We are able to track their use as well as their location."

"Oh no." I felt like Nimbisu had fallen on my head after all. I flitted back through my memories and remembered the witches telling me that the gloves could be tracked so they'd know if I threw them away. Then I remembered how I had brought them here and shown them to Paluna.

"I found it strange that you should have been at my wife's office. The location the gloves pinged from wasn't within the footprint of her office, though it was very close. Some further investigating revealed …" He looked around, making a motion with his hand.

"Fuck," Ji hissed.

I had broken out into a cold sweat. My fault, it was my fault. I had led Gladstone directly to Paluna's lair because I had forgotten … I had *forgotten* … that the gloves were trackable.

"Where is she. Where is everyone. Where is everything." I balled my hands into fists and took a step forward. Remi and Ji stepped up with me. Remi wrapped his hand around my closed fist.

Not only was I worried about Paluna and everyone who'd been here when Gladstone and his people swept in, I was deeply concerned about what they would have done with Remi's bones. We had just located them and come into a theory that we could help Remi in a different way than unbinding him and sending him to the Afterlife. We'd come here for Ziyelle's journal that Paluna said tied Memoria and Mortem magic together and could explain how the memory Milene had pulled from my mind had restored his ghost.

And now this was happening.

I felt sick, and angry. Tortuously angry.

"Do you truly believe I will provide the answer to that?" He laughed again. "You and Paluna played a very good game, I will admit. You outsmarted me several times and you almost succeeded with Vanishing me. But your upper hand is gone now. My wife will make no more moves against me, and if you value her safety, you won't move against me either."

"You despicable, disgusting, murderous, raggedy, son of a bitch!"

He laughed at my insults.

"Now, you might be thinking with nothing to stop me I can do with you as I like."

That cell, those suppression gloves. There was no fucking way I'd be going back to that. I'd Vanish Gladstone and damn the consequences.

"However," he continued before I could say anything. "My wife's plan to thrust you into the public eye, plus your elevated status after stopping that sky island has made it rather difficult to trouble you without ramifications for myself."

"Aren't you a benevolent asshole," Ji said flatly. "You won't poke at my sister because too many eyes are watching."

"You are dishonorable scum. And you will not harm a hair on Kit's head." Remi's voice was warm with anger. His hand tightened over mine.

Gladstone glanced at Remi again before returning his gaze to me.

"I want to make it very clear that while your efforts were valiant, they were no match for me," he said. "You are now mine, Kitaine Neris, and I plan to use you how I see fit."

"What the fuck do you mean by that?" The way he said that twisted something in my gut.

"In time, you will see," he whispered. "You need not look over your shoulder for officers to drag you away, your family will not be targeted, and I assure you the witch haters who were part of the recent attacks will be found and dealt with. You can remain the darling savior the witches see you to be and move about your life as you please."

He took a step closer, his eyes narrowing, a smile slanting his lips.

"But when I call on you, you will come," he said. "And what I ask of you, you shall deliver. Or else ..." He swept his gaze around the empty room and lingered on the table the box with Remi's bones had been on. When he turned back to us, I felt sure, in the pit of my stomach, that he knew exactly who Remi was and what of his he now had in his possession.

"Or else the well-being of my wife and many others cannot be guaranteed."

"You can't—"

"Of course I can," he cut in. "You may see me as the villain, but I am not a High Coven witch because I seek our downfall. It is quite the opposite. I am in service to all witches. I am just willing to utilize methods most would not. In time you will understand. You will be hearing from me in due course, Ms. Neris. Until then," he tilted his head, "this game of ours was fun, but it has come to an end at long last." His smile widened, turning into a toothy grin and turning his expression into one that would haunt my nightmares.

"Goodbye ... for now."

He exited through the fortified door and silence screamed in my ears as Remi, Ji, and I stared at the now empty space.

"Kit." Ji's voice was a harsh whisper. Remi was still holding my hand and Ji had grabbed my other. I saw fear on Ji's face, but anger burned in their eyes.

Anger had ignited within me.

"What are we going to do?" Remi whispered.

Emotions churned within me but I also had clarity. I closed my eyes and dragged in a breath, then released it and looked at Ji and Remi.

"After everything we've been through, after all we lost, all we gained, after everything Paluna did to help us—"

"We have to help her," Ji said. "Save her."

"Yes." My voice was hard and flat. I was clenched with fear at Linton's words and the fact that he had so many people in his clutches, as well as Remi's bones. But I also had firm, hard resolve.

I had not just endured the chaos my life had been for the last few weeks to cower under this son of a bitch. To allow myself to be beneath his thumb and yield to him pressing against me until I was crushed.

"Paluna has been there for us and now we will be there for her," I said resolutely. I straightened my spine and squared my shoulders. "I'm the strongest witch in the fucking world and Linton Gladstone is going to understand exactly what he will have to reckon with for fucking with me and mine."

"I will stand with you," Remi said fiercely. "My Wither magic is ready."

Remi and Ji had determined looks on their faces.

"Gladstone thinks he's executed a winning move," I said. "He thinks we're pawns on his gameboard."

"He thinks he's got us in a checkmate." Ji crossed their arms over their chest and returned my resolved look.

"Yeah," I said softly. "But we're gonna show that bastard we're playing another game entirely. One way or another, we are gonna bring the downfall of Linton Gladstone."

And I planned on making it hurt.

GLOSSARY

CHARACTERS

Arjun Bora – A Magnes Witch who works at Kiss and Hex

Arrow – An acquaintance of Marrik's from Elsewhere

Barrett Laughton – Marrik's father. Member of Normies First

Calla Loeni – A Regan Witch who works at Kiss and Hex

Conrad Belligra – Criminal who sold people into servitude

Dario Ruiz – A High Coven Repel Witch

Eldrick Neris – Kitaine and Jiano's father. A Mutans Witch

Elliot Tremal – Kit's coven-mate

Emricka Chantaro – A Mutans Witch

Fallon Laughton – Marrik's mother. Member of Normies First

Gemira Monto – Gang leader who robbed cargo trucks

Gizelle Stannik – Linton Gladstone's personal assistant

Hye-Jin Cho – A Repel Witch who works at Kiss and Hex

Indira Bava – Kit's coven-mate

Inori Yamamoto – A top journalist. A Regen Witch

Jamari Zhao – A Memoria Witch

Jeon Yoon – Kit's coven-mate

Jiano Neris – Kit's sibling. Madame of Kiss and Hex.
An Umbra Witch

Jupiter – Member of Paluna's covert operation.
An Umbra Witch

Kitaine Neris – A Vanish Witch

Linton Gladstone – A High Coven council witch.
A Magnes Witch

Marrik Laughton – Kit's boyfriend

Milene Lanson – Phinra's twin. A Memoria Witch

Namira Kimell – Marrik's cousin

Nollari Neris – Kitaine and Jiano's mother. A Regen Witch

Onyx – A witch who has a strong tie to Elsewhere

Paluna Montclair – Linton Gladstone's wife. A Regressa Witch

Phinra Lanson – Milene's twin. A Memoria Witch

Quinn Duro – Marrik and Namira's cousin
Remington Glace – A ghost bound to an amulet by one of Kit's ancestors
Reshmi Patil – Guardian of Kit's coven
Rowan Sufalo – A Mutans Witch who works at Kiss and Hex
Saffron Lomillot – A High Coven Vanish Witch
Tarena Mongue – A High Coven Memoria Witch
Tau Cherlain – Kit's coven-mate
Titan – Member of Paluna's covert operation. A Repel Witch
Valentino Romero – A Mortem Witch who works at Kiss and Hex
Ziyelle Honstrik – Kit's ancestor who bound Remi. A Mortem Witch

WITCH CLASSES

Evanescet (Vanish) – Can make people and objects disappear
Magnes – Can pull in objects and manipulate magnetic fields
Memoria – Mind reading and memory reconstruction
Mortem – Death magic and ghost binding
Mutans – Creature shapeshifting
Regen – Regeneration, regrowth, healing
Repellere (Repel) – Can repel objects and non-physical matter
Regressa – Can revert something to a previous location or state of being
Umbra – Shadow manipulation, constructs, and travel

MOON PHASE AFFILIATION

Evanescet – Aulura Waxing Crescent
Mortem – Aulura Full Moon
Regen – Aulura Waning Gibbous
Repellere – Aulura Third quarter
Magnes - Cebis Waxing Gibbous
Regressa – Cebis Full Moon
Memoria – Cebis New Moon
Mutans – Cebis First Quarter
Umbra – Cebis Waning Crescent

PLACES

The Bramble – A neighborhood of coven houses in Vonuis
Elsewhere – A parallel world full of errant magic
Hanceoh – Town in northern Sollunara
Indigaris – The name of the continent Sollunara is located on
Keltin – Town in eastern Sollunara
Kiss and Hex – Jiano's bordello
Luneso – A witch territory on Indigaris
Moonglade – An area with coven houses and a ley line well
Nimbisu – A sky island
Sollunara – A witch territory on Indigaris
Tsunsama – An island country
Vonuis – A city in Sollunara
Xislao – A Tropical island
Yarachon – Territory on the west coast of Indigaris
Youne Wilds – Forested area outside Vonuis

TERMS

Aulura – One of the world's two moons
Aura – A Vanish Witch coven
Blights – Criminals who have been Vanished
Cebis – One of the world's two moons, smaller than Aulura
Celestine – The name of Kit's coven
Evanescet Tide – The ability to Vanish something from a distance. Also known as a Vanish Tide
Evanescet Transference – The ability to transfer something from one location to another. Also known as a Vanish Shift
Hexes – Collective term for the staff at Kiss and Hex
High Coven – The governing body of witches on Indigaris
Ley Lines – Veins of magic below the earth that strengthen witch magic
Ley Line Well – A place where multiple veins of the ley lines cross and can be drawn from to strengthen witch magic
Normies – Humans without magic

Normies First – Anti-witch hate group
Relics – Items that draw in power from ley lines and allow witches to use stronger magic
Withering Touch – A ghost's ability to decay anything they touch

Evanescet Tide Incantation

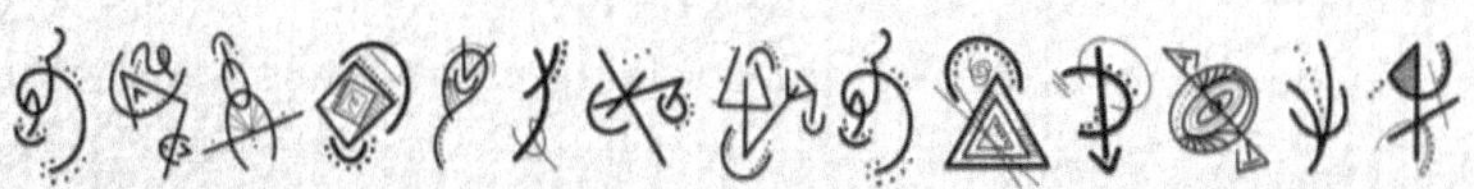

ABOUT

A.J. Locke is a young adult and adult fantasy author, and also writes and illustrates picture books. She is an artist of various mediums including oil and acrylic paint, and watercolor. When she's trying to avoid her writing projects she can be found trying to make a dent in her TBR pile, playing video games, watching anime, baking, and chasing the ever elusive eight hours of sleep. A.J. is originally from Trinidad and Tobago and now resides in NYC.

CONTACT AND SOCIAL MEDIA

Website: www.ajlockewrites.com
Twitter: @maqueripe
Instagram: art_by_ajlocke
Facebook: facebook.com/authorajlocke
TikTok: @authorajlocke

Books by A.J. Locke

Pennrae is a warrior with magical abilities who falls into an enchanted sleep for 300 years. She awakens in a magic-less world ... or so she thinks. But magic eating monsters will be the least of her problems when a nefarious plot threatens to knock her out for another three centuries.

Magical machinations are working against Penn, but she's ready to stand against them, and find time to sort out her love life with the man who's ready to fight beside her, and fall in love with her.

Entangled Publishing

EBOOK ✗ KU ✗ PAPERBACK ✗ AUDIO

Novari is a human who bartends for Luccero, an alluring incubus and the star of her fantasies. She can't have Luc, since being with an incubus will bring dire consequences, but she does have Keo, who also wouldn't mind Luc's touch. Keo, who loathes being a vampire, is in pursuit of a fabled cure that will turn Fiends human. A cure highly in demand as many Fiends crave freedom from their burdened lives.

When an unexpected discovery about the cure's location puts Novari and Keo in danger, they take refuge in Luccero's sprawling manor. There, they contemplate how to stay safe ... and succumb to each other's seduction.

But when the danger zeroes in, they'll have to figure out how to overcome it before the dream they've found together becomes a nightmare.

KINDLE   **KU**   **PAPERBACK**

As magical entities of opposing seasons, Summer and Winter, Rielle and Aden can't be together without dire consequences ... until Aden shows Rielle he can give her everything she craves.

But the primordial magic that allows Rielle and Aden to be together could also tear them apart.

Kitaine is a Vanish Witch who uses her magic to keep her city safe, until a hit goes awry and she Vanishes instead, winding up in a chaotic parallel world full of every bad soul ever Vanished. Reunited with her boyfriend Marrik, an accidental victim of her magic, they try to find their way home.

But that's easier said than done when all those bad souls want to take their vengeance out on Kit.

And once they make it home, they'll realize their problems have just begun.

KINDLE ☾ KU ☾ PAPERBACK ☾ HARDCOVER

www.ingramcontent.com/pod-product-compliance
Lightning Source LLC
Chambersburg PA
CBHW051316130726
47987CB00004B/1823